CHANGES IN LATITUDES

ALSO BY JEN MALONE

Map to the Stars
Wanderlost

Changes in Latitudes

Jen Malone

HARPER TEEN

An Imprint of HarperCollinsPublishers

HarperTeen is an imprint of HarperCollins Publishers.

ISBN 978-0-06-238017-3

Typography by Katie Klimowicz
17 18 19 20 21   PC/LSCH   10 9 8 7 6 5 4 3 2 1

First Edition

To mothers and daughters everywhere,
but most especially to mine

There are things I fully expect to encounter in my driveway.

A car. Okay, so that's a giant gimme. The Sunday newspaper. The oil stain from the time my dad decided he was tired of getting ripped off at Lube Like Lightning and demonstrated to all of us why he's far better suited for academia than auto mechanics. The garbage cans waiting for my brother, Drew, to pull them to the curb on trash day (or, more like, waiting for my mom to do it after Drew forgets . . . again).

But never—not ever—a ginormous sailboat on blocks.

Not a behemoth *thing* with a mast stretching so high that Mr. Kellerman next door could shimmy up it and finally reach above the midway point of the pine tree he wraps with lights every Christmas. (If he were about fifty years younger, sixty pounds lighter, and without the arthritic knees, that is.)

"You're seeing this, right?" I ask my two best friends, slowing my car to a stop in the middle of the road. At three o'clock in the morning on our tiny side street, I can do this without any death or dismemberment worries.

"All *I* can see down here is that you severely need to vacuum under the driver's seat . . . and be glad you didn't ask what I smell, because I could get very graphic. Were you driving Drew around recently?" Tara asks.

Jess murmurs something that sounds like, "No talk. Gonna be sick."

They're scrunched into the backseat floor wells of my hand-me-down Camry, hiding out from overzealous cops looking to bust kids like me for questionable infractions such as "driving nonfamilial minors during the first six months of holding an Oregon driver's license."

"You can get up now," I tell them, then point at the driveway. "Behold!"

Tara's mouth falls open. "Babe, your mom's lost the plot. I think the divorce has finally done her in."

She . . . might be right.

In the last six months since Mom imploded our boringly happy family, she's taken up quilting (and subsequently outfitted practically everyone in her address book with new bedding), gotten certified as a Zumba instructor (even when on good terms with each other—which we most certainly are not anymore—no child should be subjected to their mother in spandex), and run for a spot on the town council (which she lost by twelve votes, three of which I influenced).

Last year I would have helped her pick out fabrics, practiced salsa moves beside her, and canvased door-to-door collecting signatures to get her on the ballot.

This year everything's changed.

Even so . . . I thought I was at least past the point of surprise where her obsessive hobbies were concerned. But a *sailboat*? We live in central Oregon. The ocean is at least an hour and a half away on a good traffic day!

I'm forced to park on the curb, which is a new maneuver for me, and it's possible I sacrifice the rims of the tires on the left-hand side of the car. Tara and Jess spill out onto the grass and I pull them up.

We march to the boat, tripping and shushing one another as we go. I'm not physically drunk, but I am totally punch-drunk from the late hour, and sneaking into my house well past curfew somehow seems less urgent than an immediate investigation of *Sunny-Side Up* (as cheery italic script proclaims it to be). This close, the thing is even more imposing.

Jess lifts her foot. "Boost me!"

She scrambles onto a platform at the back and holds out a hand.

"Shhhh!" I whisper-yell as Tara attempts to follow us and instead collapses in giggles on the concrete. Tara might be *drunk*-drunk. Scratch that—she most definitely is.

Attempt number two goes better, and the three of us throw our legs over the top and climb into the . . . hull? That's a nautical term, right? Is that what people call the part of the boat where the steering wheel lives?

At least I know the area underneath, down a few steps, is called a cabin, and that's where we head next. I'm letting my curiosity lead, pushing all other thoughts about what it *means* that we have a boat in our driveway to the dark recesses of my mind. It's a place I've gotten very intimate with this year.

Speaking of dark. We each grab for our phones and use their flashlights to peek around, aided by a little ambient light from the street that spills in through small windowed hatches.

"This is cozy," Tara says. She's being polite. *Cramped* would be a much better description.

Jess's eyebrows are up. "Okay, if this thing is legit yours, I'm proposing right now we roll up to senior prom in it next year!"

"Are you proposing this or are you *prom*-posing it?" Tara asks, clutching at her sides as she laughs at her own bad joke. Yup, totally drunk.

"That would actually be hilarious," I say. "Or what about a joint graduation party aboard? Maybe we could push it out onto Emmet's Pond!"

"Pretty sure Emmet's Pond is all of six inches deep and covered in algae." Jess wrinkles her nose, but I put my hands on my hips.

"Hey, don't knock algae. It's very important to the ecosystem."

Tara groans. "Cass, I stand by the friendship oaths we signed in blood in third grade, but for the love of god, can we get through a night without any of your plant talk?"

I'm a little interested in (okay, maybe slightly consumed with) botany. I *might* have a few more of my mom's obsessive tendencies than I'd like to admit. But something about having your whole life turned upside down by the detonation of your previously content family unit makes the idea of a little green sprout completely rooted in the ground—thoroughly unable to up and leave—even more appealing than ever.

"Cosigned," Jess says. "We love you, but waxing nostalgic about pond scum is just wrong on so many levels."

Tara grabs my arm and does her cross-eyed zombie face, and this time we both bend over laughing. It's not even that funny, and I'm not sharing her buzz, but somehow everything becomes hilarious at three o'clock in the morning.

God, it feels *so good* to laugh. My utterly crappy junior year is only a couple of short weeks from ending. Next up is what already promises to be a less crappy summer and a way, *way* less crappy senior year.

"You guys, we should totally get some snacks and hang out here tonight, instead of having to keep it at a whisper in your room," Jess says.

"Ooh, grab your laptop too, so we can figure out more of our trip," Tara adds.

I flush with exhilaration at the reminder of the vacation we're planning together for the end of the summer. Technically speaking, it's supposed to be a week of touring college campuses with Jess's parents, but they said the three of us could set the itinerary. We're determined to hit as many cheesy roadside attractions along the way as humanly possible.

Good things are on the horizon; I can feel it in my bones. I grab Tara's arms and we both squeeze tight.

"Ugh. Stop being dorks and go find us food!" Jess orders. She's already on her knees, peering underneath the built-in table, trying to figure out how to get the folding wings to stay up.

I salute her and trip up the cabin stairs. Swinging a leg over the back edge of the boat, I prepare to lower myself onto the platform when something grabs my ankle.

I scream.

2

"Good lord, Cassandra McClure! Do you want to wake the whole neighborhood?" My mother's head appears and I snatch my leg free and drop back into the boat.

"Mom!"

Her lips purse as she pulls herself over the ledge. Tara's head sticks up from the cabin opening and Mom sighs. "Girls, it's nearly three thirty in the morning. Tara, do your parents know where you are?"

My best friend ducks her head and attempts to look ashamed. Or maybe she's just trying to hide the fact that she's stealthily slipping a breath mint into her mouth. "Sure do."

"What about you, Jess?" Even though Jess is completely hidden inside the cabin, everyone knows we travel as a pack.

"I told her I'm sleeping over here," comes the disembodied voice.

"Must be nice for *their* parents to be in the loop," my mother says, addressing me this time. "I wish I had the same courtesy extended to me. Curfew, Cass? Again?"

I plop onto a bench. As far as I'm concerned, she lost the right to weigh in on my choices six months ago, when she cheated on my dad and set their divorce in motion. Of course, she doesn't know that *I* know that juicy tidbit; she thinks I bought the "your father and I just grew apart" line my brother did. But she must be carrying hidden guilt around, or else she'd be grounding me right now instead of sighing in defeat.

I tuck my hair behind my ears and offer a mild "Sorry."

I try to stand, but the bench is slick from the dew in the air and I crash back onto my butt.

"Which is what you said last time," she says.

"Mom, why are we having this conversation on a sailboat?"

She bites her lip, then glances at the cabin opening and calls, "Tara, Jess, could you please wait for Cassie in her room?"

Mom's voice is tired. Not three thirty in the morning tired, but world-weary tired. She's usually not even a glass-half-full person but a glass-overflowing person, so it catches me by surprise, and for about half a second I feel a twinge of guilt for my role in that. But then I remind myself to put my armor back on. Old Cassie would be affected by seeing the mother she was once so close to in pain. New Cassie knows her mother brought it all on herself.

My friends climb the steps from the cabin, smile politely at my mother, and give me sympathetic looks as they wordlessly slip by and hop down from the boat. So much for cabin snacks and trip planning.

When the door to my house closes behind them, I say, "Go ahead," making a show of settling in for her explanation by leaning back and crossing my legs. Mom's smile is strained.

"Okay, then," she says. "Well, as you've probably noticed, we now own a boat. Or rather, we quasi-own a boat, for the next six months or so."

I stare at her. "But *why*?"

"Well . . . This is a good-news, bad-news scenario. Which do you want first?"

Is there ever a right answer to that question? In no universe does getting the good news second make the bad news you heard before it just melt away. And you can't enjoy the good news if it comes first because you know the other shoe's about to drop. I ignore the question and blink a few times.

My mother is quiet too, and looks nervous. This can't be good. Once she realizes I'm not answering her, she takes a deep breath and begins talking very fast. "We—you, me, and Drew—are going on a little adventure. Well, not that little, actually. The three of us are going to sail from Oregon to Land's End, at the southern tip of Baja, Mexico. For four months."

She steals a peek at me and, even though I'm not reacting one bit (processing . . . so much processing happening), her shoulders relax. This time her grin is genuine as she adds, "I really think it could be amazing."

Amazing? *Amazing?* Marooned at sea with my mother? For *four months*?

This is not real life. This is not *my* life.

"What's the good news?" I manage, subtly squeezing my eyes shut, then open, shut, then open, to see if that tilts the world back on its axis.

"That *was* the good news, sweetie."

Yeah, I was kind of afraid of that.

3

I have at least a million questions. How will we sail this thing? When do we leave? Even if it's tomorrow—which it better not be—four months would still take us into next school year, so what about classes? What about my trip with Tara and Jess? What about *sharks*? I'm a Shark Week addict and no way, no how, am I willingly putting myself in the middle of their feeding grounds on this piece of fiberglass that may look monster-sized in our driveway, but probably *not so much* bobbing in an enormous ocean.

Still I keep quiet, my mind whirring.

"Why?" is all I manage when I finally connect my brain to my speaking parts.

Mom's like a windup toy set loose, pacing the tiny open space, her words spilling out like she's been sitting on a scoop she's just gotten permission to broadcast. "Okay, so here are some basics: the sailboat's owners retired to Mexico and are looking for someone to sail it to them. There are a few others headed down the coast—three boats, including ours—so we'll have company the entire time. And then we'll hop a flight back home once we make our delivery. Honestly, the whole thing sort of dropped in my lap, and at first I thought it was ridiculous, but—"

She jerks to a stop and peers at me, trying to gauge my reaction, but I genuinely don't have one. I think I might be in shock. Is this what shock feels like? Like everything is happening on the other end of a paper-towel tube you're peering through?

She continues on with something about an online high school for the two months we'll miss in the fall, but I can't follow anymore. I used to complain that nothing interesting ever happened to me. I really did—ignorant, privileged idiot that I was. But ever since Mom cheated and Dad jetted off to another continent in retaliation, *all* I've wanted is to get my normal, boring life back. I crave BD (Before Divorce) like a sugar fiend craves cake pops with rainbow sprinkles.

And if I can't have that—I *do know* I can't have that—then I want BD, Version 2.0: a new kind of normal I can control myself. My friends, my job scooping ice cream at Heavenly Licks (which sounds so porny, and I don't understand why the owner won't hear me out about it), a crazy-fun vacation with Tara and Jess, and a killer senior year to remember. And then to graduate and *really* do things on my own terms. Is that too much to hope for? It seemed a thousand percent reasonable until about three minutes ago.

There is no version of BD that takes place at sea.

Now my mother is staring at me again. "Cass? Honey, are you paying attention to any of this?"

I look up at her, and all I can manage—*again*—is "Why?"

Then she says, so quietly I have to strain to hear her, "Well, partly because we need to put what's left of our family back together, before you go off to college and it's too late."

I fight the prickle of tears that spring up behind my eyelids. She's not going to disarm me with a few soft words. She's not. We're no longer the unstoppable mother-daughter duo of Cassie-and-Elise.

I hit the "anger" preset button on my brain. All I have to do is rewind to the argument between her and Dad, the one that she still doesn't know I overheard. The one where I learned the real reason behind my parents' split.

"What about finding a new job?" I ask. My mother was a bank manager until she got laid off a couple of months ago, after her company was sold to a new one.

She picks at her cuticles. "That's the other reason. The severance they gave me will eventually end, and there just isn't a whole lot out there right now. I'll be able to continue sending résumés from the boat, but in the meantime, this sailing gig is a bird-in-the-hand scenario. Any little bit would help at the moment, and this can offer more than that."

"But you don't sail."

"Of course I do!"

She sounds offended, and okay, yes, she's mentioned being

on the sailing team when she was in high school in San Diego, and she's told us stories about the summers in college and grad school when she crewed on catamarans for rich people chartering in the Caribbean. But that was a whole lifetime ago. *My* whole lifetime. How do I know those experiences make her capable of taking our lives in her hands now?

"Right, but you haven't done it in *forever*," I say.

"Pretty sure the ocean hasn't changed. Or the principles of maneuvering sails through wind," Mom answers calmly.

Okay, but *I* don't know how to sail. Before tonight, I'd never even set foot on a sailboat.

This is crazy. Normal people just don't *do* this kind of thing!

"What did Drew have to say?" I mumble, though I can already guess. If I inherited my mom's obsessive-hobby gene, my fourteen-year-old brother got her optimism. Drew's a roll-with-the-punches kind of kid who's always the first one packed for any vacation. As long as he has access to junk food and/or his laptop for *Star Wars* movies and video games, a tsunami could hit Oregon and he'd shrug it off.

Oh my god, what if we're out in this thing when a tsunami hits? When was the last time a tsunami hit the West Coast? Is that a possibility?

My mother snorts, oblivious to the cliff my thoughts have fallen over. "Drew's first question was whether we could rename the boat *Minecraft*. Since it's a small craft and it's ours, at least for now . . ."

Of course he's on board, no pun intended.

Mom sobers. "It would be great to have your support here too. Meet me halfway?"

Meet her halfway? How? By saying "Oooh, sounds fun! Hey, I get to be captain!"? Sure, that'll happen.

Because when you'd love nothing more than to put as much distance as possible between yourself and the mother who took a crap on your blissful life, purely out of her own selfishness, the thing you'd *most* want in the world is to be stranded at sea with her.

For *four freaking months.*

She can't pull the rug out from under me. Not again.

"I'm not going," I state. "I'm old enough to live here on my own until you get back."

"That option is completely off the table, so put it out of your mind right this second."

I can tell by her tone of voice she won't budge on that, so I tuck my knees up under my chin, wrapping my arms around my legs. I lower my eyes and voice and try another tactic. "Mom. You don't understand. I have my own plans for the summer. Tara, Jess, and I are getting all of the details of *our* trip in order! And with everything that happened this year, what I really need more than anything is to be with my friends in my familiar surroundings. I need my own bed in my own room and—"

Mom cuts me off. "About that . . ."

I yank my head up. "What?"

"Honey, this is the bad-news part. I'm sorry. This trip pays well, but we can't overlook any opportunity to shore up our savings right now, so—"

She breaks off and reaches for my hand, but I snatch it away and tuck it under my butt.

Holding eye contact with me, she continues, "I'm still in touch with the dean of Dad's department, and she mentioned a new professor they've hired for the fall semester. He and his family need a short-term rental while they house hunt, so I told them . . . well . . . they'll be subletting our house while we're away."

Not only can't *I* stay here, but she's invited strangers to live among all our things?

No.

No, no, no, no, *no*.

My eyes fill, and I'm riding a crazy-fine line between heartbreak and rage. I'm like one of those blow-up balloon people outside car dealerships, with the bodies that wave around as they fill with air from beneath. When the wind knocks their torsos over, they fold in half, then bounce back. Hit with a wind gust, bounce back. Hit, bounce back.

When do *my* hits stop coming?

"Another family in our house?" If my words were printed instead of spoken, they'd be in six-point type, that's how small my voice is.

Mom slides up close and puts her arms around me, my folded knees between us. I consider jerking free, but I'm so defeated by this plot twist that I don't even bother. She caresses my hair.

"I'm so sorry, baby. I know it's weird to think of other people living here, but this is what the situation requires. When Dad and I got divorced, we never expected I'd lose my job so soon after, and maintaining two households on a single income is outrageously expensive. We've already cut back on a bunch, and Dad's doing all he can to conserve on his end, but with the cost of living in Hong Kong . . ." She sighs, then adds, "It's only temporary—they'll be all moved out before we get home."

But I'll know they were here. This house is the keeper of 99.9 percent of my memories of life BD. It's bad enough that living in it without Dad feels unnatural, but to think of some other girl's foot dangling off the side of *my* bed as she sleeps, or of her spending an afternoon reading graphic novels in the window seat on the landing of the stairs, or happening upon the heart-shaped rock collection I arranged in a hidden circle at the very base of my favorite forsythia bush, or—

My thoughts skid to a stop.

"What about my garden?" I ask.

My backyard is my sanctuary these days. It's calming, digging in the dirt and cradling the new plants as I nestle them into the ground, experimenting with different fertilizers and charting their growth. I've devoted countless hours to maintaining it. I can create order there, and I can keep it that way. No sudden surprises.

"We'll have to leave very detailed instructions for taking care of it," Mom says, not sounding reassuring at all.

And just like that, I can tell that my garden will become the next casualty of the Divorce That Just Keeps Taking. I press my fingers into the corners of my eyes, trying not to let my emotions circle the drain.

"I don't understand why we can't stay here and figure out some alternate plan. I can pitch in with my earnings from Heavenly Licks—"

That would mean giving up my August vacation with Tara and Jess, since my summer job was funding my portion of our expenses. Either way, I'd be missing my trip. But at least in this scenario we'd have the *rest* of the summer to hang out. That would almost—*almost*—make up for not being with them to witness the World's Largest Ball of Yarn.

My mother sighs. "I appreciate the offer, sweetheart, but I have to think beyond just getting us through the summer. This sailing fee *plus* having our living expenses covered for four months *plus* the money from the sublet will buy us a lot more time."

"My college fund, then," I offer. "I can take out student loans. If it means getting to stay here . . ."

I'm clearly desperate, but I mean every word.

"Absolutely not. We're not touching that account. Besides, the money's a motivator, but it's not the only one. I honestly, truly believe I'm offering you and Drew something special with this adventure. Once you're out there on the water and you see how amazing it can be to live that kind of lifestyle, things back here won't seem as all-consuming as they do right now. I think you, especially, could use a break after the last six months, Cass."

But not from my life and my friends and my plans with them. What I need is a break from *her*. Not *more* of her, in my face, 24-7.

She brushes a strand of hair from my cheek, waiting for a response, but I don't answer.

Mom is silent too, and I can tell she's searching for the right words. I could save her the effort. There *are* no right words for when you turn your daughter's life completely upside down.

Again.

If she hadn't cheated in the first place, none of this—*none* of this—would be happening.

"Maybe I'll leave you alone to process for a bit," she says, ending her words on a sigh. She puts her hands on her knees and pushes to a stand. "It's a lot to take in, and I'm really sorry to spring it on you, Cass." Her voice catches. "I just wanted to wait until all the plans were solidly in place before I said anything. I really do think this'll be an incredible experience for all of us."

Solidly in place. Ha!

The Pacific Ocean is the very opposite of solid.

4

The only freezer on board is . . . under my mattress. On a long list of recent injustices, beginning with "you have to leave the only home you've ever known to move onto a sailboat the size of your bedroom in said home, which, oh, by the way, someone else will be enjoying" and including "you'll miss the first two months of your senior year of high school, which is supposed to be the exact time everything magical happens to you, if every teen movie ever made is to be believed," the freezer thing isn't the worst offense.

But still.

Let's say we're under sail somewhere off the coast of California and Drew decides he wants a Hot Pocket. His big sister, Cassie, will then have to go into her stateroom (which makes it sound like it might actually be stately, instead of postage-stamp-sized), pull up the piece of foam that is supposed to pass for a mattress, lift a wooden hatch on the frame, and dig into an ice-cold compartment.

I will, quite literally, be reenacting "The Princess and the Pea" every time I go to bed. Except there will be an entire *bag* of peas under me, instead of just one. And they will be frozen.

Mom keeps going on about how clever the boat designer was to utilize every square foot of space, but I'm busy wishing he or she had thought to include about a thousand more of them.

I refold a fuzzy sweater and squeeze it against my chest to flatten it. There's hardly room to stand in here, and everything I brought has to fit into a series of small cubbies built in above and beside my bed/freezer. Not only that, but since Drew has to sleep in the main cabin, on the cushioned seats that run alongside the built-in table, he'll be using half my cubbies for his own clothes.

"Cass! Come up! We're getting ready to leave the dock!" Drew calls.

I sigh. Poor kid. He's treating this like one big vacation, even though he's the one stuck sleeping on a glorified bench for four months. And I really don't think he's thought through the ramifications of missing the beginning of his freshman year. Our high school has three middle school populations feeding into it, and those initial months include an epic reshuffling of the social order. He'll practically be the new kid come November, and there's only so much a big sister will be able to help with that.

I'm hoping my *own* classmates won't forget my name by the time I get back. Okay, I may be exaggerating, but it's one thing to be away for part of the summer—plenty of kids go to camp, their grandparents' place, or beach houses. Missing the start of school is something else entirely. Everyone will be settled into new routines by the time I reenter the scene.

"Cassie!" my mother yells. "We're about to christen our voyage. You don't want to miss this!"

Oh, but I do. I want to miss all of it.

I drop the sweater and climb the few steps up to the cockpit (turns out the hull is the entire underbody of the boat, whereas the cockpit is the area in the back of the boat where we sit and steer. I hate that I now know this).

Drew and my mother are beaming in the bright sunshine, but I can't work up more than a scowl. Mom chooses to ignore my dark mood the same way she's been ignoring it for the last six weeks, since she first sprang this trip on us.

I hang behind them as they crack a bottle of cheap Champagne (encased in a plastic bag so no shards of glass pollute the riverbed) against the boat's hull, while a guy on a yacht in the next slip takes a picture on Mom's cell.

"Bon voyage!" he wishes us, handing her phone across the narrow strip of wooden dock dividing our boats.

Mom's answering laugh seems to hold all the sparkles dancing on the water right now.

"I can't believe we're doing this!" she tells him before turning to toss her arm over Drew's shoulder. "Okay, gotta hit the seas if we're gonna meet up with the other sailboats by dinnertime. Ready, first mate?"

"Ready, cap'n," he answers, hopping onto the dock and unwinding the rope to free *Sunny-Side Up*. He's so into this trip, he's been practicing tying and untying different nautical knots night and day for the past several weeks.

"And we're off," Mom says, breathing deeply. She glances in my direction again, but I pretend to be absorbed in picking at a thread on my yoga pants. As soon as I feel her gaze leave me, I return below deck to finish unpacking my "room."

I'm here, but I don't have to like it.

This boat may not have all the comforts of home—or even half of them—but at least it has a Wi-Fi hot spot. I'd planned to take full advantage of this to at least maintain all aspects of life back in Pleasant Hill that don't require an actual physical presence. In fact, one of my tearful good-bye promises to Tara and Jess was that we wouldn't have to be out of texting range from one another for more than five seconds. But not thirty minutes into our trip, I've had to abandon scrolling through Instagram on my phone and am instead digging in the dreaded freezer under my mattress for that bag of peas. I place it on my forehead, but even the soothing cold on my skin can't stop my stomach from rolling worse than the waves passing beneath our boat.

Oh god. Oh god, oh god, oh god. I can't take four more minutes of this, much less four more months.

The diesel fumes of the engine stick in my nostrils, and the vibrations of the motor are especially torturous on top of the back-and-forth motions of the entire cabin.

I stand, but it takes both hands to steady myself as I lurch from my room into the vertical box that passes for a bathroom. A mist of seawater sprays through the open hatch when we encounter another wave. My stomach heaves and I bend over, aiming for the toilet, except the boat rocks again and I miss. Now I see the merit of the entire room being the shower "stall," with a drain in the center of the floor.

When I emerge a few minutes later, Mom is waiting outside the door with a lollipop and a box of Dramamine. Because, *of course*, she heard everything. There's zero privacy when you live in a shoe box.

"You'll feel better if you come up into the fresh air," she says quietly. "Focusing on the horizon is the best cure for seasickness. The waves are always worse where the river meets the ocean; once we're in open water, the seas should calm down."

I don't answer, but I do grab the lollipop and peel off the wrapper as Mom returns above to reclaim steering duties from Drew. It's lemon-flavored and goes a long way toward getting the taste of vomit out of my mouth. I hang at the bottom of the stairs for a minute or two, debating whether I'd rather have my stomach hurt down here or my heart hurt up there, but the next lurch sends me climbing in search of relief.

Mom is standing at the wheel. She gives me a small smile and nods at the bench that contains our life jackets. I grab one and fasten it around myself, something Mom has decreed nonnegotiable any time we're on deck and not at anchor.

I ease myself into a seat and take in my surroundings as I allow my lungs to fill with the cooling sea breeze. My stomach thanks me by unclenching just a tiny bit.

We're still in the river, but only barely, as our boat enters its mouth and aims for the expanse of Pacific Ocean just beyond. The wide sea stretches to the horizon, where it meets with the wispy clouds. I gulp at the endlessness of it. It's cold out here, with the wind and the fact that coastal Oregon—even in July—is far from tropical, but the bright sun makes the whitecaps appear as if they're dusted with glitter. It *looks* magical, though it feels menacing. Vast. Bleak. Just like the time stretching before me until we're back home.

Drew is at the very front of the bow now, and when he spots me he gestures. "Come!"

My first inclination is to shake my head, but my stomach wonders if standing and stretching might not be the worst thing. I stumble up the narrow pathway along the side of the boat, the fiberglass below my feet angled to shed water. Every so often I encounter a rope coming off the sails and connecting to the deck, and I have to maneuver around it. I'm basically left with no choice but to clutch at the waist-high metal bars that line the perimeter like a fence; they're the only thing keeping me from sliding into the yawning water below. It doesn't help that the boat is pitching from side to side, and that my belly has clearly scored an invite to the dance party too.

When I reach Drew at the very front, I grasp the railing

just below his hand. After a few gulps of air to push down the queasiness, I say, "I'm *not* reenacting that 'king of the world' scene from *Titanic*, if that's what you have in mind. . . ."

He makes a face. "Eww, don't be gross. You're my *sister*. Anyway, that was the annoying kissy-kissy part of the movie. The sinking scenes were the only ones worth watching."

"Yeah, maybe we can skip talking about sinking ships while *out to sea on one*?" I request blandly.

Drew snorts. "Only if *you* stop referencing romances that are super shi—" He cuts off as we both steal a quick glance back at the Language Police.

My brother is about as enamored with curse words as every other freshman boy the world over. Which is to say: a whole lot. He's usually pretty good at restraining himself around my mother and other authority figures though. Luckily, Mom is blissfully steering, her eyes hidden behind sunglasses. She's oblivious to us as the wind whips her hair around.

For a second, I'm struck by how intent but relaxed she seems. I haven't seen her look like this in a while, though it used to be beyond familiar. When I was in elementary school, she let me read her the entire Harry Potter series, half a chapter at a time, night after night. *Order of the Phoenix* alone took an entire winter. And every bedtime she'd lie curled next to me, rubbing circles on my back and wearing this exact expression anytime I glanced up from the page.

I ignore the sudden tightness in my chest and turn back to my brother, poking his arm. "So. First mate, huh?"

He ducks his head. "Whatever. Just 'cause I don't feel like having a four-month pity party doesn't mean you need to be on my case about it."

"I'm not on your case. I'm merely trying to get how you're so totally into this."

"You mean sailing around like pirates, something new and different to look at every single day, learning to surf on Mexican beaches while everyone else is stuck in algebra? I don't get what *you* don't get. No offense."

I turn my face to the sun and close my eyes to avoid answering. (Note to self: don't close eyes while seasick.) I wonder how I'd have felt about this trip last year, back when I used to be glass-half-full too. I wish more than anything I was still as ignorant as Drew, so I could be that way again. Of course, he might also be different if he knew about Mom's betrayal . . . which is exactly why I'll never tell him. I'm perfectly fine having it be my cross to bear, if it means he gets to stay happy-go-lucky Drew as long as possible. There's no reason for us both to wallow in this muck.

"Oh crap! I almost forgot!" he says, scrambling up and nearly losing his balance. He rights himself and laughs. "Whoa. Gotta work on my sea legs. Be right back."

He drops his narrow hips easily through the open hatch and onto Mom's bed beneath, then disappears. I take unsuccessful steadying breaths to counteract the motion of the waves. A minute later, heavy metal blasts through the cabin and filters up. Drew's grinning face appears below me.

"I made a playlist! Starting with 'Rime of the Ancient Mariner' by Iron Maiden. Sea references plus it's our *maiden* voyage. Get it?"

"Impressive symbolism, Roo." Despite my stomach woes, I can't help teasing him with the nickname I gave him as a toddler, when he was way into Winnie-the-Pooh. "No offense, but I'm not sure death metal is helping my seasickness. Got anything on there that's a little more mellow?"

Drew makes a face. "Fine. No one appreciates a good electric guitar solo these days. How about Jimmy Buffett? King of the boat jam?"

I shrug, and his head ducks under again. A minute later soft acoustic strumming spills out from below. I don't recognize the song, but I lie back on the deck and let the happy melody wash over me.

It's those changes in latitudes, changes in attitudes, nothing remains quite the same, Jimmy Buffett sings.

Ha! How many latitudes will we cross on this trip? I can't speak for any changes in attitude, because I certainly don't have any plans for those, but the "nothing remains quite the same"? You sure got that right, Buffett.

Mom calls from the cockpit, "Hey, Drew, come back up. Let's trim the sails and get this baby racing!"

Um, yes, because nausea at whatever number of knots we're going now isn't enough fun—let's make things interesting.

But at least she's keeping up her end of our bargain and only asking Drew for help. In Mom's attempt to make me believe she valued my input about this trip she's forcing on me, she allowed me to strike a deal with her. My terms: I don't have to help with any sailing. Hers: Fine, but you do have to know enough to stay safe.

That mandate bought me a boating safety course last month, where I learned the parts of a boat; to watch out for the boom, a long metal bar that holds the bottom of the bigger sail and swings when we're changing direction; to wear my life jacket; and that you always pass green buoys on the port side and red buoys on the starboard side. I also learned which sides the port and starboard are. Left = port. Which I can remember because both words have four letters. Right = starboard. Which is kind of like Starburst, and it is very, very *right* to like all Starbursts (except the orange ones).

But we were in the middle of Oregon for the class. We didn't actually *sail*. No one bothered to mention how difficult it is to move around up here, with all these rope and cleat booby-traps everywhere on deck. I clumsily retreat to the bench seats of the cockpit and sneak peeks as my brother takes the wheel. Mom is pulling on ropes like she last did this yesterday, instead of however many years ago. The sails billow with air as the boat angles south and begins to skim—*fast*—along the coastline.

Another helpful tidbit the class didn't mention: how much every single wave would send us—and the contents of my stomach—rolling around. On a long list of things Mom has been wrong about lately is the insistence that the waves would calm down once we hit open water. If anything, they're tossing us even more than before. My mother and Drew don't appear the least bit affected, but in a supreme analogy to how *everything* this year has somehow managed to hit me ten times harder than anyone else, my body revolts.

I lean over the stern and regurgitate my lunch into the choppy waters below.

This is gonna be one hell of a trip, all right.

5

By the time, hours later, that Mom adjusts the sails again to turn us toward the inlet river where we'll "pull in" to meet and spend the night with the two other sailboats making the trip with us, my stomach is so empty it's hollow.

There's nothing I wouldn't give right now to be home in my soft bed in my cozy house.

Except someone else has laid temporary claim to that soft bed *and* the cozy house.

Although we've stayed within distant sight of it all day, the coastline looms closer now. It's not escaping me that our journey is a whole day under way and we're actually nearer to home now than when we started. The marina where *Sunny-Side Up* got her seaworthy checkup and was lowered into the water was far up the coast, and we've now sailed to a point almost *exactly* parallel to Pleasant Hill. A quick jaunt across the 126 and I could be hanging with my friends tonight.

Which is a thought. A definite thought. My phone is clipped to my waist in its new bulky, plastic waterproof case. I subtly slip it out and send a series of quick texts to Tara.

With Mom shouting instructions, she and Drew wrestle the sails down, and Mom switches on the motor as we approach shore. Soon we're chugging along a narrow river, winding our way inland the few miles to the town of Florence, where we're supposed to drop anchor and meet with the others. Mom sends Drew up front to keep a lookout for any old deck pilings hiding just under the surface, because apparently one of those could do a number on our hull.

"Cass, I know we had a deal," she says, "but would you mind just keeping an eye out on the port side, so Drew can cover starboard? It would be hugely helpful. And not technically sailing."

I sigh, but I'm secretly glad to have a role of my own. While I would never give Mom the satisfaction of asking for anything to do, it's a little boring just observing, especially since my seasick woes won't allow me to curl up in the cabin with a book or my laptop. I stake out a spot on the railing and peer into the faded-denim waters, trying to train my eyes to see below the surface like a sailor a hundred years ago on iceberg duty. I'm deep into a fantasy that my superior eyesight would have saved the *Titanic* when Drew calls out, "Piling!"

Damn. I wanted to do that.

Mom swings the wheel. I peer below me, but all I see is the sandy bottom. It . . . looks kind of close, actually.

"Um, how much clearance do—" I begin, but the

horrible skidding-to-a-stop sound of boat meeting riverbed silences us all.

Mom stares at one of the computer screens on the dash above the steering wheel in disbelief and whispers, "That can't be."

I choose to peer at the actual visible evidence that we have run into a sandbar camouflaged just below the water's surface and whisper my own, "Oh yes, it can."

Drew dangles over the railing. "Well, sheeeeeeeeeeet."

There is no stiff sea wind masking his curse from Mom this time, but she chooses to ignore it, leaning over the side herself. "How—but—"

The boat is at a dead stop, which feels strange (and not as tummy-soothing as I'd have expected) after so many hours of having constant movement under us. Mom plops onto the bench and puts her face in her hands. It's the silence that follows that turns me from perplexed to scared. She doesn't speak or move; she just sits clutching at her head. Drew and I exchange worried glances.

Is this worse than maybe I'm making it out to be? I mean, there *are* ways to get boats unstuck from sandbars, right? Or could we have somehow messed up the hull so badly we'll have to abandon the trip and head home? Am I a terrible person for wishing this could be true?

"Um, Mom?" I venture, after a bit.

She raises her head. Her eyes look haunted. "I got us grounded."

Uh, yeah. We know.

"I was so preoccupied with avoiding the piling that I stopped paying attention to the depth meter and I knew—I *knew*—this river had shifting sandbars all over the place. I can't believe I was so *stupid*!"

Drew rushes to her defense. "You were trying to keep from hitting something. Anyone would have done the same thing. What if I hop in and see if I can push us free?"

He strips off his shirt, climbs to the narrow lip of decking on the outside of the railing, and balances there for a second before jumping. He treads water, trying to find a place to stand so he can leverage his pushing efforts, but while the bottom of the boat is wedged into the sandbar, it's still too far below Drew's feet for him to touch.

He eyes the current and calls up, "Get changed! Maybe the three of us working together can find a way to budge it."

If it was Mom asking, I might resist, but I know how much it would mean to Drew to save the day, so I trail my mother into the cabin and tug on my bathing suit. Ten minutes later, all three of us are floundering in the murky water, trying to push a who-knows-how-many-tons sailboat out of the sand. Not. Gonna. Happen.

Twenty minutes after *that*, the water has receded so much that the boat is basically beached, and Mom declares us stuck until the next high tide rolls in overnight to flood the riverbed and lift us back into the water.

Despite the fact that someone will have to wake up at two

thirty in the morning to drop an anchor once that happens, it sounds like a pretty low-key solution that certainly won't derail the whole trip or anything. The entire situation would almost be comical if Mom weren't acting like we'd just gotten word of the zombie apocalypse. I mean, we're only one day into our trip and we're already freaking grounded. It's sitcom-funny, right?

Not to her.

We slump in the cockpit, exhausted from our efforts and smelling like slimy river gunk. It's bad enough to be trapped in such close quarters with a "remind me what deodorant is again?" pubescent boy, but now we all stink like rotting fish.

"What's the plan?" I ask. "The other boats are probably waiting upriver by now, right? Do we need to let them know we're gonna be really, *really* late to dinner? Should I use the radio thingy?"

I admit, my tone might be a little smug. After all, this trip was Mom's brilliant idea, and it's not totally the worst thing to see her discouraged so early on. Even though the problem has a simple fix, maybe realizing her ineptitude will be enough to make her change her mind, and we can go home.

However, I'm 100 percent taken aback when she bursts into tears. My mom *never* cries. Like, ever. She watched completely dry-eyed as my dad packed up every last belonging and got on a plane to the other side of the world, for a visiting professorship he'd turned down a dozen times before. In fact, that little incident is number three on my List of Things That

I Currently Hate about My Mother. (Number one being the cheating that caused him to leave in the first place. Number two: insisting on this trip.)

As much as her usual stoicism baffles and annoys me, I also kind of count on it. If Mom's in charge, everything will be handled. Simple McClure family fact.

But this? This is not Mom in charge.

"Umm . . . ," I venture, as Drew disappears below deck.

"I'm sorry," she says, pressing her eyelids with the heels of her hands.

I have no clue how to act in this situation.

"I'm so . . . embarrassed," my mother finally says, swiping at her cheeks. "I just—I just needed this *one thing* to go right for us. Is that too much to ask?" She raises her eyes to the sky like she's addressing the heavens. "I thought, I *really thought*, if I could get us all on this boat, I could fix everything. I wanted to have my feet firmly under me and feel in control again."

It's almost amusing to hear her use the words "feet firmly under me" in relation to sailing, now that I know full well what it's like to try to maneuver on deck with waves pitching us left and right.

"I'm no expert, but I'm pretty sure an ocean isn't something that can be controlled, Mom." I don't bother to mention that she's got some nerve complaining to *me* about not being in control of anything.

I hate to admit, though, that seeing her like this is throwing me off guard.

She uses the thin shoulder strap of her bathing suit to wipe her nose. "This isn't the ocean, Cass," she says. "This is the piddlydunk Siuslaw River Bar. Oh my god, I'm in so far over my head."

Drew returns with some wadded-up toilet paper, which he hands to Mom in place of tissues. "If we were in over our heads right now, we wouldn't be beached on a sandbar. I'd say the problem is more that we're under our heads. Or at least the water is."

Leave it to Drew to make jokes at a time like this, but it totally works. Mom cracks a tiny smile and reaches for his hand. "Hardy-har. I'm serious, though. If I can't keep it together here, what does that say for us once we get out there?" She gestures in the direction of the ocean.

Drew catches my eye and widens his, in a plea for me to help.

Crap. He obviously knows I'm beyond upset about the divorce. We've both vented plenty to each other about it. He also knows I'm more upset with Mom than Dad. He's seen me act out around her, even if he doesn't understand the reasons behind it. But I've tried really hard to reign in the worst of my rage whenever he's around to bear witness—mostly by staying away from her altogether.

Being confined to just forty feet of boat doesn't allow for many avoidance tactics though, and he would *not* understand my refusing to help cheer her up now.

So I take a deep breath. Then I stroke my chin with my

hand comically and offer in the goofy "Australian commentator" accent my dad and I spent the last summer Olympics perfecting, "She's right, Roo. We're pretty much doomed. No doubt *Sunny-Side Up* is going sunny-side down before this trip is over. Looks like it's gonna be watery graves for all of us."

Drew grins and plays along. "I'll start drafting our wills. Does anyone have a bottle I can send them to shore in?"

"Fresh out of bottles," I say. "Al*though*, if you toss them over the port side, they'd stay perfectly dry. In fact, if you throw hard enough, you could probably reach a mailbox on the other side of that dune."

Mom picks her head up and looks between us. A tiny smile teases the corners of her mouth.

"You two are goofs."

She's right. We are. Inappropriate joking is another staple ingredient in the McClure Family recipe, even if we haven't exactly done a ton of it lately. If the divorce hadn't happened and Dad were on this boat with us, he'd probably be belting off-tune sea shanties right about now.

Before the thought has even fully formed in my head, Drew stands and tugs Mom up. He turns her in a circle as he sings in a horribly off-pitch voice:

What would I give, if I could live
Out of these waters?

Okay, so sea shanties, *Little Mermaid* soundtrack, same same. I have to give him credit for remembering the words, even if I did force him to listen to that song with me approximately four billion times when I was ten, after Mom and I went on a Girls Weekend to see a traveling production of the show in Portland.

In the last six months, Drew's grown a full head taller than both Mom and me, and although he's still "awkward teen boy" in his too-big feet, he's doing a pretty good job of breaking down my mother's defenses as he dances her around. Watching them starts a warmth fizzing in my chest, much as I'd like to pretend it doesn't.

I've missed this so much.

Missed us being us.

Drew finishes with a bellowed *"PART OF THAT WORRRRRRRRRRLD"* that sends a few seagulls into the air, and I swallow, wishing I could let go and be part of his and Mom's world right now. Wishing I could unknow everything I learned about my mother and just enjoy this silly moment with them.

Mom grins and straightens her shoulders. "Okay, I guess it's possible I'm completely overreacting. So what if I'm meeting the rest of our merry band of travelers after making the most ridiculous rookie mistake there is? Maybe it will ensure they don't attempt any techniques that are outside our depth." Her eyes twinkle. "Get it? Outside our depth? Little pun on this whole situation?"

It's such a quintessential Mom reaction—the one I expected when this whole thing first happened—that I can't stop from cracking a small smile, even though I'm groaning.

Mom steals a glance at me, but doesn't comment.

Beside me, Drew snorts. "Nice one."

Mom winks. "Still got it, kiddos." She brushes sand off her legs. "Okay, so we clearly can't abandon ship to go to a restaurant. Let's go radio a big, fat N-O RSVP to the group meal that was planned. Cass, time to try on your chef's hat."

Ah, yes. In exchange for not having to take on any sailing duties, I'm designated Spoon, which is some military term for the cook on a ship.

Drew's still humming Ariel's song to himself as he follows Mom down the stairs. I give a long last look at our boat, jauntily propped at a precipitous angle on a sandbar surrounded by water, and follow.

The downside to this development is that, if it only takes a few Mom tears to crack my defenses this much, what does that say for my hopes of surviving this trip with my righteous anger intact?

The upside to this development is that, as firmly as we're wedged into the sand, at least there's no chance of getting seasick down below.

6

"Mama says you either encountered a redhead before departing or you have bananas on board, because it's the only way to explain luck like this on the very first day!" A small girl of maybe eight or nine, with white-blond hair straight out of a Nordic tale, swings a leg over the back of the boat and slides into our cockpit like she's been executing this exact move her whole life.

My eyebrows go up, but before I can think of a suitable response, a woman's laughing, wind-burned face appears behind her. "Sorry about Abigail. She's nine-tenths precocious and one-tenth egomaniacal. Doesn't always make for the best first impression."

The girl tilts her head and squints. "What's egomaniacal, Mama?"

The woman, who has only slightly darker blond hair than her daughter, climbs aboard. She squeezes Abigail's shoulder and answers, "It's another word for utterly lovable, my kitten."

Her smile stays in place as she holds out her hand to me. "Hi there. I'm Amy, and you must be Cassandra."

"Cassie," I reply, shaking her hand. The palm she slides into mine is covered in calluses, and her grip is firm. I guess living full-time on a sailboat means never having to ask for help loosening the lid on a jar of tomato sauce.

When we radioed the others to explain why we couldn't make our meet-up, it was somehow decided that the party would come to us instead. I'm wondering how it's going to be possible to fit five more people into our cabin for dinner, but also really curious about the group we'll be spending every day of the next four months with. So far, so good. Amy seems completely normal and friendly.

"Cassie it is, then," she says. "My wife and our other daughter, Grace, are catching a ride with Christian, the third boat owner. He won them over with his Zodiac, which is far fancier than *Liki Tiki* down there."

She gestures with a grin to their dinghy, tied up alongside the one we're towing behind our boat. I don't know what qualifies one as being any better than another—after all, they're not much bigger than a kayak and are basically glorified inflatable rafts with sides and small outboard engines, as far as I can tell—but I also don't want to reveal my ignorance of all things nautical just yet, so I settle for a nod and a smile.

She leans closer, darting a glance to make sure Abigail isn't paying attention, and stage-whispers, "Between you and me, if I were ten years older and straight, Christian could give me a ride on his Zodiac anytime, if you know what I mean."

Um, I *do* know what she means, but I'm not exactly used to adults (especially ones I've known for two-point-three seconds) talking to me so casually on the topic of sex, and the best I can manage is a cough and another nod.

Amy's grin gets wider. "Oh, now I've embarrassed you. Miranda—that's my wife—would kill me. I'm seriously the worst. No filter. She's convinced our kids are going to spend all their future earnings on therapy sessions. Between my big mouth and them growing up out here . . ." She passes a hand vaguely through the air in the direction of the sea, then turns and calls, "Abigail, did you leave the salad in *Tiki*?"

Abigail scrambles over the side and drops out of sight. By now, my mom and Drew are climbing the steps up from the cabin, and Mom's smile of greeting is huge. My mother considers every stranger a friend she just hasn't met yet. Reference: brief political aspirations. I'm only about 30 percent her and the other 70 percent my dad, who far prefers to meet new people inside the pages of books.

While they introduce themselves, Abigail passes up a bowl covered in plastic wrap and hops inside the cockpit again. Immediately she moves to where Drew took the tail end of a rope that extended off one of the sails and wrapped it around a cleat using some weird crazy-eight pattern. Wordlessly, she begins unwinding and expertly retying it; the whole process takes her about six seconds.

"You did this backward," she states.

Drew gets a pucker between his eyebrows and leans in closer. "Really? But it matched the picture on my iPad perfectly."

"Backward." She lifts her chin, daring him to argue, before saying, "I can fix the rest of them if you want."

"Show me," orders Drew, and the two of them take off for the bow, my brother looking like a giant next to the tiny girl. Abigail scrambles along the narrow deck like a sea monkey and I grimace, remembering the full five minutes of clutching at railings it took me to maneuver the same path. Granted, we were rocking some waves at the time, but still.

"So what was that your daughter said about redheads and bananas? I could only hear a snippet from down below," Mom is saying to Amy as I move closer to them.

"Old sailors' superstitions. It's supposed to be bad luck to encounter a redhead before boarding. Except if you speak to them first it negates everything."

My mother's eyebrows rise and her lips twitch in amusement as she asks, "And the bananas?"

Amy smiles too. "There may have actually been something to that. Most of the ships that disappeared at the height of the trading empire between Spain and the Caribbean were carrying a cargo of bananas. There are some rationales for that, though. One is that ships with bananas tried to make faster time so the fruit wouldn't rot before landing. Another theory suggests that the heat where they were stored caused the bananas to produce toxic fumes. Or that a species of deadly spiders caught a ride in the bunches and bit sailors during the journey."

I shudder as Mom and Amy share a laugh.

"But I'm sure there's nothing to those bad omens besides silly superstition." Amy bites her lip and peeks comically over the rail of *Sunny-Side Up*, whose name would be more apt at the moment if it were *Belly Up*.

Mom laughs again. "Either way, we'll be tossing our bananas at the next port of call."

"Meh. Welcome to a life at sea. Nonstop adventure," Amy says. "Seriously, don't worry about the grounding. The sandbars in this river are notorious for their constant shifting, so it's next to impossible to chart them. Trust me, it could happen to the best of us."

Mom makes a face. "I think you're being too kind, but let me assure you I am far from 'the best of us.' I'm counting on you guys to help guide us down to Mexico in one piece."

"Challenge accepted," replies Amy, shading her eyes with her hand and peering over Mom's shoulder. "Oh! I see the rest of our crew coming!"

A few minutes later, three more people climb aboard and the cockpit becomes standing room only. Amy's wife, Miranda, turns out to be another blond, tanned bubbly type. With her is Abigail's little sister, Grace, an adorable girl with Asian features who looks about four and who refuses to unwind her arms from Miranda's legs.

The last to board is Christian. The first thing I notice is

that his irises are the color of the forget-me-nots I planted this spring—jarring in contrast with his sunbaked skin and hair as black as a newly paved road. I can see what Amy meant about his, er, Zodiac. He's pretty easy on the eyes, even for a guy who must be in his fifties, at least.

"Where's Beatriz?" Abigail demands of him.

"Ah. Well. I had to leave her on the yacht. I was worried it would be too crowded."

"Is Beatriz your wife?" I ask, confused.

"Beatriz is my golden retriever," Christian replies with a smile, before addressing an indignant Abigail. "My deckhand, Tommy, agreed to stay behind to keep her company and he's promised her a long game of Frisbee this evening."

He turns to me again and holds out his hand. "*Buenas tardes*, lovely Cassandra. In Venezuela you would have all the boys trailing after you."

I hate that my cheeks go hot, but I compensate by smiling nonchalantly and offering a confident "Nice to meet you, sir," which makes him smile.

"I come bearing gifts," he says, reaching into the large canvas bag he carried aboard and pulling out something tall and conical, wrapped in green tissue paper. He gestures that I should take it by the base, and I raise surprised eyebrows at my mother, who shrugs.

I gently peel away the paper and gasp at the perfect bonsai tree I'm holding.

Seeing my dazed expression, Christian laughs. "Your mother mentioned how much you love to garden. It's not so possible on a ship, but perhaps with this . . ."

He trails off as I examine each delicate branch of the miniature tree. It's planted in a small green pot covered in lighter green polka dots. It's like he's been inside my brain—I love polka dots. On the bottom, a giant suction cup is affixed to the ceramic.

As I run my fingers over it, Christian says, "Ah! So you can stick it in place on your table and the turbulence of the sea won't send it crashing to the floor. There are instructions and scissors for grooming it."

"Thank you so much. It's amazing." I give him a smile before returning to my every-angle examination of the little treasure in my hands.

It's basically the perfect gift.

But wait.

He said my mother told him about my gardening? I mean, I assumed Mom had been coordinating details of the trip with Christian, Amy, and Miranda, but I didn't realize they were trading personal information too. What else has she told him? Were the polka dots maybe not such a coincidence? I suddenly wonder if Mom's oversharing about the details of our lives included mention of her newly single status.

She steps behind me and puts a hand on my shoulder, addressing Christian. "This is so nice, but you really didn't need to bring any gifts—"

He interrupts her with, "I derive such pleasure from it though. I wasn't always in a position to be generous with others, so please indulge me."

I swear I feel Mom's knees buckle when he adds a help-less shrug to his killer grin. I jerk my shoulder from her grasp and step aside. She glances at me in confusion, then returns her attention to him, saying, "Well, that's really sweet of you. Thanks. I guess we should get dinner going, huh?"

If things were cramped above, they're even worse below. The table occupies most of the cabin. With the sides folded down, there are narrow alleys between it and its cushioned benches, allowing someone to pass through to where Mom's berth is built into the V-shaped bow. Opened up, it completely fills the space.

To the immediate left at the bottom of the steps is a tiny kitchen. Obviously there's a sink. There's also an oven, barely wide enough for one brownie pan, framed by two upper and two lower cabinets—except behind one of the bottom doors is actually a dorm-sized refrigerator. Which is just fine for a dorm because there's, you know, an entire dining hall to back it up. But for three people who each use a different type of milk on our cereal? Not so much. And then, of course, we all know where the freezer is. . . .

To the right of the steps is a small built-in desk and "navi-gation center." The VHF marine radio is there, along with a whole wall of buttons that make zero sense to me, even when I read the labels below them. They go far beyond the scope of what our safety class covered and into "serious sailor" territory. Two words that will never apply to me.

My bunk and the only bathroom are both underneath

the cockpit, at the stern of the boat.

The whole tour takes all of five seconds; one 360-degree turn and you've seen the entire place.

Christian drags his bag down with him and produces *Star Wars*–themed Monopoly for Drew, claiming to be a bigger fanboy than my brother, though I wonder if that's possible. He also has coloring books and fancy markers for Abigail and Grace, and Mom sends the girls into her bunk to play with them while the rest of us set up our potluck meal.

Our previous plan was to meet at a restaurant in the town of Florence, to take advantage of dining-out options that won't be available to us for whole chunks of this trip. Instead, everyone brought what they had on hand.

Amy and Miranda produce a giant salad with chicken, and Christian provides fresh loaves of bread and a couple of bottles of wine the adults *ooh* and *aah* over, so I guess maybe they're decent.

We stocked up on groceries before leaving port this morning, but that's a relative term when you factor in the limited amount of storage space we have on board; what we'll eat at sea will consist primarily of canned goods. The best we can come up with as dessert for a group this size is a package of Double Stuf Oreos. No one seems to mind, which gives me the impression that boat meals are held to lesser standards.

All the adults are laughing, pouring wine, and turning this into a party atmosphere as they set the table. I can't help but be annoyed when I see my mother toasting with them.

Any thawing I felt toward her earlier flies out the hatches as she smiles up into Christian's face when they clink glasses.

Why should she get to have fun and do whatever she wants when I have so little say in making my own happiness? When *she's* the one to blame for upending our lives. I'll bet my dad's not having nearly as much fun tonight, grading papers in a lonely Hong Kong apartment, half a world away from his family.

I'm oddly grateful to have the sour taste back in my mouth; its familiarity over the last year has made it almost a comfort, and I need the reminder to stand my ground. Even when there's not much ground around (present circumstances excepted).

I can't let her unhinge me out here. I won't.

"We have a tradition whenever we start a new leg of our trip," Amy says, once most of us are squeezed thigh-to-thigh around the table. Abigail and Grace are cross-legged on the floor in front of the stairs and Drew opted to stretch his long legs under the navigation desk. "Do you guys know those six-word novels?" she asks.

Christian nods, while Mom, Drew, and I shake our heads.

"Okay, so I'm not sure if this is true or not, but the story goes that over lunch one day, Hemingway bet a group of his writer friends ten bucks he could craft an entire story in six words," Miranda says, picking up for Amy. "Obviously they all took the bet, figuring it was impossible. Then he writes on a paper napkin *For sale: baby shoes, never worn.* They all paid up."

I mull the sentence. "That's so sad."

"Exactly! But you get a whole narrative right in those six words, don't you?" Amy asks.

I nod.

"Why didn't the baby wear the shoes, Mama?" Abigail asks. Miranda shakes her head at Amy, who'd opened her mouth to answer.

"Uh, maybe she took a really long time learning to walk and by the time she needed shoes, she'd outgrown that pair," Drew suggests, and Abigail thinks this over for a second before nodding, satisfied.

Miranda and I both give Drew a smile. Hers is grateful; mine is proud.

"Obviously, we don't want anything as morbid as that example, so the challenge before you is to come up with six words that encapsulate either why you're here or what your hopes are for the trip we have ahead of us. Whoever's ready first can go." Amy sits back, looking very pleased with herself.

There's a hush around the table as we formulate sentences, but it isn't long before Christian starts us off. *"Worked hard, cashed in, relaxation awaits."*

Mom, Amy, and Miranda applaud.

"Hear, hear," Mom says. "I'll go next!" She smiles softly at me, and then at Drew, before saying, *"Trying hard to rebuild and renew."*

The sour taste slides into my throat when Miranda reaches over and squeezes Mom's hand. Do they *all* know *everything* about us? It's one thing to fill strangers in on my love of plants, but bringing them into our personal stuff before we've even met them? Not cool. I avoid eye contact and stab a piece of chicken.

Abigail pops up from the floor. "I have one! Can I play?"

Miranda smiles. "Of course, honey. Whatcha got?"

Abigail waits for everyone to turn to her. When she's satisfied she has the stage, she says, *"Gonna see the whole wide world!"*

She laps up our praise and applause before declaring, "Now Gracie has to go."

Grace looks like she'd rather run upstairs and dive overboard, but she manages to squeak out, "I just want to see a real live mermaid."

"That was nine words!" Abigail accuses, ticking each off on her fingers to confirm.

Miranda says, "Your sister just needs to work on her counting, the same way you did when you were four. Maybe you could help her. And, Grace, I think that's an excellent goal. I'll help you look for one."

Grace smiles and goes right back to ignoring her dinner in favor of coloring. Abigail murmurs sulkily, "I wanna see a mermaid too," but soon returns to her picture, too.

Amy rolls her eyes as if to say "Kids!" but aloud she voices, "Okay, I've got mine: *Challenge accepted: go big or surrender.*"

Miranda adds a "Hells, yeah!" and there's laughter in response.

Drew is next, and his is: "*Surf, sand, sun: living the life.*"

So very Drew-like.

All eyes turn to me, next in line. Other than Mom's, they've all been adventure-y and cheerful, but I can't get there. I just . . . don't feel that way about this whole thing. I stare at my hands in my lap. "*Four more months until I'm home.*"

I steal a glance at Mom in time to see her lips purse tight. I don't know what she expected from me. I can't fake enthusiasm for this trip and I don't think she should force me to.

"Poor Cassie had a bad bout of seasickness today," Mom says.

"That's merely the cherry on top," I snap.

If she's going to fill them in on our personal lives, let's not hold back. I don't need her making excuses for me. I know I'm being rude in front of company, which must drive Mom crazy because she drilled manners into us from the second we could keep a napkin in place on our laps. And, okay, maybe I'm not acting terribly mature.

But.

I know Mom hopes I'll simply get over it now that our trip is under way, but she needs to know you can't just kidnap someone from their *life*, force them onto a sailboat for months, and expect them to be upbeat and *polite* about it. You just can't.

It's tense and quiet for a few beats, until Miranda clears her throat and jumps into the sudden silence with, "Okay, I guess I'm last, then. Here's mine: *Adventure awaits on the seven seas.*"

"Are you guys really going to sail all seven seas?" Drew asks.

Mom is still stealing glances at me with narrowed eyes.

"That is the plan, my friend," Miranda says, sharing an excited smile with Amy. "We've been bopping around the Pacific Northwest for the past eighteen months or so, getting used to life aboard, learning to do our own repairs, and making sure we're fully prepared for an ocean crossing. Now it's time for the big go-round."

She grins at her wife, who picks up right where Miranda left off. I kind of love how they do that.

"This is the big one, all right," Amy says. "From Mexico to the Panama Canal, then across the Atlantic to England, down the western coast of Europe, through the Strait of Gibraltar, and along the top of Africa to the Indian Ocean. From there we'll skirt the bottom of Asia before heading south to Australia." She pauses to catch her breath before adding, "And finally, we'll cross the Pacific to South America and head up here again."

"Whoa," Drew breathes. "How long will all that take?"

"We figure maybe three years. There are entire seasons we have to plan around—hurricane months in the Atlantic and such. But we're in no hurry. There's really no final destination because, once we get all the way around, we'll probably just do it again. This is our life for the foreseeable future."

Everyone is awed for a moment, thinking about the scope of their plans, when my phone finally buzzes with the text

I've been waiting for. I peek into my lap to check it, smile to myself, then take a deep breath.

"Hey, Mom? I texted Tara and Jess earlier about how we got stuck right outside of Florence, and guess what? They drove over to hang out for one last night! Can I take the dinghy and follow everyone back to the town dock?"

My mother's brow furrows. "I don't understand. They drove *here*? Why would they do that?"

I shrug. "I guess to see me again before I disappear from their lives for four months? You *know* how devastated we are about being apart for the rest of summer and the start of school and all."

The others at the table become very preoccupied with rearranging forks and knives around their empty plates, until Mom, in an obvious attempt to deflect attention, begins gathering the dirty dishes to her. Too bad she's trapped on the opposite side of the table from the kitchen sink.

Her voice is we-have-company fake as she asks, "What exactly did you think you were going to do in Florence with them?"

"Tara said there's a cute downtown. We'll probably walk around and grab some coffee or dessert at one of the restaurants. We just want a chance to hang out together."

"I'm sorry they came all this way, Cassie, but you're not leaving this boat. For one thing, you don't know how to start the outboard engine on the dinghy, which you've never even sat in. And how would you propose maneuvering it back up an unfamiliar river in the dark?"

"But they drove all the way here already! What am I supposed to tell them?"

Miranda slides off the bench and settles next to Grace on the floor, prodding her to finish her salad. Christian pulls out his own phone and buries his face in it. For her part, Amy leans back and throws an arm across Miranda's empty seat, clearly enjoying the show.

Mom is obviously embarrassed. "I can't believe you would pull this, Cass. I really can't."

I glare back. "*I* can't believe you won't let me see my friends when they're driving three hours round trip just to hang out with me. It's bad enough you're forcing me to spend the next four months away from them."

She isn't backing down. "It's nice that they wanted to surprise you, but they should have asked you first so you could have discussed it with me. Then we would have avoided all of this."

Yeah, well. Let's just say it wasn't *totally* a surprise to me. It might have even been my idea to begin with.

"They knew it would make me happy. That's what people who care about each other do—consider the happiness of their loved ones."

Mom sucks in a breath just as Christian clears his throat. "I don't wish to intrude here, but if it would be helpful, I would be pleased to offer Cassandra a ride to the dock, and then either I or my deckhand could return her when she's through in town. We both keep late hours, so it would be no trouble at all."

I grin triumphantly. "See, Mom? Perfect solution."

Mom flutters her hands helplessly before pasting on a smile and turning to Christian.

"That's a really lovely offer. I know it would mean a lot to Cassie to have one more night with her friends. She's a little less, er, enthusiastic about this trip than the rest of us, as you might have guessed by now. If you're sure you wouldn't mind?"

"My pleasure," he responds, closing his eyes briefly as he inclines his head.

Mom's smile grows in return. "Thank you," she answers, blushing slightly.

I'm going to have to keep tabs on *that* situation, but for now . . . freedom! Before she can reconsider, I rush into my berth to change for my stolen night out.

7

"**This is not** real life!" My laughter is breathless as I watch a second dolphin join the first in leaping through the wake our boat is creating. We're free of the sandbar and back in the ocean . . . and the universe is *not* playing fair.

I'm trying really hard to hold my ground—and last night's argument with Mom helped tremendously, as did having to say good-bye to my best friends all over again. But how am I supposed to harden my black, shriveled heart against all things boat-trip-related when there are adorable sea creatures, with their playful jumping and their smiley faces and their silky-looking skin. It's impossible—*impossible*—to be cranky when freaking *dolphins* are cavorting alongside your boat.

"There's another one!" Drew points to his left and I see it too. And a fourth! Four dolphins are crisscrossing behind our boat. I lean as far over the side as I dare, so I can watch.

"Can you believe this?" I ask, inhaling deeply. Thanks to the motion sickness bands Amy dropped off this morning when we met up with them at the river's mouth, my breaths are full from wonder and not from trying to keep my stomach contents in their proper compartments.

"Most sailors encounter pods at some point in their travels," Mom replies. "But it *is* pretty amazing we're experiencing it on day two of our trip."

I don't want to look away for even a second, but I really want my phone right now, so I can get this on video. No one will believe me otherwise.

"Grab the binoculars too," Drew says when I tell him where I'm headed. I slide across the sea-sprayed deck as quickly as possible to retrieve both and race back.

"I think I see more over there." Drew points a few hundred yards off our stern, where *Tide Drifter*, Amy's and Miranda's boat, has its bright red sails pulled tight.

"Here, check this out." Drew passes me the binoculars. "Does it look like there are people in their dinghy?"

I squint hard at the tiny boat being pulled behind the bigger one. "Yeah . . . yes! Definitely!" I shift the lenses. "Okay, someone's on the platform at the back, and there's another person up by the mast. Both look tallish. Do you think the girls are in the dinghy?"

"I'd guess they wanted to get closer to the dolphins," Mom says.

I lower the binoculars in time to catch Drew's smile. We stare at each other for a beat before we both exclaim, "*I* want to be closer to the dolphins!"

"Jinx, you owe me a Coke," Drew says.

I punch his arm and he fake falls against the railing like he's in a boxing ring.

"Hey!" Mom yelps. "I don't need one of you going overboard."

"Unless it's in a dinghy, right? We can do that, can't we?" I ask, even though I hate to have her thinking she has the power to grant me any favors.

Mom looks between us and bites her lip before casting another glance down at the dolphins. "I—"

"Pleeeeeaassse." Apparently I have no shame where dolphins are concerned. "Who knows how long they'll hang out, and what if this chance never comes again? Grace and Abigail are doing it and they're, like, one-fourth our ages."

My mother glances at *Tide Drifter*. "I guess. But you do know you're going to freeze out there, right?"

Coastal Oregon summers are more like New England winters. We're currently bundled in about ten layers each and I'm still fantasizing about hot soup for dinner.

"Who cares!" Drew says. He's right. What's a little frostbite when weighed against dolphin encounters?

We lock eyes again before grabbing each other's arms and squealing. Then we scramble down to the platform.

It takes all three of us to haul in *Minecraft*, so christened by Drew when Mom refused to let him temporarily paint over *Sunny-Side Up*'s italic lettering. She insists on triple-checking our life jackets and makes us repeat back the procedure for starting the outboard engine, in case we're not able to pull ourselves along the attached rope to get back to the platform when we've had enough.

When it's my turn to climb in, I hesitate for a moment. We're going fairly fast right now, and I'm about to step off a relatively stable platform into something tiny, wobbly, and more or less inflatable, no matter how sturdy the rubber sides feel.

Am I crazy?

But . . . *dolphins*.

Right next to us.

One surfaces so close I can hear the puff of air through its blowhole and I'm sold. I grab Drew's hand and let him pull me aboard.

When we both make "okay" signs with our fingers, Mom nods and pushes us off. We jerk backward across the wake until all the slack is out of the rope. It's like tubing, but better because . . . *dolphins*!

I push up the sleeves on my many layers and dip my hand just beneath the surface of the frigid water, fantasizing that one will come nose it with its snout. That doesn't happen, but two appear just to our right, er, starboard side, and crest the surface mere feet from us. I clasp Drew's arm. "Holy crap!"

"Damn straight," he agrees, in a tone every bit as awed as mine. We both giggle like hyenas.

Even after our new friends abandon us for a different watery playground, we stay out for another forty-five minutes, straining to see any last glimpses of them and then just relaxing and enjoying the different perspective. As expected, it *is* ridiculously cold—I'd put the temperature in the fifties, and factoring in the wind and the frequent spray from the freezing water, well, let's just say I won't be breaking out my bikini any time soon. Eventually, and with some help from Mom, we pull our dinghy back in.

"I got some great shots of you with the dolphins," Mom says. "I'm thinking we have this year's Christmas card all sewn up."

As I brush past her, she settles her hand on my shoulder and I freeze.

"I know I've been upset with you over the whole thing with Tara and Jess yesterday, but I'm really happy you were enjoying yourself out there. It's nice to get a glimpse of this side of you again."

I nod once, then move away.

That may have been an incredible, once-in-a-lifetime experience and, okay, I can be big enough to admit it wouldn't have happened if she hadn't forced this trip on us, but let's not get carried away with the mother-daughter bonding here. It doesn't change the fact that a whole lot of *other* things wouldn't have happened—like our entire family falling apart—if not for her either.

8

"**The problem is,** Dad, a critical competent to reaching Mexico is to actually set sail in a southerly direction."

My father's eyes crinkle in the corners, the way they always do when he's amused, and I get a sharp pang in my chest over how accustomed I'm getting to only seeing his face on my computer screen.

"Where are you now?" he asks.

"Same place as yesterday, which is the same place as the day before. We had two days of sailing and then got totally stuck in Middle of Nowheresville, Oregon. We're 'weathered in,' meaning we have to wait for the winds to pick up enough for our run down the coast to the next stop."

Without the proper winds, we go nowhere. Yes, technically speaking, we could motor, but gasoline is costly. Our boat's owners are covering our expenses, but Amy and Miranda's budget is truly bare-bones, and Christian maintains, "If I wanted to motor there, I'd have bought a speedboat."

"You've been in the same cove for *four* days?" Dad asks.

I make a face. The wonder of our dolphin adventure has long since worn off, and I'm almost grateful the actual experience of this trip has gone back to mirroring my nightmares about it. It's definitely helping me keep my defenses up.

"Yep," I answer. "Apparently this is the main reason it takes months to sail somewhere you could reach by car in thirty-six hours."

"About that. I still don't understand why the owners couldn't have had their boat driven down on a trailer. Wouldn't that have cost a whole lot less?"

"Oh, believe me, I even volunteered to play chauffeur. But it turns out it's crazy expensive and a huge hassle. Oversized loads can only use certain roads at special times of the day, there are all kinds of permits, the mast has to be removed . . . and a bunch of other stuff."

"Got it." Dad shakes his head sympathetically.

"Being stuck in Oregon would actually be *fine* if Mom would let me see Tara and Jess again, but no."

Now Dad's eyes crinkle in a very different way and lines appear on his forehead. "Yeah, well, she filled me in on your little rebellion the other night. Not cool, Cass."

"What do you mean she filled you in?" I ask.

"She emailed me. That surprises you?"

I roll my eyes. "Uh, *yeah*. Considering you're divorced now."

Dad winces nearly imperceptibly, but I see it. And now I

feel terrible. It's not like he asked for my mom to cheat on him.

"Sorry," I mumble.

"Look, things aren't perfect between your mom and me right now. . . ." His voice has an edge to it, and he huffs out an annoyed breath before continuing. "But we're ex-spouses, not ex-parents. Obviously she's going to keep me filled in on anything related to you guys, just like she's been doing all along and just like I'm sure *you know* she has. Causing a scene in front of a group of people you'd just met for the first time? C'mon, Cass. That's not my girl."

I swallow over the lump in my throat. "Mom's exaggerating."

"Cassandra . . ." His voice holds a warning I'm all too familiar with. I'm about to get his famous "Don't sweet talk a sweet talker" lecture, the same one I used to get when I'd try to convince him I hadn't snuck any of my Halloween candy up to my room, despite the crumpled wrappers peeking out from under my bed.

Maybe I could've handled things differently the other night. I might not care as much these days about upsetting my mom, but my father doesn't deserve it. It's bad enough he felt he had to move to the other side of the world to escape the situation. And when his visiting professorship ends next year, he'll probably have to sign a lease at one of those sad single-dad apartments by the highway. When *he* did nothing wrong. When none of us did anything wrong, except the one person who gets to live exactly as she pleases and do exactly what she wants. How is that the least bit fair?

"I think I've been unbelievably patient about your acting out these last few months," he says, "but it's time to man up, young lady."

"Dad, that's super sexist. Why doesn't anyone ever say 'woman up'? We're tougher than guys about most things anyway."

"Fair point. Consider your old man schooled. Only I wish *you'd* stop being so tough and maybe realize you're bringing a lot of this on yourself, sweets. Look, I understand the divorce threw you for a loop, and you have a right to be upset. But maybe if you'd stop fighting your mom tooth and nail, your life would get easier, you know?"

"I'd still be stuck on this boat though, wouldn't I? So, no. My life wouldn't be easier. At all." I swipe at a few bitter tears in the corners of my eyes.

"I appreciate that you feel that way, but what would happen if you gave this whole sailing thing a chance? It wouldn't have been my first choice for you guys either—and you know very well that I said as much to your mother—but you're there now, so . . ."

I will *not* give it a chance. I *hate* chance.

Chance is like the good news first or the bad news first question. Chance is the card in Monopoly that might be *Advance to Go, Collect $200*, but could just as easily be *Go Directly to Jail*. Chance is not steady and normal and predictable and routine and all the other things my life quite happily was BD.

And Dad is supposed to be on my side here. We share a common enemy, after all. I'm annoyed that he's even suggesting I go along with her whole agenda.

I shake my head. "*You'd* still be over there. I'd still be missing the start of my senior year, and strangers would still be living in our house, and—"

Dad cuts me off with his palm to the camera. "Point taken. I wish like hell you didn't have to deal with any of this. I know it's a lot to ask of any kid."

I want to bark at him that I'm *not* a kid, that I'll be eighteen in a few months, that I'm graduating high school soon! Only, the truth is, I actually do feel like a child these days. Like everything is happening *to* me and not *because* of me or *with* me and doesn't even require my input in the least. It sucks big-time.

"Okay, let's try another angle here," he says after I'm quiet for a stretch. "How about your favorite professor gives you a little homework assignment?"

I raise my eyes to his with an expression of doubt, to which he replies, "Humor me, okay? It's my job to assign homework, and at the end of every semester, my students always agree it helped them learn. Or at least I think they do; I try not to read my evaluations because all that entitled whining throws me off my game."

I fight a grin, and Dad catches it and winks before continuing. "Every day you get to email me one picture of something truly terrible or annoying about the trip. Sound doable?"

Sounds like the easiest assignment ever.

Until he adds, "*But*, you also have to send me one picture per day of something pretty great. Think you can handle that?"

I shrug with as little enthusiasm as I can muster. Odds are we won't be escorted by dolphins the whole way to Mexico, and I haven't seen much else these past few days to get shutter-happy over.

"Lassie?" he prods. Damn. He pulled out the big guns. His special nickname for me.

I sigh. "Fine. I guess. The terrible one will be a cinch. Although, lucky for you, no picture could capture the particularly rank scent of a poop tank in desperate need of emptying."

"Poop tank?" my dad asks, and I'm glad he's every bit as clueless about sailing as I am. It's just one more thing that bonds us.

I wrinkle my nose. "Yeah, well, it turns out when you, uh, *do your business* on a boat, it doesn't just flush out into the ocean, because that's illegal. It all gets stored in a holding tank and you have to find something called a pumping station at a marina to empty it."

"Wait, wait, wait! So you have your own Cousin Eddie scenario going on right now?" Dad's whole face lights up with glee, and I grin.

He's referring to a scene from *Christmas Vacation*. Since I turned ten, Mom, Dad, and I have watched that movie every December, snuggled under the sick-day blanket, this crocheted afghan my grandmother made that we all swear has secret healing powers woven into the ugly avocado-green yarn. When Drew reached double digits, he joined in the tradition.

I try not to let my smile fade as the realization hits that we won't be watching Randy Quaid empty the RV's sewage into the Griswolds' storm drain together this year. I mean, I guess I can watch it with Dad at whatever hotel he'll be staying in when he comes home for his semester break, but that just sounds sad.

He clears his throat and my attention returns to the screen.

"Yeah, somehow it's not as funny in real life," I say. "Between the gasoline smell when we run the generator to cook or charge our laptops, and the scent coming off that tank, I'm about to send away for some of that stuff that medical examiners put under their noses when they do autopsies. And maybe you could have 'the talk' again with Drew, about puberty and the body odors that accompany it? At home it was easy enough to steer clear of his bedroom, but when his 'room' is the same cabin we all have to live and eat in . . ."

I wrinkle my nose once again.

"Hey! I heard that!" Drew calls from the other side of my closed door.

"Drew, leave Cassie alone to talk to Dad." Even though my mother's speaking at her normal volume, I can hear her as clearly as if she were right next to me. I suck in a breath.

There is no such thing as privacy on this stupid boat! I'm suddenly embarrassed about opening up to Dad. I didn't stop to consider I'd have an audience.

"Dad, I should hang up. Certain *people* just can't help being nosy." I speak loudly for my mother's benefit, but it's not like I even need to raise my voice. This boat is the *worst*.

"Pictures. Two a day. I'll be expecting them in my in-box."

"Yeah, yeah."

"And, Lassie? New mantra to inform all decisions going forward: ask yourself first, 'Would my dad want me doing this?' Answer yes to eating raw cookie dough from the package but no to making anyone who gave birth to you walk the plank. Got it?"

I roll my eyes at him.

His voice grows serious. "I was trying to give you a little space to work things out on your own, but my leniency stops now. This is your opportunity to get yourself under control, and I expect that to happen. We clear?"

I grimace but nod, and his face relaxes.

"Good. Love you, baby girl."

"Love you too, Daddy."

I sign off Skype and wish for the millionth time that he were here. If he was and this were last year, before everything went down, this trip might almost feel like an adventure. Even though we'd have a whole other body taking up space, his Dad-ness would make the quarters feel more cozy than cramped, I just know it.

The very last thing I want to do now is face my mother, so I turn my attention to Instagram. Tara's posted pictures of

Omar Abergel's pool party, and I spend way too much time poring over them, trying to keep completely in the loop despite my physical absence. Tara, Jess, and I did a whole preparty lead-up text session yesterday. I'm about to group-message them to find out how the blue streaks in Jess's hair went over when a primal yell from outside sounds across the water, followed by the noise of a motor roaring to life.

Garbled screamed words follow, and as I run from my room to investigate, I practically crash into Mom and Drew. We all jockey for position on the steps. When we get above deck, it's just in time to see Christian dive off his boat, anchored about a hundred feet from ours. He swims at a furious pace across the inlet, but if he's trying to chase down the dinghy that's tearing toward the open water at top speed, he'll need Aquaman's fins for that. A few strokes later, he stops and treads water, shouting Spanish words into the sky that I'm guessing are *not* PG-rated. Drew's probably taking notes to add to his arsenal.

"Christian? What's going on?" my mother calls to him. He glances over at us, seeming to suddenly remember his surroundings.

"I am so sorry. I—I just—" He gestures helplessly at the faraway Zodiac before paddling over and swinging a leg onto our platform, easily pulling himself from the water in one fluid motion. My mother's jaw drops open as he stands bare-chested and dripping water like some romance-novel cover model. I give her a sharp look and she snaps her mouth shut, then opens it again to ask, "What's going on?"

Drew tosses him a towel that was draped over our side rails, and Christian dries himself off, all the while staring darkly into the distance, where the dinghy disappears around a bend.

"I believe I have been both robbed and deserted."

9

"So your deckhand took your watch and a wad of bills and peeled off in the getaway, er, dinghy?" Drew asks.

"And a few bottles of very, *very* expensive wine I was saving for the right occasion," Christian adds.

"Should we try to go after him?" Mom asks.

Christian ventures a dubious look at *Minecraft*. Next to his sleek Zodiac, custom-outfitted with a high-powered engine, we might as well have Huck Finn's log raft tied up behind us.

I follow his gaze. "In your yacht, then?"

Christian looks confused and Mom fills in quietly, "Something as small as the Zodiac, with such a powerful motor, could be miles away before we even got the anchor raised on any of our boats."

Oh. Well, I never pretended to know the first thing about this sailing stuff, so . . .

Mom turns back to Christian. "What if we radioed the authorities?"

"He'll be long gone before anyone could even take a report. It's likely he has an accomplice waiting for him. He's been on his phone quite a bit over the last few days, but always out of earshot, and always hanging up any time he spotted me. I should have suspected something like this."

Out of earshot. What would that be like? Christian's yacht must be at least double the size of ours. I guess that kind of square footage buys you privacy alongside floor-to-ceiling closets and a freezer housed in the actual cooking space, where kitchen appliances rightly belong.

Tommy seemed nice enough when he and Christian gave me a ride back to *Sunny-Side Up* the night Tara, Jess, and I explored Florence. Guess you never can tell.

Drew stares at the spot on the horizon where the Zodiac was last visible. "Wow. We've been living next door to an actual pirate and I barely even got to know him."

"Next door?" I raise an eyebrow and Drew slugs my arm.

"You know what I mean."

"Drew, I hardly think this situation needs romanticizing," Mom warns.

Christian pulls the towel tighter around his shoulders. "I should have trusted my intuition about him. He knew far less about sailing than he claimed to in our email exchanges before the trip."

"I really am so sorry," Mom repeats. Her hand hovers over his shoulder before she reconsiders and withdraws it. "Can I get you anything? Do anything?"

I cut her a dark look. What does she have in mind exactly? Mom squints at me, puzzled, and I relax. Her thoughts don't seem to be in the gutter with mine.

"You are very kind, but no. Luckily, he didn't touch the safe in my bunk, and I have cash in reserve there. The rest are only *things* I've lost, and items are easily replaced. My trust, on the other hand . . ." He hands the towel back to Drew. "Thank you for your kindness. I'd better go fill Amy and Miranda in on the situation, as this changes things a bit for all of us."

Changes things?

Mom says, "Amy radioed earlier to say they were taking the girls to build a fairy garden in the woods."

Christian's lips turn up in the corners. "So sweet."

"Um, excuse me, you said this changes things?" I can't help asking.

He turns to me with a rueful smile. "I'm afraid I can't handle a yacht the size of *Reality Bytes* on my own. But I will try to procure a new deckhand right away."

The words vibrate through my head as I grasp their meaning.

"Does that mean we're . . ." I can't even speak the next part out loud.

"Stranded here even longer?" Christian apparently can. "I'm terribly sorry, but I'm afraid so, *plantita*."

He's taken to calling me "little plant" after my obvious enthusiasm for my bonsai tree, but no silly nickname can redeem this situation. Snatching the towel from Mom's hand,

I run below before balling it up and stuffing it against my mouth. It only partly muffles my scream.

I never considered how much about living on a sailboat would be basic survival stuff.

Aside from being completely at the whim of the weather, our space is so limited we can only store enough fresh food to feed three people for a couple of days. So if we don't want to be stuck eating canned tomatoes and soup for *every* meal, we need to stick near to land. And not just any land, but close enough to a town to make grocery shopping possible.

And then there are the matters of the poop tank needing periodic emptying and of having enough fresh water to drink, shower, flush, and brush our teeth with.

On day eight of our trip, we're running low on all those things. Plus, for six days in this remote inlet cove, we've had the same scrubby patch of dirt "beach" to stare at, the same grating bird calls to listen to, and the same marshy smells to inhale. I'm running low on hope we'll ever finish this trip and get home.

Cabin fever? It's no joke, y'all.

Yesterday and today I emailed Dad a picture of our location on the map, showing us in the exact same spot both times. For the good ones, all I could find was a shot of Drew drooling in his sleep and another of the starry sky, unblemished by any nearby light pollution. To be honest, the stars *are* pretty fantastic out here. But that only goes so far.

I tried texting Tara and Jess to rescue me from monotony. To hell with Mom's threats—how much worse could she make my life anyway? But Jess's mom doesn't want her putting too many miles on their car, since it's a lease, and Tara doesn't have her driver's license. She's convinced that she'll be finding an apartment in New York City two minutes after graduation, so what's the point of learning to drive? We all know she's actually just freaked out at the thought of operating heavy machinery after a slight incident with a riding mower in middle school.

I'm also sensing that after two rounds of heartfelt, tearful good-byes, it's becoming a little anticlimactic when I keep reappearing again a couple of days later.

My whole life is stalled, and no one seems appropriately sympathetic.

Drew's been keeping busy teaching himself common boat repairs, and he can still play his multiperson shooter games remotely with his friends on his laptop (which is mostly all he ever did at home anyway), so he's perfectly content.

Mom's worked her way through *The Essentials of Living Aboard a Boat* (item number one of which should read: a reliable deckhand who won't leave your whole boating party at a standstill when he steals away in broad daylight) and has now resumed submitting résumés to every halfway-promising bank job posting within a certain radius of Pleasant Hill.

Me . . . I'm still spending most of my time on Instagram, trying helplessly to keep up with everything at home. I even go to Heavenly Licks' website several times a day, just to smile at the logo. Who would have thought I could ever miss dishing out ice cream? My left bicep (my scooping arm) used to be bigger than my right, but after being off work for less than two weeks, it already feels like it's shrinking.

I feel like *I'm* shrinking. What if nothing is the same when I get back? What if I never *get* back because it takes us ten years to sail down there?

I'm lying on the bench in the cabin, tossing a tennis ball up in the air, when the radio screeches to life, startling me.

Christian's voice echoes in the small space. *"Grocery run, anyone? Over."*

Drew grabs the transmitter before I can even react. *"When? Over."*

"You should have asked *where*," I say. "There's not a town for, like, twenty miles. Believe me, I've researched."

"Seven miles," Drew corrects.

Meh. Seven, twenty. Either might as well be a hundred.

"Now. Planning to bicycle slowly if you'd like to jog alongside, Drew. Over."

"Mom?" Drew calls. "I could use my skateboard."

"I guess if you're going with Christian, it's fine," she answers. "I can drop you both ashore in the dinghy."

Drew finalizes plans with Christian and replaces the transmitter before spying my doubtful expression.

"Seven miles is nothing," he tells me. "Before we left, I was running ten miles a day on Mom's treadmill to get ready for basketball."

And that's another thing. Drew is dying to go out for JV basketball at our high school. He was *training*. What fourteen-year-old trains for a team he's not even on yet? Yes, we'll be back in time for tryouts, but does Mom even realize she stole four months of practice time from him? He can't dribble on a slanted deck and we're not likely to encounter many hoops at sea. Did Drew even speak up about that?

"Seven miles *each way*," I point out. "And half of it while carrying groceries balanced on a skateboard. Are you crazy?"

"Crazy for Cocoa Puffs." When I make a face, he adds, "Or *anything* that doesn't come in a can. And milk that isn't powdered."

Oh god, just the thought. "Okay, you might be onto something. Fresh bread . . ."

"Chocolate chip cookies," he says.

"Swedish fish. Strawberries. Salad. *Slurpees*."

"Are we going alliterative now?" Drew asks. "Okay. Potato chips, pumpkin pie, pancakes, and . . . uh . . . peaches!"

"A: totally unintentional on my part. B: I'm impressed you know the word alliterative *and* can pronounce it. C: you cannot convince me that you, of all people, are dying for anything as healthy as fruit. And D: a thousand times yes to potato chips. Get many bags of those."

"Twenty-five percent increase in allowance to anyone who brings me real cream for my coffee," Mom adds from behind her bunk door.

"I would have done it for fifteen!" Drew answers.

As soon as they leave in the dinghy, I retreat to my berth, so I don't have to engage with Mom once it's just the two of us. I'm deleting old messages off my phone when she returns, but happily she ignores me and goes right back to her bunk.

Shockingly enough, it doesn't take long to clean up years' worth of text threads, even when you've never bothered to do it before. I'm sprawled across my bed, waiting for a better boredom buster to present itself, when my eyes land on a hanging bag.

There's one other survival necessity we've been neglecting: laundry.

It's not like I'm trying to impress anyone out here—I've mostly been living in yoga pants and sweatshirts—but there's still the matter of my, um, delicates. I can rough it as well as the next girl, but I have my limits, and clean underwear is one of them.

Even if I wanted to hand wash in the sink and hang them up in my room, my berth is so damp, they'd take a year to dry. Not to mention it also serves as my brother's closet and changing room, so . . . no. And anyway, we're on the strictest of rations until we can get to a marina and refill the bladder tanks that store our fresh water supply. Who knows when that will be, since the closest one is days away by boat.

We've been meeting on *Reality Bytes* after dinner most nights—and sometimes *for* dinner, since (until now, I guess) Christian has way more provisions, and the space to store them. He's also been nice enough to let Amy and Miranda shower the girls there, since their boat is even tinier than ours, with smaller tanks and more people. But even his giganto-yacht doesn't have a washer-dryer.

Although thinking of his boat reminds me that last night when we gathered post-SpaghettiOs, Amy mentioned a nearby stream she'd found while hiking. If I can reach it relatively quickly, I should have plenty of time to rinse out my things and let them dry in the sun before the dinghy would be needed to bring groceries to the boat.

I don't know how long fourteen miles on a bike and skateboard will take, but I'm guessing somewhere between three hours and the length of time between *Avengers* movies.

I quietly gather up my stuff and leave a note for Mom, because the fewer words I have to exchange with her the better, and sneak off to the dinghy. I don't want to alert her to my exit, so instead of starting the engine, I grab the paddle from underneath the bench seat and work my way over to *Tide Drifter*.

"Hallllll-oooo?" I call up softly.

Abigail's face peers out of an open hatch.

"Did you come to play with us?" She looks hopeful.

"Maybe later, okay?" I think it's totally barbaric of Mom to force this trip on me against my will, but is it borderline abusive to make two little kids live aboard a sailboat? I mean, there's barely any room to move around. What about their developing bones and stuff?

"Okay! We're doing an obstacle course! You have to get all

the way through the cabin and up to the bow following one piece of rope and you can't let go EVER! Grace figured out how to somersault through a knot on Mommy and Mama's bed. You should see her all twisty like a pretzel! You could try it if you want."

So much for calling Child Protective Services.

"Hey, Cassie!" The edge of Miranda's face appears in the hatch next to Abigail's. "Wanna come in for a bit? Promise not to make you turn yourself into a human bowline knot. We're breaking soon for science class anyway. We found some moss on the creek bed yesterday and we're gonna see if we can use it to make live graffiti."

Okay, seriously. How do they manage to make a childhood at sea seem so magical?

"Thanks, but I was actually hoping Amy could give me directions to that creek. I need to do some laundry." I gesture at the bag beside me in the dinghy.

"Sure thing! Hey, could you bring back more moss with you, in case our first attempt is a flop?"

"Check on our fairy garden too!" Abigail says.

I agree to both conditions, and Amy points out the clearing in the trees where the path to the stream begins. It takes me less than ten minutes to paddle over and land the dinghy on a small bank of dirt.

As I step onto the first patch of land I've stood on since going out with Tara and Jess in Florence a week ago, the earth sways under me. Or rather, it doesn't. My body has gotten so used to subtly balancing out the constant rocking motion of the water—gentle in this protected cove, but still there—that not having it underneath me feels like that first moment after exiting the Tilt-A-Whirl at the state fair. I have to grab on to a tree trunk while I wait for the sensation to pass.

I should have come ashore sooner. I don't know why I haven't, except, I guess, stubbornness. If Mom was going to force me to be on the boat, then I was going to be on the boat, right in her face with all my miserableness.

But now, surrounded by ferns and all the other lush green plants that grow next to the water in Oregon's rainforest climate, I'm suddenly buying Abigail's insistence that fairies truly do live here.

I use a rope in the well of *Minecraft* to tie it to a nearby tree, pausing to inhale the pine scent. Our backyard in Pleasant Hill is full of evergreens, so to me this smell is croquet tournaments with Dad, and running through the sprinkler, and harvesting pinecones with Mom to make birdseed hangers as teacher gifts. It's stifling giggles in the front bushes while Mom and Dad tried to scare trick-or-treaters by sitting stock still in hooded ghoul costumes on the porch before coming to life the second a kid reached into the basket for a Snickers.

It's the smell of home and safety and good things . . . and I need it like I need oxygen. I step eagerly into all the beautiful, beautiful flora and fauna.

10

Now, this. This is so *me*.

The ground is every shade of brown and a million more iterations of green: avocado, moss, mint, olive, shamrock. The only blue I see is faint glimpses of sky through the treetops. We've been within sight of land for most of the trip, but there's been endless sea in all other directions this entire time. Now, tucked in safely among the ferns and the branches, with dirt underneath my feet, I feel sheltered and solid.

The stream, when I find it, is clear straight to its bottom, which is littered with river stones that make the water gurgle and gush and drown out the other forest sounds. The cove, the boat, my mother—they all feel far, far away, and I am completely loving this moment.

Even if it happens to involve scrubbing my bras together with powdered soap flakes.

It's not exactly dignified, but it does lend to the feeling

that I've traveled into a fairy tale. I mean, surely Little Red Riding Hood's cottage didn't have a Kenmore Elite front-loading washer, right?

I don't mind that I have to crisscross up and down a whole section of the stream to find enough small boulders that meet my optimal drying requirements (flat-topped and exposed to at least dappled sunlight, so Mother Nature can do her thing). I would happily spend whole days here. I would happily spend the next four months *here*. Maybe Mom and Drew could swing by for me on their return trip.

As soon as everything is laid out across a patchwork of rocks, I allow myself to play. I spend who knows how long exploring the creek bed, peering at leaves and the tiny plants that curl toward the places where light breathes into small clearings. We're not so far from home that the flora is entirely different, but this close to the ocean and the salt air, there are some variances, and I geek out over them.

When I've collected my fair share of leafy samples, I retreat to the cluster of boulders currently drying my favorite bra-and-underwear combo in a single ray of sun. There's a crevice that molds perfectly to my back, and I snuggle in and wiggle my toes into the squishy mud. Bliss.

I reach into the laundry bag for my sketchbook and the colored pencils I tossed in. My set is labeled "earthen," and that's just perfect for this location. Perfect for me. *Earthen* is maybe my new favorite word.

I'm not all that great at drawing, but I love creating my

own botany reference materials. Soon enough, I'm lost in the task of capturing tiny vein formations and patterns.

"So there *is* such a thing as wood sprites! I thought Shakespeare was taking license with his fiction."

My arm spasms with shock, jerking a hard line of Verdant Green across my page, and I yank my head up.

A tall guy, close to my age, wearing hiking boots and one of those serious backpacks with the metal frames on the outside, covers his mouth.

"I'm so sorry! I didn't mean to scare you. Did I make you mess up your drawing?"

His eyes trail to the sketchbook dangling in my hands and I follow them, staring at it stupidly.

"I—what?" I'm still reeling from the sudden return to reality, and now my brain starts wrestling with its fight-or-flight response and stranger-danger thoughts: alone in the woods, miles from people, no cell signal.

The guy shifts his backpack on his hips and half cringes, half smiles. "I guess I should have made more noise when I approached."

Still processing: apologetic, referenced Shakespeare, not wearing a hockey mask or carting a chain saw. All hopeful signs he's not a mass murderer. Plus he's way too attractive to be a serial killer.

"Laundry day, huh?" he asks, his cheerful smile turning up at one corner and his eyes flashing amusement.

My brain finishes assessing the situation, then blares: *HOLY CRAP, THIS HOT GUY IS SEEING A TRAIL OF YOUR UNDERWEAR UP AND DOWN THE STREAM!*

Additional urgent incoming message from brain: *React in some manner, Cassie. Say something, Cassie. Do something, Cassie.*

"I—uh—" I yank my toes out of the mud and stand, flailing my arm behind me to grab the bra-and-thong set off the rock closest to me. I crumple them in my hand. Then I sigh when I spot my bag on the ground, just out of reach, before forcing my eyes back to his, which are still dancing all along the creek.

"R-right. Laundry d-day," I stammer. I'm not usually one of those girls who can't hold her own around members of the opposite sex, but come *on*. . . .

He puts his arms up in a "surrender" gesture and takes two tentative steps in my direction, smiling all the while. "Permission to approach?"

When he reaches me, he sticks out his hand. "Jonah Abrahmson, apologetic hiker."

I blink at him once and then reach to shake, but I yank my arm back when I realize my fingers are still curled around my balled-up underwear. *Why is this my life?* Earlier today I wanted nothing more than the ground under my feet, but at the moment I'd actually rather be on a boat with a full poop tank and dwindling provisions. Maybe.

My complexion is surely going all luck-o'-the-Irish on me.

I have skin that, at the smallest embarrassment, doesn't delicately blush so much as . . . splotch red like I've been hit with a dozen paintballs. I awkwardly transfer both items to my other fist, breathe deeply, and offer a glance to the heavens.

"Cassie McClure, humiliated wood sprite," I say, shaking his hand firmly.

Okay, not so bad, Cass. I'm recovering my senses. He startled me, that's all.

Jonah's grin grows wider and, seriously, his teeth should be in a toothpaste commercial or something. "No, no. I *like* that even wood sprites have to wash their underwear every now and again. Makes the whole spritely profession read much less mystical and really more, I don't know . . . salt of the earth. It's too bad Shakespeare cut the Wash Day scene from *A Midsummer Night's Dream*. Just think if he hadn't. Maybe the guy could have been famous for centuries after his death or something."

I try to fight the giggle, but here it comes. At least Jonah laughs too.

"So, can I see them?" He gestures with his chin to my hand, and my mouth falls open. His brow comes together in confusion, and after a beat, his eyes widen. Even though he has a deep tan that would hide any sign of a blush, his horrified expression says it's definitely there.

Embarrassment is in his voice too. "Um, I swear I meant your sketches."

Ooooh. My curled fingers are also holding my sketchbook, and now the cardboard cover is starting to soften where I've pressed my still-wet, balled-up bra and underwear against it. My arms go splotchy again, and I can only imagine my face is doing the same. Wordlessly extracting the more humiliating items, I step to where my bag lies on the ground. I shove them inside before straightening with another deep breath.

Showing my drawings to a total stranger is only minimally preferable to showing my underwear to one, but it's not as if I'm ever going to see this random hiker guy again, and he seems like he's trying really hard to be nice, so . . . what the hell. I pass the sketchbook into his outstretched palm.

"I'm not, like, an artist or anything. These are just for, um, reference."

He takes a long time flipping through the pages, and I'm alternately puzzled and flattered as I watch his face examine each picture. I mean, they're poorly rendered drawings of leaves and trees. I totally get that botany's not the most exciting of subject matters to the average person. My friends' eyes glaze over after two seconds, and even my professor dad, who's forever buried in boring academic papers, only lasts a few minutes longer.

But Jonah is thoughtful and thorough, not looking up until he reaches the final sketch, which has the jagged pencil mark from where I startled. He grimaces slightly and passes the book back to me.

"They're great. Sorry again about that last one. I hope you can still use it to study from."

I flip the cover closed. "Oh, I'm—I'm not studying from

them. I mean, not for a class or anything. Um, not yet anyway. It's kind of more of a hobby."

"Ah. I assumed they were for a course. But, hey, what better hobby for a wood sprite? It fits you perfectly."

Huh. That's what I think too, but no one has ever come right out and agreed with me; they tolerate it or tease me about it. His easy acceptance feels really nice.

A cloud passes over the sun, casting deep shadows, and we both glance up at the sky. Jonah checks his watch.

"Well, Sprite, much as I'd love to stay and offer my washing services to aid your own—purely out of the goodness of my heart and not to get my hands on a girl's unmentionables, mind you"—he places a hand on his chest and opens his eyes wide in pretend innocence—"I'm afraid I'm on a schedule."

Of course he is. It must be late afternoon by now, and I'll bet he needs to make camp somewhere before nightfall. He has Serious Outdoorsman written all over him.

"Right, sure." So much for my one good line of banter earlier. All my attempts at acting like a normal human since deserve a label less Bewitching Wood Sprite and more Village Idiot.

To further prove my point, I'm also at a loss for how to react as Jonah steps ridiculously close. He gestures, raising his eyebrows in a question. At my flustered nod, he drops a palm onto my shoulder, using me for balance to stretch one foot onto a rock protruding from the creek's center. His hand lingers lightly on me as he presses down a few times on the stone with his hiking boot, testing how well it's lodged into the mud below. After a beat, he places his weight and gently pushes off me.

From the center of the stream, he glances back. "Thanks. Nice meeting you, Sprite! And sorry again for disturbing your sketching."

"Er, you too." I wave limply, still a little dazed at how surreal it is to happen upon a stranger in the forest and then share sketches with him that no one else in the world has seen. But Jonah must be used to odd woodland encounters, because he continues to pick his way merrily downstream, balancing nimbly on the tops of rocks. I force myself to turn away and begin gathering the pencils that scattered when he startled me.

The secluded setting, which was so perfect for its solitude twenty minutes ago, feels oddly empty now, and I almost wish my clothes were drier so I could scoop them all up and return to the boat.

I peek over my shoulder. Jonah is at least half a football field away, his red shirt a shock of color against the green-and-brown backdrop. As if he senses my eyes on him, he turns and points to a flat rock beside him.

"*Purple polka-dotted* thong! Not bad, Sprite. Not bad at all!"

At least he's not close enough to witness my jaw drop, nor will he be ever again. Thank god for small miracles.

When I get back to the shoreline an hour or so later with a bag of clean delicates and an armful of moss for the girls, the first thing that hits me is the bright sunlight. I step from the leafy protection of the woods and onto the scrap of muddied sand that passes for beach around these parts.

The second thing that hits me is a definitive absence of a dinghy.

What kind of an asshat would steal *Minecraft*? I have to believe it can barely be worth the parts it's made up of, unlike Christian's fancy Zodiac. I cup a hand over my eyes and squint at the three sailboats in the center of the cove. The wind is such that *Sunny-Side Up* faces the ocean, and the space behind it, where *Minecraft* usually bobs merrily, contains nothing but gently rippling water. So much for my glimmer of hope that Drew and Christian beat me back with the groceries and happened upon the dinghy.

I move my gaze to *Tide Drifter* and spot *Liki Tiki* tied up behind it, all alone. I know *Reality Bytes* will be dinghy-less, since Christian can't replace his hijacked Zodiac until we get to some marina near San Francisco where he's having another custom-outfitted one delivered.

But instead of the empty space I expect to see, there *is* something behind the yacht. I can't tell if it's *my* something because of the sun's glare, but what else would be tied up there? They must be unloading food after all.

I make a megaphone out of my hands and yell "Drew!" sending my voice echoing across the water.

There's no movement, and I'm about to yell again when I spy a flash by the back platform. Then a motor roars to life and I exhale. Not that I'm in a particular hurry to leave solid land behind, but it was kind of disconcerting to be stranded all alone over here, even for a few minutes.

The dinghy headed toward me is in silhouette against the sun, meaning I can only see shadows of a shape, but the body type of the person inside tells me it's not Christian. Christian is toned yet compact, and this figure is clearly taller and loose-limbed. Drew? And then a cloud passes in front of the sun and I catch sight of a red T-shirt.

Why, why, *why* is Jonah, Apologetic Hiker, suddenly Jonah, Driver of My Dinghy?

Okay, that sounds way more porny than even Heavenly Licks. But still. Why is Jonah waving at me like it's no big deal that he's taken the boat?? Maybe *borrowed* is more accurate—but still. Why is he *here*?

As he approaches shore, he calls, "Ahoy there, matey!"

I give a halfhearted wave and, as soon as he cuts the motor, wade into the water to meet him.

"So, enchanting wood sprite moonlights as a water nymph, is that how it is?" he asks with a laugh in his voice.

Something witty, Cass. Something witty that does not involve uttering the phrase "driver of my dinghy" out loud, for the love of god.

"And somewhere-to-be hiker has nautical secrets of his own, I see," I manage.

He cocks his head. "Nautical secrets? Hmm. I like it. Not as much as your Victoria's Secrets, of course." He glances obviously at my laundry bag, both of us knowing just what it contains, and I instantly remember that this guy has seen exactly how much padding is in my padded bras. Beyond embarrassing.

To avoid a response, I pretend to be absorbed in the task of situating myself in the dinghy without capsizing us both or dropping the moss. Jonah casually starts up the engine again and turns us back toward open water.

"Sorry I stranded you—I was trying to get Chris's attention from shore when a lady on that boat with the red sails yelled over and said I should borrow this. I figured I could get a jump on unloading my gear while keeping an ear out for whoever owned this to return." He pats the side of *Minecraft* before gesturing at the sailboats and asking, "So, which one are you?"

I point to *Sunny-Side Up* and he nods, driving full-throttle toward it. The wind whips my hair against my cheeks.

"What *are* you doing here?" I ask, raising my voice against the engine noise. Who's Chris? And what does he mean by "unloading my gear"?

Jonah leans toward me as far as he can manage while still keeping a hand on the tiller, presumably so I can hear his reply over the wind.

"I'm crewing for Uncle Chris."

"Uncle—? Wait, *Christian's your uncle?*"

He raises one shoulder and lets it drop. "Not by blood. He's one of my dad's oldest business partners and I grew up calling him that."

"Oh!" I nod, trying to hold my flyaway hair back with one hand and failing. Then the other piece of information falls into place. "Crewing?"

"Yep. Down to Mexico." He bites his lip in concentration as he slows and approaches *Sunny-Side Up* at the perfect angle to leave me aligned with the platform.

Mexico. This guy who's seen my underwear *and* my sketchbook is coming with us all the way *to Mexico*?

Jonah stands in the center of the dinghy on steady feet and holds a hand out, first for the moss, and then to help me onto the platform. He hops off after me, quickly ties our dinghy to *Sunny*, and strips off his shirt. He tosses it onto the dinghy's bench seat and faces me, smiling. *Hello, abs.*

"Hey, would you mind bringing that with you next time you swing by Uncle Chris's yacht? I'd rather not get it wet. You of all people know how long things take to air-dry around here."

Keeping his mischievous grin in place, he steps backward off the platform and disappears into the ocean. When he surfaces, he cuts easy strokes across the water to *Reality Bytes*.

I force myself to look away before he climbs aboard.

Crewing.

To Mexico.

Huh.

11

Mom is waiting for me when I step down into the cabin. I'm distracted by thoughts of Jonah joining our caravan, so it takes me a second to grasp that her mood could best be described as Furious with a capital *F*.

"I'm fifteen feet away and you didn't think it would make sense to talk to me about your plans, rather than sneak out with a note that says only *Off to do laundry, back soon?*"

"I don't see what the big deal is. You let Drew go fourteen miles into town and back and he's three years younger than me. I only went maybe *one* mile."

Mom grabs the towel from next to the sink and begins roughly drying a plate. Since *Sunny* has the potential to tilt at steep angles while under sail, all our dishes are plastic, and I'm surprised this one doesn't snap in half with the effort she's putting into the task.

"Yes, Cassie, but the difference is that he's with an adult, and I've been told exactly which route they'll take, so if they aren't back at a reasonable hour, I'll know precisely where to go looking for them. Tell me which part of *Off to do laundry* includes any of those reassurances? I had no idea where you were or what you even meant. Were you looking for a Laundromat? How am I supposed to interpret *Back soon*? Five minutes? Five hours? Not to mention that you took the dinghy and left me stranded here, so if I did need to help Drew, I couldn't! Did you think of that?"

She tosses the plate on the counter, where we both watch it wobble out of control before settling. Okay, so no, I didn't, but she's exaggerating just a little bit.

I cross behind her to my berth and begin taking my clean laundry out of my bag, laying things on my bed to fold.

"You could have used the radio to call Amy and Miranda if you needed anything," I tell her. "They would have come over in *Liki Tiki* to get you. They *also* could have told you which path I'd followed into the woods since Amy's the one who gave me directions." I'm speaking the words to my quilt, but I can sense Mom in the doorway.

"Oh. Well, then. As long as *Amy and Miranda* were in on the plan."

I guess there's no question who I get my mastery of sarcasm from.

"Did you not think your own mother had a right to know where her child is?"

"That's just it, Mom. I'm *not a child*! I'm seventeen years old, so you can quit trying to micromanage me. It's bad

97

enough you have me cooped up in this cabin like I'm freaking Rapunzel. You don't need to know where I am every second of every day! What are you going to do next year when I'm off at college?"

"Know what, young lady? Keep acting like you're the only person on this planet with feelings worth considering and you might *not* be going away to college. Oregon State's a perfectly good school."

"You can't control where I go," I spit.

"Oh? Which of us is paying the tuition bill?"

I see red. That's hitting way below the belt. The surge of anger coursing through me is Hulk level, and I feel every bit as volatile as the big green dude. And since Drew's not here, there's no reason to hold back. It's so incredibly hard not to fling the cheating in her face right now, to *really* hammer home my argument. I'd love to watch her expression when she realizes that, oh yes, I know ev-er-y-thing. There have been a million opportunities like this over the past months to confront her with it, but I always clamp my jaw shut and grind my teeth together instead. Like I'll do now too.

I have reasons. Many of them.

The thing is, I don't know *everything*. I know I overheard Dad hiss, "If you hadn't cheated, we might not be in this position," and I know that was the last night he spent in our house. I know that a week later he accepted a yearlong visiting fellowship overseas, something he'd been offered many times before and claimed he'd never consider because he didn't want to uproot our family. I'd say that's telling enough.

I don't think I can handle any nitty-gritty details. No one wants to picture their parents having sex, but trying to imagine Mom doing the nasty with someone else? It makes my head thud and my stomach heave.

I also don't think I can handle the awkwardness of confronting my own mother about something as *adult* as this. I used to think I could talk to her about anything, but not *this* anything. Not "please defend all your screwups to me, your child who previously looked up to you as someone worth emulating." What kid wants to be placed in that position? It's not only embarrassing, it's *humiliating*. For her, probably . . . but also for me.

The whole *thing* is humiliating, not just the idea of confronting Mom about it. I couldn't even bring myself to confide in my very best friends in the world. I know that's not logical, and that they love me no matter what, and that my mom's actions don't reflect on me . . . but they do, on some level. I couldn't bear to see Tara and Jess try to act like what happened was fine and normal when they came over, when we'd all know deep down that my family *isn't* normal anymore. No one else we know has a cheating mom.

And then there's my even bigger fear. What if whoever he was is still in the picture? I don't *think* he is. I've avoided my house a lot since the split, but whenever I *have* been there, so has Mom. Alone, or with Drew. And would she really have instigated a four-month trip if it meant leaving the new love of her life behind?

But.

She fooled us all once.

I don't know what it's going to take for me to forgive her for that, but I do know finding out he's still around—or, worse, that I might be getting a new stepdad—would plummet our mother-daughter relationship into an abyss we'd never climb out of.

So I keep the little I do know held tight to my chest.

Instead I spit out a tamer version that fits both our narratives. "You think *I* act like the only person on this planet with feelings worth considering? Where do you think I could have learned that, Mom? It's *real* obvious you considered all of our feelings when you and Dad called it quits."

Not that tame, I guess, because she winces like I've slapped her. A millisecond later, she turns and retreats to her berth, slamming the door. I throw myself onto my bed and land directly on the pile of clean laundry, but I don't care.

Where does she get off looking so hurt? I only said the truth. She *didn't* consider us. And she wants to say *I'm* only concerned with *my* feelings? Hey, pot, it's kettle. You're black.

If I were in Pleasant Hill, I could escape to blow off steam. I could come home after she was already asleep and I wouldn't have to worry about a huge blowout with her. It's not like I *want* to feel this way about my own mother, and I've been doing a pretty damned good job over the last six months of avoiding arguments like this, especially since Drew's always around and I don't want to drag him into it.

But now she's trapped me in this floating jail cell.

How exactly does she expect me to avoid saying all the horrible things I've been shoving down when I'm cornered in this . . . this pressure cooker?

12

I blink awake, early the next morning, to my mother settling gingerly on my bed.

"I'm sorry, Cassie," she whispers.

I'm bleary-eyed and my brain's not functioning yet. After our fight yesterday, I fell asleep and woke to an empty boat and a note (ah, the irony!). It said they were having dinner on Christian's boat and to call if I wanted to join them; otherwise there were plenty of groceries to choose from.

Plenty is a relative term, given Drew's carrying capabilities and the size of our "pantry" under the floorboards, but at least I scored my potato chips. The distance back must have kept Drew from getting anything frozen, because no one had disturbed me to get under my mattress.

I made myself dinner, took it into my berth, and watched a movie on my laptop. When I heard them return, I faked sleep.

Now it's morning, my head is fuzzy, and my mother is stroking my hair like she used to every time I'd have my recurring nightmare about being at a funeral and being unable to see who's in the casket. I tug my blanket around my neck, curl my legs to my chest. I don't look at her.

She sighs. "Look, I feel terrible about our fight yesterday. I wanted this trip to be about setting things right between us, but it feels like they're getting worse instead of better. I was hoping . . ."

She trails off and I don't move. After a second she exhales deeply and says, "I was hoping you might start to feel differently about things once a little time had passed and you'd settled in. *But*, I can acknowledge I'm probably not helping things much, and that's on me. I heard what you said yesterday, and I'm going to try harder to treat you more like the grown-up you're becoming." She pauses, then asks, "Okay?"

I lie perfectly still and hide the one tear that sneaks out of the corner of my eye and onto my pillow.

God, I miss my mom.

I miss my dad because he's thousands of miles away, but I think I miss my mom, who's all of two feet away, more.

Except I don't see any way back to how things used to be with us this time last year. If I give in now and start being my regular self with her, that would be like acknowledging that what she did to us was okay. It's *not* okay.

"Cass?" she asks, and her voice cracks.

I shrug, causing the covers to slip down. "Sure, whatever," I whisper, my head still turned to the wall.

She puts a hand on my back. "All I ask in return is that

you try to put in an effort too, okay?"

When I don't answer, she settles my blanket back into place, squeezes my shoulder, and stands.

"I'll let you get some more sleep. We're finally setting sail, in about an hour."

In reply, I curl up tighter.

"Now that Jonah's here, things are about to get interesting, huh?" my mother says.

I whip my head to face her. She's perched at the steering wheel, while Drew's in the bow and I fulfill my simply-an-observer role on a bench in the cockpit.

Despite it being only a few hours after her possibly heart-felt apology, her question instantly puts me on the defensive.

"Why? What do you mean?"

It's just like my mother to assume that the mere appearance of a guy my age on this trip would catapult me into a schoolgirl crush. I'd like to think I'm slightly more mature than someone who would fall into instalove, thank you very much.

"What's with the tone?" she asks. "I meant that now we can finally put some coastline between us and our starting point. Why? What'd you think I was saying?"

Oh.

I don't respond, instead returning my gaze to our wake. I may be annoyed with her, but I'm thrilled that we're finally back under sail, cutting through the choppy whitecaps like we're the boss of them. This time my stomach is only slightly queasy, which is a bonus.

A minute later, Mom asks, "Wait, did you think I was suggesting something about *you and Jonah*?"

Her laugh suggests she considers the mere idea of it preposterous. Okay, so, I'm not exactly thinking about Jonah *like that*. Sure, he's cute. More than cute. But in the first ten seconds we spent together, I could tell he's a giant flirt, and past experience has taught me not to mess with giant flirts—they're nearly always players. Plus, my head is enough of a mess without bringing any guy drama into it, least of all over one who's seen my entire underwear collection. *Nothing* could be more mortifying.

But still. My mother doesn't know any of those deterrents, and it's not *that* crazy to imagine two teens forced to spend months together at sea eventually hooking up. Is she saying there's no way he'd be interested in me? What must she think of her daughter for the idea not to have even crossed her mind?

I ignore her question and continue to study the wake we're leaving behind us, until Mom says, "Well, I really hope you're smarter than to go there, Cassandra."

I turn to face her. "What? Go where?"

"Jonah. He seems directionless; he told us last night at dinner that he recently dropped out of college. Trust me, you *don't* want to get involved with a grotty yachty."

"*What* is a grotty yachty?"

My mother shrugs. "Like a beach bum, but the sailing version."

I roll my eyes. "That's a super-lame term. Anyway, I think he's kind of cute," I say, a challenge in my voice. Regardless of my own feelings on the matter, where does she get off telling me who I can like? I dart a glance at Drew, who's far in the front of the boat with wind whipping around him, before lowering my voice and saying, "And thank you so much for your new efforts to treat me like an adult capable of making my own decisions. I can tell you're trying really hard."

Mom's shoulders drop. After a few seconds she nods and says, "You know what, you're right. You should make your own decisions when it comes to who you like. I'll keep my mouth shut."

I never said I liked him; I said I thought he was cute. But wow. I'm impressed with her total 180, despite myself.

"Thank you," I murmur.

"You're welcome," she says, offering a half smile.

"Mom, should I hoist the jib now?" Drew calls.

She turns her attention to the bow and I open my phone. I finally managed to guilt Tara into planning a spy mission to my house so she can text me pictures of my garden. I need to make sure the tenants are watering and weeding it according to the detailed instructions I left, before it passes the point of no return. It's gonna be hard enough getting *me* back into the swing of things come November; I don't need my garden to be equally out of sorts.

No updates from Tara yet, so I switch to the GPS app. I want to know exactly where we are and how much progress we're making.

"Think we'll cross the California border tomorrow?" I ask, studying the map. Both sails are now filling with wind, and Drew joins us in the cockpit.

"Tomorrow, if all goes well," Mom replies. "We anchor in Hunters Cove tonight, then on to Cali in the morning."

Cali. That's almost as bad as *grotty yachty*. Parents should not use slang. Like, ever. I catch Drew's eyes, roll mine, and smile when he has to bite his lip to keep from laughing.

"So by tomorrow night we'll be docking in an actual marina," I say, amazed at how giddy this makes me. "Actual laundry facilities. Actual showers that don't have to end after two minutes, to conserve the fresh water in the tanks."

"Maybe even a burger joint!" Drew adds, and I smile. A burger would be heaven.

The thought of creature comforts to come breathes life into me. I creep along the ropes until I reach the front, where I dangle off it like one of those mermaid torsos carved into the front of Viking ships so I can take pictures of us zooming along for Dad.

I still need to find the negative one for today, but I push that aside because I'm tired of being all angsty. The water is green and we're finally headed in the right direction, which means this trip is getting closer to being over by the nautical mile.

Things have to be looking up, right?

"Hey, check it out," Drew says, joining me and pointing to the shoreline in the distance. "Cape Blanco."

"Westernmost point in the state of Oregon!" we singsong in unison, grinning at each other. Cape Blanco is a national park where we used to go camping. Every time we'd pull up to the entrance, Dad would say, "Here we are, kids. Westernmost point in the state of Oregon," until it got to be a family joke.

I wish we were close enough to snap a picture for Dad. Although even at this distance and in the bright sunshine, I can see the flashing of the familiar lighthouse beacon every few seconds. It's strange to view it from this perspective, versus being on land. We're far enough out to sea that I'd need the binoculars to discern the mossy green covering the top parts of the chalky cliffs that Mom and I spent countless hours walking beneath, chatting about stuff at school, or what plants I wanted to add to the garden that year, or, well, anything.

Dad had his precious lighthouse, but my favorite part was always exploring the tidal pools formed by all the rocks along the water's edge. Mom and I would spend whole afternoons crouched down, peering in at the mini "aquariums" formed by crevices in the rocks. I loved watching the hermit crabs scurry along the tops of mussel shells and brainstorming with her about what kinds of weird things we could put on our s'mores that night at the campfire. (For the record, melted Hot Tamales candy s'mores are not as bad as they sound.)

I steal a glance at her now, standing at the helm of our boat, and my heart sighs. I swallow the memory away.

"I'm gonna go read for a while," I tell Drew.

I'm barely downstairs when I hear:

"Reality Bytes *to* Sunny-Side Up. *Come in,* Sunny-Side Up. Sunny-Side Up, *do you copy? Over.*"

Okay, I'm no willing participant in this life at sea, but talking into the VHF radio makes me feel like a wartime spy, and I'm all over it anytime it squawks.

"Sunny-Side Up, *we copy. Over.*"

"Plantita? *Is your mother available? Over.*"

No fun radio time for me; Christian sounds all business. *"I'll grab her. Over."*

Drew takes the wheel and Mom comes down to the navigation center. *"This is Elise. Go ahead, Christian. Over."*

"I'm worried about a change in the weather report. It forecasts a small system hitting our area overnight and I don't like the idea of being anchored in Hunters Cove during it. Over."

I watch Mom's face for a reaction, but she doesn't give anything away. *"What are you proposing? We pass Port Orford first, right? Should we try to stick it out there for a couple days and wait for the storm to pass? Over."*

Oh dear god, no. I can't do any more "sticking it out." I swear, I could *walk* to the tip of Mexico faster than this.

"I'd rather try to outrun it, so we don't get any farther behind schedule. It would mean sailing straight through to Crescent City, but that's a protected harbor. If the storm tracks south, it's a better spot to wait things out. Plus it has the marina. Over."

Getting to a marina sooner? Unloading trash? Emptying

out the waste tank? Being able to take a shower long enough to use my deep conditioner? Creeping closer to the finish line? Yes, please. Let's go!

Mom has frown lines between her eyes. *"I don't know. I thought we were committed to avoiding overnight sail-throughs? Have you checked with Amy and Miranda? Over."*

The radio is crackly for a second, and then Christian's voice is clear as he says, *"They said they're good either way, but I'll wait and watch the forecast. We can assess again in a couple of hours when we're approaching Port Orford. Over and out."*

As far as I'm concerned, we can sail straight through to Mexico with only a couple of quick stops to replenish gas/water/food, but Mom looks nervous as she hangs up the radio. She returns upstairs without a word.

The forecast is still concerning when Christian radios again a few hours later.

"I guess I have to defer to your expertise here. But I'm—" Mom pauses and steals a glance at me. I'm pretending to play solitaire at the table, but obviously eavesdropping. She turns her back and cups her hand over the radio transmitter as she speaks in a lowered voice. Her words still echo clearly through the cabin. *"I'm just not thrilled about sailing through Gale Alley at night. Over."*

Gale Alley? What the hell is Gale Alley?

Christian's voice is calm as he replies. *"Copy that. We need to make the call now though. Hunters Cove is too exposed to the open sea, which means once we pass Port Orford, we're committed to staying the course until we reach Crescent City. Over."*

Mom is still turned away from me, so I can't see her face, but the way she tugs a hand through her hair is a tell. She wants to stop. Instead she says, *"Let's aim for Crescent City, then. I trust your judgment. Over and out."*

Once again she climbs the steps without a glance in my direction, but I swear I can feel tension coming off her in waves.

I have my computer fired up when Drew bounds down a minute later. "Did you hear? Night sailing! Pulling an all-nighter. Effing A, huh?"

"Uh, did *you* hear the Gale Alley part? I just Googled it, and check this out: 'The area stretching three hundred nautical miles between Cape Blanco and San Francisco has the most consistent big waves of any area on the West Coast, and high sustained winds, earning it the nickname "Gale Alley." Winds build quickly and create steep breaking waves.'"

I don't read him the next part, which talks about the one to two sailboats per year typically lost in storms along this stretch. I wish I could unsee that myself. At home when there's bad weather, you close the windows or grab an umbrella. You complain about how frizzy your hair gets. But out at sea, it's life or death. And not *just* life or death. *My* life or *my* death. Or Drew's. I can't *believe* my mother would put us in this position.

I climb the steps and confront her. "Are you sure about this? Because I just went online and Gale Alley sounds pretty freaking terrifying."

Mom schools her face into a smile, but I'm sure I'm seeing strain in the corners of her lips. "Oh, honey. You can't believe everything you read on the internet."

"So it's *not* true that one or two sailboats are lost every year? What if *we're* the statistic for this season?"

She relaxes. "Sweetheart, that's in a storm. We're adjusting our schedule so we can *avoid* sailing in a weather system or any of its aftermath. It will be totally fine."

I'm not so sure. I peer over her shoulder at whitecaps that suddenly look more menacing than they did when I was up here a few hours ago. The water isn't deep green anymore. It's blue-gray and steely. Is it my imagination or do the swells look bigger too?

A hard pit forms in my stomach. I learned the tough way that getting broadsided by the bad stuff is terrifying, but getting hints that something's coming is its own kind of scary.

In the distance is the faint outline of *Tide Drifter*, and somewhere behind that is *Reality Bytes*, but otherwise it's only open water in three directions and a far-off, fuzzy, and barren coastline in the other.

We're all alone out here. Tiny and vulnerable. Which is exactly how I feel right now. This time last year I was safe in Pleasant Hill, spending my summer afternoons at the pool or scooping Rocky Road, secure in the knowledge that my parents were in love. And it was perfect. Really perfect.

I get—*I honestly do get*—how relatively nontragic this divorce stuff could all sound. Believe me, I do. I know there are kids out there with way worse problems. *Way, way* worse.

It's just that when you have something special one day and then it's taken away the next, it's a tragedy whether it fits the criteria for others or not.

And now I could legitimately die out here.

13

As darkness falls, the winds pick up and whistle ominously, even over the hum of the motor, which we're using because it's too intense out here for the sails. Even after I shut all the hatches, I can still hear the gusts calling, *"You're not safe, you're not safe."*

Conditions seem to be worsening by the hour, despite Mom's hollow-sounding reassurances that these are regular Southern Oregon seas, and the breaking waves and wind have nothing to do with Christian's storm forecast.

She and Drew have worked out shifts for the night, so one can steer while the other naps. Or, in Mom's case, dozes in five-minute spurts on the bench in the cockpit, since she can't exactly leave someone who learned to sail two weeks ago in charge. The boat's autopilot is set, but in weather like this, someone needs to be standing by, alert.

It wouldn't make any sense for *me* to offer to help with the sailing tasks for the first time ever in these seas, but I want to contribute. I won't admit this out loud, but Mom and Drew have this whole "we're gonna get through this night together" camaraderie thing going on and I need to be part of it because otherwise I will go out of my mind.

Without prompting, I make soup and grilled cheese for everyone for dinner, fill the coffeemaker, and prepare plenty of peanut butter and jelly sandwiches, so whoever's on duty can eat easily while keeping a hand on the wheel. I drink plenty of the coffee myself, so I can stay awake. I may not be able to sail, but I can follow simple instructions and fetch things. And I can provide moral support. That I can do.

If Mom's surprised at my sudden willing participation, she doesn't make a big deal about it, which is a relief.

I also offer Drew my berth to catch a nap, so he'll be rested enough to take over for Mom. It takes about thirty seconds before he's snoring loud enough to drown out some of the wind. I set up camp in the cabin, keeping one ear out for the radio and another out for any calls for help from Mom above. I fervently wish I'd never watched *A Perfect Storm*.

I send a quick group text to Jess and Tara. If I die tonight, you can have my Toledo Sunrise concert tee to share.

Neither answers, which means they're probably at the movie theater where Jess works. It's a Monday night, which is when the employees get a sneak peek at a film set to open that weekend. If I were with them, which I would be, I'd be trying to make my Raisinets last through the opening credits and turning around to glare at Jess's coworker Brad, who finds it highly amusing to try to land popcorn down the girls' shirts.

I would gladly endure a thousand kernels in my bra right now, if it meant being there instead of here. Even the Zen art of bonsai cultivation is not doing anything to lower my stress levels.

Abigail has been saying hi by radio now and again, and it sounds like a party in their cabin every time she does. I know they're way more used to life at sea, but doesn't anything rattle them? I expect Abby again, but when the radio crackles to life around midnight, it's Christian's voice that sounds loudly.

I grab the transmitter. "Sunny-Side Up, *we copy. Over.*"

"*How's your evening? Over.*"

He sounds relaxed, as if he's waiting on a corner for a bus.

"*We're hanging in, I guess. But a little freaked out. Over.*"

"*Freaked out? Over.*"

"*Yeah. The pitch black, with these winds and the waves and . . . everything. Over.*"

"*Is your mother sharing these concerns,* plantita? *Over.*"

I went up to refill her coffee before Drew came down to nap, and she was joking around with him, but I noticed her knuckles were white on the steering wheel. I'm positive she's only putting on a brave face for us. After all, I now know what a master she is at keeping her true nature concealed.

"*Yes. Over.*"

The radio is quiet for a long time, and I wonder if something's gone wrong. What if *Reality Bytes* was taken out by a rogue wave? Oh god, why didn't I consider the possibility of rogue waves before? Now I have something new to worry about.

I'm about to go on deck to investigate when his voice returns. *"I have a suggestion. Over."*

"Oh, okay. Over."

Drew peeks out from my room. I mouth "sorry," because obviously the radio screeching woke him, but he shakes his head and crosses the cabin to stand next to me.

"It seems unbalanced to have two extremely experienced sailors here and three less-experienced ones there. What about swapping Drew and Jonah for the night? Over."

I nearly laugh that he would term me "less experienced." How about "no experienced"? Drew snatches the transmitter from my hand, grinning ear to ear. *"Yes! How do we make that happen? Over."*

"Drewwwwww," I hiss.

He's all innocence. "What? Sounds totally logical." But he can't keep the smile off his face. "Oh man, I can't believe I get to sail a real yacht. Like a giant-ass one!"

The radio crackles, and Beatriz barks in the background. *"I doubt your mother would want Drew out in your dinghy, so we'll pull up alongside and make the transfer. Tell her to hold course and cut the engine. Be there shortly. Over and out."*

Drew begins racing around, stuffing items into his backpack. It's like he just scored tickets to the Super Bowl or something. He finishes in seconds, and I follow him above to deliver the news.

"Who was on the radio?" Mom asks. "I could hear it

squawking, but this stupid wind . . ."

I expected her to welcome the help of a seasoned pro, but after I fill her in on the plan, she frowns and asks, "This was Christian's suggestion? He thinks I need help?"

Kinda. Sorta. Well, the *suggestion* was his, anyway. It just may have been prompted by me. But I can't trust her to be honest with me, so what choice do I have but to take my and Drew's safety into my own hands?

When I nod, she squints into the dark. "Wow, I thought I was proving myself better than that with my sailing today."

The wind leaves her sails (and now that I've seen that happen in real life, I totally get the metaphor). I feel a little bad. I genuinely thought she was freaked out. It definitely *felt* like she was tense underneath all her bravado.

We all peer through the darkness as *Reality Bytes* closes in. Some of the waves are big enough that its cabin lights disappear temporarily at times, but it grows steadily closer until we can make out the yacht's outline. Soon the indistinct shapes take form to reveal a mast, a hull, and furled sails.

It isn't until it's bearing down on us that I give real thought to the logistics of transferring two people between the boats. The only reference point I have is scenes from films where a puffy-sleeved pirate, wearing an excess of guyliner, swings on a braided rope from the mast of his black-sailed ship onto the deck of the innocent sailors', where he lands effortlessly on two feet. I try to picture my brother wearing a puffy blouse. Nope.

"How are we going to do this?" Mom asks, and adds, "That was a rhetorical question" when both Drew and I shake our heads. *Reality Bytes* is close enough now that I can identify Jonah at the wheel and Christian tying barrel-shaped objects to the outer side of the railing running along their port side.

"Foam-padded bumpers," Drew says, interpreting my confused expression. "You use them when at dock, when there isn't decking between you and the crafts on either side, to keep from scratching each other's paint jobs."

How does this kid know so much about sailing already? He's like a freaking sponge.

"So he's gonna get close enough for us to bump each other, and then what? You just step across?" I ask.

"Looks that way," Drew replies.

"I don't know about this," Mom says, eyeing the waves slapping our hull. We're riding them down and up more than left to right at the moment, but every so often one breaks in a different direction and sends our boat tilting to the side. My stomach must really be adjusting to life at sea because it's hardly been revolting, but it does a flip at the thought of keeping two vessels aligned enough for someone to cross from one deck to the other.

It's almost a comical proposition, except there's nothing funny about it, because we're talking about my baby brother here.

"Hello there!" calls Christian. The wind whips his words past.

"Is this necessary?" Mom shouts back, but he cups his hand to his ear to indicate he hasn't heard her. We're almost parallel, but there's still a good twenty feet of open water between the two boats. Forget comical; this is insanity.

Christian and Jonah trade places. Beatriz stands a ways back from the railing, wagging her tail and wearing a doggy life jacket that's clipped to a short tether of some sort. Animals are supposed to be good at sensing danger, so maybe the wagging is a good sign. Then again, how could a dog know what we have planned?

They reverse, back across a wave, and approach again. This time they're much closer, but nowhere near close enough. A third attempt brings them right alongside us.

A wave sends us dipping low, and the railings of the two boats clink loudly, well above the bumpers. I witness Christian's cringe before a spray of seawater catches me in the face.

Christian tosses a rope onto our boat and instructs Drew, "Use a cleat hitch knot and tie it down to your deck." Although our engines are off and the sails are down, the boats are still being tossed by the waves, and Mom tries to steer us straight again whenever one turns us to the side. Jonah's doing the same in his cockpit. I can't see his face because he's got the hood pulled up on a yellow rain slicker identical to the one the Gorton's Fisherman wears on the packages of frozen fish sticks my mom made on nights Dad had faculty dinners. But his wide-legged stance is relaxed, and he's not even wearing a life jacket. Mom would die if any of us were ever up above without ours, but in *this* weather? I'd meld mine to my skin if that were an option.

"Okay, Drew, step to the outside of the rails and hang tight. When the next wave rocks you this way, grab on to my hand."

Ummmmmmmm? I peer at the good six feet of inky-black, angry sea between our boats. He wants Drew on the *other side* of the railing? The only thing separating us from *that* ocean?

Mom leans away from the wheel and yells, "Christian, I don't think—"

But Drew has already followed instructions. One leg is over, then the other. Both arms extend behind him, hands grasping the metal rail, as he leans out over the expanse of the black, ominous water. His face looks a little green in the deck lights, but he's hesitating a whole lot less than I would be. In fact, I'm not even sure I can *watch.* Christian has one hand out and a life ring in the other. Not exactly the most soothing of sights.

The boat tilts, and before I can even react, Drew steps off into nothingness.

14

Beatriz barks and my heart jumps to my throat.

Drew's fingers close over *Reality Bytes'* railing, but one hand slips. Christian's arm shoots out and grabs Drew's wrist as my brother scrambles to get a foot onto their deck. He dangles from the side of the boat for a second and then his leg is up and over the railing.

Mom thumps a palm against her chest and yells, "You almost gave me a heart attack!"

Drew waves and smiles like he didn't just do the scariest thing ever. Christian passes the life ring off and switches places with Jonah at the helm as I realize, with a sick feeling, that we have to do it all over again. Well, not *we* exactly, but . . .

I tense as Jonah approaches the edge, finally buckling a life jacket around his chest before climbing to the outside of the railing. He watches the waves for a minute and then, as a swell dips both boats toward each other, jumps easily from one deck to the next like he's a cat hopping between couches or something. Grinning at me, he says, "Hey there, Sprite. Mind if I pop over for a bit?"

He confidently unwinds the rope from the cleat, tosses it onto *Reality Bytes* to separate us, and somehow manages to sweet-talk Mom into taking a break below to warm up with some tea.

Then he flashes another easygoing grin at me as he grabs the wheel and expertly steers us over a wave. Christian called Jonah an "extremely experienced sailor" and he clearly wasn't kidding. I'm so relieved to have someone in charge whose competency I trust that I slump onto the bench and *finally* allow myself to relax.

"Second star to the right and straight on till morning," Jonah says, hours later. The autopilot is steering us, and the wind and seas have both calmed considerably. He plops down next to my mother on a bench in the cockpit and puts his elbows behind his head before leaning back and stretching his legs in front of him.

"It already *is* morning," my mother replies.

From my perch on the opposite bench, I peer up at the vast expanse of sky, searching for hints of dawn. "What time is it, anyway?"

Jonah pushes up a sleeve to check the fancy-looking watch on his wrist.

"Four forty-three," he answers. "Almost an hour past when you were supposed to take a sleeping shift, Mrs. McClure."

"Elise. Remember?" my mother answers drowsily. I can tell she's exhausted.

"Like I said before, don't feel like you have to stay up here on my account," he says. "I'm used to pulling all-nighters and everything's under control."

For all Mom's earlier opinions on Jonah, there's no way she can say he's been anything but courteous and respectful. She must feel the same, because she says, "We really appreciate your help, Jonah. I think we'll take you up on your offer."

She stands and stretches her fingers to me. "C'mon, Cass, let's go get a few hours of rest; then I can relieve our intrepid sailor here."

"That's okay. I'm good for now," I answer, ignoring her hand and instead adjusting the balled-up beach towel I'm using as a pillow.

What started out with my wanting to be up here so I could see any bad stuff coming has turned into me being way too lazy to move a muscle. Plus, though I hate to admit it, Jonah has me a tiny bit intrigued. I'm telling myself it's just the novelty of someone new on our trip, when we've had only the same seven faces to stare at for so many days.

She hesitates before finally making her way down the stairs, calling, "I'm only a few feet away if you two need anything."

Her words are innocent, but the way she stresses "a few feet away" is not. Ha! For someone who didn't even seem to consider the possibility of a Jonah-Cass hookup this morning, she's sure making a point to let me know she's nearby now.

"Interesting," Jonah says.

"What's that?" I ask.

"The way your mom's mind works," Jonah replies, grinning.

Oh god. He picked up on her innuendo too. I try to hide my mortification, rolling my eyes and saying, "Yeah, she's a gem all right."

He just laughs. "Seriously though, you sure you don't want to crash too?"

"Nope. Wide awake," I answer, discrediting my words with a giant yawn.

It's contagious, and Jonah's mouth opens so wide I glimpse a few fillings in his molar teeth. He catches me staring and I turn away, pretending to study the sea. It's definitely much calmer, but I'm still eager for the sun to come up and eliminate the creep factor of not being able to see what's out there in the inky darkness. Gimme a little horizon, please and thank you.

As if sensing my thoughts, Jonah says, "I promise I'm not trying to give you a hard time, but you do know those waves last night were no big deal, right, Sprite? I get the feeling your mom knew too—she seemed pretty composed moving around the deck."

She did actually. Could I have been imagining her tense expressions earlier in the evening?

"Yeah, well, they were a pretty big deal to me," I reply, turning my head to look at him.

The corners of his mouth twitch as he obviously fights a smile. "Fair enough."

We're quiet with our own thoughts for a long time after that, and although the sky gradually lightens, when it does a fog creeps in and envelops our boat in white wisps. A long, low trumpet sound rumbles across the water, followed a second later by two shorter, crisper blasts. Jonah sits up straighter.

"Figured that was coming," he says.

"Was that a foghorn?" I ask.

"Yup. Christian has an electric one on *Bytes*. I would have held off until it got soupier out here, but if he's starting his, we might as well. Since you missed your chance to sleep, mind if I ask for some help?"

I hope he's gotten the correct impression over the last several hours, that I know zero things about sailing. I shrug. "Sure. What do you need?"

"First it would be great if you could warn your mom that we're about to intrude on her sleep every two minutes until the sun burns this off."

For all her "I'm only a few feet away" bravado, my mom is so dead to the world she's barely coherent as I deliver the news. When I come back above, the air seems even thicker and the damp tendrils invade my nostrils and my throat, so that I'm almost suffocating. From the cockpit I can only make out the hazy form of our bow . . . and absolutely nothing beyond it. So much for holding off for soupier—we're there now.

"Are we in any danger of crashing into rocks or a beach or

anything?" I ask, fighting to keep panic from my voice.

Jonah has one hand holding up the lid of the bench I vacated and his head and torso inside, searching for something. He stays bent, but turns his face so his surprised eyes meet mine. "Crashing?"

He emerges with what looks like a fire extinguisher with a megaphone attached to its top and allows the lid to fall closed.

"Well, yeah." I gesture at the curtain of white surrounding us. "There are peninsulas all along this coast, right? Are we out far enough to avoid them?"

He laughs, then immediately claps a hand over his mouth. "Sorry. Okay, so you *really* don't know anything about sailing, huh?"

"Uh, I'm pretty sure I said as much once or twice last night." I try for attitude in my voice, to cover my embarrassment at having asked an obviously idiotic question.

"I guess I just didn't realize the level of novice. No worries, Sprite. Sailing isn't everyone's bag. The thing it teaches you, though, is that sometimes there are other ways to see than with your eyes."

"Very New Agey."

Jonah's laugh rumbles in his chest and echoes around the fog-enclosed space. "All depends on whether you consider hard science New Agey or not. Here, c'mere."

He gestures for me to move to the wheel, where he points at a series of electronic screens mounted on a dash above it. Obviously, I've noticed them before now, but the lines and random blobs of color they display are such gibberish I never paid close attention.

"The instrumentation here is acting as our eyes right now," he says. "This one's a chart plotter that uses GPS to show our course. It's controlling the autopilot's steering, and monitors the different depths we'll cross along the way. So, see? We're ten miles off the coast with no pesky peninsulas in our path. Rest easy."

"What's this one?" I ask, and earn myself a look of approval from Jonah.

"Ha! I knew you were the curious type. I predict the lure of sailing's gonna grab you by the throat any day now."

I bite my lip, fighting a smile. "No chance."

"We'll see. I like a good challenge. To answer your question though, that's the radar, which tracks objects around us and, equally important, lets them track us. Look. This blip here is us. And those two over there are *Reality Bytes* and *Tide Drifter*. Otherwise, the coast is clear. Or I guess I should say 'the sea is clear,' since we can't actually make out the coast."

I roll my eyes at his lame joke. "Ba dum bum."

Jonah grins, and I have to admit that I do feel much better. When he turns back to fiddling with the foghorn, I pause. "If there's nothing around us, why do we need that?"

He glances at me, clearly considering something. Then he sighs. "Okay, so this really isn't *anything* to be alarmed about, but even with the instruments helping, we do need to be alert because not all vessels broadcast radar signals, so the screen can be a little hit or miss."

I raise my eyebrows and he groans. "Bad choice of words. Sorry. Uh, might as well add that we also cross shipping lanes out here, and by the time we appear on a container ship's radar, it's next to impossible for it to change direction fast enough to avoid us. Meaning it's more on us to steer clear of them versus the other way around. Usually they're pretty easy to spot, being that they're gigantic and all, but in fog like this . . ."

Oh, perfect. One more thing to add to my list of worries. Falling overboard, capsizing, rogue waves, shark attacks . . . and now, being mowed down by something the size of an aircraft carrier. Or maybe even an actual aircraft carrier!

My eyes must be wide because Jonah touches my arm lightly. "Don't worry, I've been at this a very long time. We're fine."

When I nod, he says, "Okay, need you on lookout, Sprite."

I settle halfway between the bow and the stern with my back propped up by the mast, and stare into the wall of fog off the starboard side. Still standing at the wheel, Jonah raises the horn and sounds one long blast, followed by two short ones. They make my eardrums weep, but I'm willing to accept a little hearing loss to avoid being chopped into pieces by a tanker's giant propeller. It deserves pointing out that no one in Pleasant Hill was ever obliterated by a container ship while biking to school.

When the ringing in my ears stops, I turn my head slightly in Jonah's direction, keeping my eyes trained on the hints of water I can make out through the mist.

"You said you've been doing this a long time?" I ask.

"Forever."

"Oh really, Father Time? You hide your age well, then."

"Is that your super-crafty way of asking how old I am?"

When I steal a quick peek, the corners of his lips are doing that twitchy thing again. Damn. Busted.

"Maybe," I answer, glancing away and pretending I'm not totally curious.

"I'm twenty. How about you?"

"Eighteen in November."

"Hmm."

Hmm? What does "hmm" mean?

When he doesn't elaborate, I ask, "How many of those twenty years have you been sailing?"

"All of them."

I laugh. "Well, you probably weren't tying any clove hitch knots as an infant."

"If you believe my dad, I was. Also, I'm very impressed you know what a clove hitch knot is."

"Oh. I don't, exactly. Drew's been practicing all the different types over and over, and I guess I retained the name somehow."

He bends closer to the screens, scribbling something on a piece of paper as he says, "You're funny. Ignorance is bliss? You don't think learning to sail yourself might make the trip more memorable?"

I snort. "The only thing I want to remember about this trip is how fast it was over."

He jerks his head up to look at me. "Ah. Okay, then. Care to share?"

My smile is tight and I stare hard at the fog. The last thing I want is to drag a stranger into my drama. "It's kind of complicated. Maybe some other time?"

I feel his eyes linger on me for another few beats, and then he issues a casual, "Yeah, sure."

I steer us to a safer topic. "You were saying about your dad?"

Now it's Jonah's turn to snort. "Speaking of complicated . . ." He trails off, then adds, "Although he did teach me to sail, so I have to give him credit there. I have no early memories that don't involve a boat."

"Did you live on one, like Grace and Abigail?" I ask.

He holds up a hand to pause us for a second while he squeezes the horn: one long, two short. It does not get any easier on the ears with repeat performances. In the distance, another boat sounds its own call, then another does. Our little caravan, all accounted for.

When the echo dissolves, Jonah answers, "Nah, nothing like that. I grew up on Nob Hill. But my dad kept a racing yacht at our weekend place in Sausalito, and he took me out on the water all the time."

Nob Hill? Racing yacht? Weekend place? I flash back on his fancy watch. Now it's my turn to say "Hmm."

He slides his eyes to me but doesn't comment.

When he stays quiet, I ask, "So what's San Francisco like?"

"Wait, are you saying you've never been?"

When I shake my head, he leans forward, and even a good ten feet away and with very little sun penetrating the mist, I can tell his eyes are lit up. "You have to let me show you around when we dock there. I *love* watching people experience my city for the first time."

"Oh . . . um . . . sure, okay."

His grin is self-satisfied, like he's just scored a point, and I duck my head to hide my own smirk. I don't think so, buddy. I'm not that easily won over.

I pretend to be so consumed by my lookout duties that I don't notice him moving along the deck, stepping over ropes, until he's just opposite me. He sits without comment, settling his back against the other side of the mast.

"Needed someone keeping an eye off the port side," he says casually.

"Cool," I mumble, before clearing my throat. "So I was asking what San Francisco is like. . . ."

Jonah answers quickly. "Water, water, everywhere."

I groan. "No, not what *this* is like."

"Ha! Not quite like this." He turns his torso so he's halfway facing me, our shoulders nearly touching. "The city's built on hills, meaning most everywhere you go, you're gonna at least catch glimpses down to the bay. You get so used to being near the water that after a while, it becomes part of you. I seriously don't know how I let my dad talk me into Cornell. Can't knock an Ivy League education, but being landlocked in the middle of New York State was probably the thing I hated most about college. Well, that and the crap-tons of snow."

"Hated. Past tense. Mom mentioned something about you leaving school."

He lowers his head and coughs. "Yeah, well. I was supposed to be on a plane back to campus yesterday, to work with my advisor on an independent study, so . . . I guess it's done now."

I mutter a quiet, "Wow."

"Yup. Wow."

"Are you dropping out for good?"

His voice retains its usual confidence. "I only deferred, for now. Even if I do end up withdrawing, I can take a few semesters as a leave of absence before I'd have to reapply. And I get to keep the credits I already earned, so . . ."

"Right. That's cool."

As someone who's counting the days until college, I'm not sure I can relate to anyone wanting to leave it behind, but I do fully support the practice of free will. Especially since it's been denied to me so much lately.

"So what's your plan in the meantime?" I ask.

"Not sure. I'm gonna hang around Mexico for a bit to try to figure that out. I've been on kind of a predetermined path since around, oh, say, *birth* and it, uh, it was time for a detour and some reassessing."

I open my mouth to ask a follow-up question, but Jonah picks just then to sound the foghorn. He stands and crosses to the instrument panel. When he returns a few minutes later, he doesn't seem all that eager to resume our conversation.

We're both quiet, other than Jonah continuing to blare the horn every two minutes. Eventually, to keep from nodding off—because holy hell am I tired, and being wrapped in a blanket of fog is not helping matters—I bring my knees under my chin and turn to face him. "What is it you like so much about sailing?"

He thinks it over for a second, and then he answers, "I don't know who to attribute this to, but some poet once said, 'the sea makes a man suspect he's homeless and has no roof but dreams,' and something about that's always resonated with me."

Okay, seriously? First he's all over-the-top flirty and now he's quoting poetry. Epic eye roll.

I would never say anything that rude to his face, but he must see something in my expression, because his eyes get wide and he shakes his head. "Wait. No. I swear I'm not *that guy*."

I raise my eyebrows. "That guy?"

"You know," he says. "The pretentious private school brat who wears a sweater knotted around his neck and snaps his fingers at waiters or checks out your best friend's ass while his arm's around *your* shoulder."

My eyebrows remain up.

"Look! I can't even snap." He holds out his hand and

demonstrates. His thumb slips noiselessly across his middle finger. "Honestly. It's like a weird defect of mine. And I own exactly one sweater, which has *never* had its sleeves tied together."

"What about the best friend's ass?" I ask, earning a laugh and an appreciative look from him.

"Okay, I wasn't going to go there, but since you did . . . I'm more of a leg guy, if you must know." He gives me a wicked grin.

"Oh, I'll bet you are."

"What's that supposed to mean?" he asks, all wide-eyed and innocent.

"Nothing. I'm just guessing you do okay with the ladies."

He looks scandalized, but the hint of laughter in his eyes betrays him. "I take offense to that characterization, I'll have you know."

"Mmm-hmm," I answer.

He bops me playfully on the head as he stands to check the instruments once more before returning to sit beside me.

"Okay," I say, once he's settled. "Let's go with your insistence that you're not *that guy*. What's with the poetry quoting, then?"

"I don't like to admit it," he says, with an exaggerated sigh, "but it's possible there's a note of truth in the private school brat thing."

"Um, I believe you said *pretentious* private school brat."

He smiles his appreciation again. "Way to call me on my

crap, Sprite. I knew there was something I liked about you."

I will myself not to blush, instead giving him a "what can I say" shrug that makes him laugh.

"Well, if I am, I don't *mean* to be," he says. "I can't exactly unlearn all the knowledge that was imparted to me, can I?"

"Well, you probably *could* refrain from trotting it out to impress the girls."

He makes a show of looking around. "Wait, there's more than one girl here?"

When I just shake my head in exasperated amusement, he asks, "Does that mean it's not working?"

I roll my eyes. "Do you have an answer to my question about the ocean that doesn't involve unknown poets?"

He smirks. "Do you have an answer to *my* question about whether I'm making an impression on you?"

I level him with a look, and he laughs. "Okay, you want a genuine, heartfelt answer, I get it. If I tell you what I love about the sea, in my own words, would that be satisfactory?"

I feign indifference. "For starters."

He smiles, then gestures out to the expanse of water beyond the wall of fog. "I love how small and insignificant I feel out here."

"That's a *good thing*?" I'm stunned. "That's what's most terrifying to me, being all vulnerable and, like, completely at the whim of this crazy, uncontrollable, massive ocean."

He nods. "Yeah, I get that it could feel that way. But it's a matter of perspective, I think. I look at it as more of a big-picture thing. If I'm just this teeny tiny dot on the sea, it makes my problems seem kind of ridiculous in the grand scope. Know what I mean? Sailing sort of . . . lets me get out of my own way."

He makes some sense, I guess.

But what if the person responsible for all your problems is *with* you at sea?

What then?

I try to fight a yawn, but Jonah catches me. "You look like you're about to fall asleep sitting up. You ready to call it a night?"

I hesitate, but my lids are reaching the point where I'll need toothpicks to prop them open soon. As much as I like talking to Jonah, I have to give in to my exhaustion.

"Would you mind? I'm really sorry, but my eyeballs are stinging."

He stands and holds out a hand to help me up. "Stinging eyeballs is probably not great criteria for a lookout."

"What about you? Aren't you dead on your feet too?"

"The captain always goes down with the ship," he jokes. When I squint at him in reply, he says, "I'm one of those freaks who only need a few hours of sleep a night. I'm completely fine, honest. Get some rest—you're totally safe under my command."

You're never *totally safe*, I badly want to tell him. Although at the moment, I actually do feel pretty okay.

"Thanks. Good night, then. Or . . . good morning, I

guess." I pass behind him, suddenly feeling a little shy, which is silly.

Even with my back to him, I can hear the smile in his voice when he says, "Night, Sprite. Don't let the bedbugs bite. Hey, did you catch that rhyme? I didn't even mean to do that. Must be my fancy private school education."

I'm still half groaning, half laughing as I retreat to my berth and fall onto my bed.

15

"Okay, check this out," Drew says, reading off his laptop as we lounge aboard *Tide Drifter*. "This is from the Pier 39 Marina's website: 'We have a sea lion herder on the docks every day to keep the sea lions from hauling out on guest areas. . . . If you find a sea lion on your dock, contact the marina staff.'"

I cross my ankles under me and break off a piece of turkey sandwich. "So, what, like, a pretty decent-sized animal could be flopping around on our boat and we're supposed to casually call for the herder?"

At the moment, we're docked at the oh so romantically named Spud Point Marina in Bodega Bay, where Christian and Jonah are off picking up the new Zodiac. But all our thoughts and planning are on San Francisco, which we'll be setting sail for tomorrow and will be able to explore the day after that.

I'm so ridiculously excited. After seventeen days at sea,

we'll finally be in a city! People! Buildings! Restaurants! SOLID LAND!!! Absolutely anything civilized a person who's been living on a sailboat for weeks could want!

"What kind of background do you think is necessary to become a sea lion herder?" Amy asks, passing Grace a napkin mere seconds before the Popsicle she's eating drips onto the deck.

"And who sets out to become one?" Miranda adds.

"*I* want to be a sea lion herder," Abigail pronounces.

We all share a smile over her head.

"Well. Then we should be asking you these questions," my mother says. She holds her fist like a microphone under Abigail's chin. "Just what makes you determined to be a sea lion herder when you grow up, young lady?"

Abigail squints at Mom's hand and then leans over to me. "What's she doing?" she whispers.

I swallow around a piece of sandwich that suddenly sticks in my throat. "She's, um—" I take a deep breath and avoid looking at Mom. "It's a game she and I used to play when I was your age, Abs. I would be so tired out from school that I would only give one-word answers to questions about my day, so she invented this game where she was a news reporter and I was her interview subject, to get me talking."

Abigail looks doubtful. "Did it work?"

I smile. "I was kind of obsessed with the idea of being on TV back then, so yeah, pretty much."

Abigail leans over Mom's hand and says, "I want to be a herder because sea lions are cute and bald and wrinkly like my gramps."

My mother ruffles her hair.

"Do *you* still play the TV game?" Grace asks me, her eyes big and round.

I have to take a second before I can get out, "Nope. Not anymore, Gracie."

Now I do glance up at Mom, only to find her eyes on me. They're hauntingly sad, and I drop my gaze immediately before she sees my own fill with tears.

I gather a shaky breath and make my voice as cheerful as possible. "You know what? *You guys* are pretty lucky. You can take a nap in the middle of the school day whenever you want. How cool is that?"

Mom clears her throat and begins busily taking our paper plates.

"We'll be finding out for ourselves soon enough," Drew says.

Even though it's only July and back home we don't start school until the end of August, we're planning to start our online courses any day now. They're pre-ordered courses, so we can bang them out anytime, and because we both want shorter school days, we're planning to spread two months' worth of classes over three.

A motor draws near, and Jonah's voice sounds across the water.

"We're back in business!" he says, pulling up in the brand-new Zodiac.

Everyone hops up to *ooh* and *aah* over it, while I take the advantage of the relative privacy to glance at a text I get from Tara.

Tara: Picture. ASAP. You promised yesterday.

I type a quick reply.

Me: Haven't had opportunity to take without him noticing.

Tara: No time like the present. Where is he?

Me: Here.

Tara: Do it. Now. I'll loop Jess into our convo.

She's been bugging me for a photo of Jonah since I told her about him joining us. If I don't deliver soon, she'll probably resort to texting Drew. I peek at Jonah helping Abigail aboard the Zodiac.

I tuck my phone next to my hip, my finger on the camera button, and call down, "Hey, Abby!"

As hoped, they both look up at me. I snap the shot, then slide my cell farther out of view.

"Yeah?" she asks.

"Oh. Um, I just wondered if you wanted the rest of your chips?"

She gives me a weird look. "No. You can have them."

Jonah smiles and waves, and I return the gesture before slinking back to my seat. I shield my eyes from the sun and check out my paparazzi work. Jonah has a quizzical look on his face, but the guy is pretty undeniably cute no matter what expression he's making, so I attach it to a text. Within seconds, they both reply.

Tara: Um, holy hotness! You should hit that.

Jess: If you don't, I might.

Me: Hit that? Are we frat boys now?

Jess: Ooh—can I be president? I christen us Eta Alpha Theta Me.

Me: I miss you guys!! Why aren't you here?!??

Tara: Because four's a crowd and you have Pirate Sexytimes to bag.

Me: Negative. Dealing w/enough drama already on the Elise front. Besides, he's a GIANT flirt. Flirt = player. Been there, done that.

Jess: Player = fling. Don't see a problem. Go get you some pirate's booty, my sweets!

Me: Until fling fizzles out and we're stuck in a boat caravan together for next 3 months! Hella awkward!

Tara: She may have a point.

Of course I have a point. Jonah is adorable and fun and . . . well, adorable. But there's no way I believe that he's flirting with me specifically. He would be chatting up *any* girl in front of him on this trip; I just happen to be the only one in his path right now.

Besides, even if I wanted to add more drama to my life, I'm not sure I'm built for casual, so why bother going there and risking heartache when I'm already feeling fragile enough emotionally?

There's not much about this trip that's in my control, but this one thing *is*.

I tap my screen to type a response to my friends.

"Hey, Sprite."

Aaaah! I was so absorbed in the *thought* of Jonah that I didn't notice his actual person climbing the ladder to board the boat. I jump, and the phone falls from my hand and skitters across the deck, landing practically at his feet. He bends and scoops it up, turning it over in his hand and glancing down.

Please let it have shut off, please let it have shut off.

But even in the bright sun, I can see the green word bubbles of my text conversation with Tara and Jess.

Please don't let him have read, please don't let him have read.

Jonah passes it to me, and I swear there's a tiny smirk on his face. "You got lucky—doesn't look like the screen cracked."

Lucky, my ass. I'm not feeling anything remotely like lucky.

My skin burns, and I'm torn between wanting to check which parts of our conversation might have been visible and wanting to get the thing out of sight/out of mind as quickly as possible. I stuff it into the pocket of my shorts.

"Thanks," I mumble.

"My pleasure," he replies, and there is definite amusement in his eyes.

We're close enough to the San Andreas fault line, right? Where is a non-damage-causing-but-very-distracting earthquake when you need one?

I lean over the side of *Tide Drifter* and call to my mother and Drew. "Are you guys ready to head back to *Sunny*?"

"Sure," my mom replies. "I've got a phone interview to prep for—the one and only bite I got on all those résumés I've been sending out. But it only takes one, right?"

My mother, ladies and gentlemen. Eternal optimist.

"I'm staying with Jonah," Drew says. "He's gonna show me a hack he knows for my game."

I hop down and climb into *Minecraft*, tossing off a quick "bye" to Jonah. Ordinarily I would not relish the idea of being alone with my mother, but I'm pretty desperate to escape at the moment.

It could also be the perfect opportunity to ask her about touring San Francisco with Jonah. Wondering whether he did or did not see the texts wouldn't keep me from exploring with him . . . but my mother could. I'm dying to be free of her for a whole day, especially when it means checking out the city with someone my own age who is also pretty fun. But I haven't been able to work up the courage to ask. I wanted to have it to look forward to for as long as possible, without opening myself up to the risk of her ruining everything by saying no.

As far as I'm concerned, this is the first big test as to whether she really means it when she says she's going to start treating me like an adult and giving me more freedom on this trip.

There hasn't been much chance for that so far. In Crescent City, where we landed following our sail through Gale Alley, we spent most of our time at dock restocking, refueling, refilling our water supplies, and repairing. Oh, and pumping out the poop tank. Let's not forget that. The marina was practically five-star accommodations after our remote anchorages, so I didn't really mind that we were still more or less confined to it. None of us has access to wheels (apart from Drew's skateboard and Christian's bike) and there wasn't all that much to do in the walkable vicinity.

Same with today's stop.

But in San Francisco we'll be docked right in the heart of things, and there will be *everything* to explore.

Once *Minecraft* is motoring toward our sailboat, I collect my breath and then spit out the words fast. "Hey, so, Jonah kind of asked if I wanted to go around San Fran with him. You know, get the lay of the land from the hometown kid . . ."

I trail off and wait for all the excuses for why she'd prefer I stay with her and Drew and do the family thing. After that, she'll probably restate her feelings about Jonah's life choices, and then she'll most likely—

"Sure, honey. Sounds fun," she says.

I startle. "Really?"

We reach *Sunny-Side Up*, and she hops out to tie us on.

She glances over the rope at me. "I told you I'd make more of an effort."

I force my jaw not to drop. "Yeah, okay. Cool."

"All I ask is that you bring your phone and check in now and then, 'kay?"

"Done."

Freedom? A whole city to explore? With Jonah as a guide? San Francisco, here I come!

16

Jonah is waiting at the end of the dock, wearing a pair of frayed khaki shorts, a navy Henley shirt, and a Giants cap that leaves his hair curling around its edges.

"So you're *really* a virgin, huh?" he asks with a goofy eyebrow waggle, once I'm close enough to hear him over the constant barking of the sea lions lining the docks.

I blush, despite knowing perfectly well he's talking about the fact that I've never been to San Francisco before. But, skin reactions aside, I'm ready for any Jonah-patented witty banter. I may not be willing to let things progress past that, but I'm totally gonna enjoy myself with it.

"Be gentle with me," I purr, fluttering my eyelashes. I'm rewarded with his laugh.

We wave at Amy, who's trying to pry Grace and Abigail away from a railing overlooking a platform where a massive quantity of sea lions are flopping across one another. They call guttural *ark, ark, ark*s, and I have to admit, they're completely endearing. Except if one comes aboard my boat while I'm on it. Then I'm going ninja on its ass, no matter how cute it is.

Jonah places his hand at the small of my back and steers me around a street performer dressed as a bride who's setting up a box in the center of the sidewalk. We're docked right on Pier 39, which has to be stop one for all the sightseers, judging by the gimmicky shops and the kiosks hawking harbor tours. There's an energy that buzzes through the air, and I wonder if I can feel it so acutely because it's been forever since I've been around this many people at once.

"Okay, so we're close to Fisherman's Wharf," Jonah says as we pass the aquarium and turn right (actual right, not "to our starboard side," because we're on *land*, praise the gods). "This area of town has the best provisions to get our day started, despite being a tourist trap. But after that, I show you your San Francisco this morning, then this afternoon I show you mine. Sound good?"

"*My* San Francisco? I've never been here before. How can I have my own version?"

Jonah laughs easily. "I may not know you that well yet, but I've gleaned enough. I predict I'll be able to make you fall head over heels in love in three hours flat."

My jaw drops open, and Jonah playfully nudges my shoulder with his. "I meant with the *city*, Sprite. Take it easy there."

I knew that. I nudge him back, not quite as gently, and he laughs.

"Inhale," he orders as we approach a two-story glass structure with its own silo that has the words "Boudin Sourdough" printed on it. He nods in satisfaction when I follow his instruction and sigh happily.

I may not have wanted to come on this trip, but I'd be crazy to let that stop me from embracing everything about today, starting with the turtle-shaped loaf of bread Jonah buys us. It would go better with coffee, but he refuses to let me order any. Instead, he tugs me down the street and up a short hill, where we bypass the crowds waiting to board a cable car and duck into Ghirardelli's.

"Screw Rice-A-Roni. *This* is the San Francisco treat," Jonah says, snagging us each a free sample square of chocolate from the greeter and steering me straight to the café. "Trust me?"

"I'm pretty sure you sailing us through those waves last week established that, and besides, we're talking about a chocolate bar. How wrong could it go?"

Turns out, not wrong at all. At *all*. Jonah orders a latte for me with swirls of caramel sauce the barista drizzles on top in an elaborate design. He chooses a peppermint bark mocha that smells like Christmas in a cup (and tastes even better, when he offers me a sip). I snap a close-up of a giant bin filled with wrapped candy to send to Dad as today's "plus" picture, although I suspect I'll have my pick of shots to choose from before the day is out. San Francisco is making a *very* good first impression.

Once we're properly caffeinated, with some bonus chocolate boosters and a bit of sourdough to soak it all up, we head back into the pale sunshine.

Jonah practically bounces on his heels. "Ready for this, Sprite?"

I don't know what he has planned, but I'm game. "Bring it, Abrahmson."

He steps to the curb and whistles for a nearby cab.

"I'm good with walking," I protest as I slide across the seat anyway.

"We'll be doing tons of that today, but for now I just want to be there." He turns to the driver. "JFK and Conservatory."

I stare out the window, taking in views of the iconic bridge, the crazy bicyclists zooming by, and the pastel-colored buildings. We leave the streetscapes behind and enter a huge wooded area.

"What is this place?" I ask Jonah.

"Golden Gate Park," he answers, looking out his own window.

"Is it good to be home? Are you planning to see your family?" I ask, watching him ogle all the eye candy San Francisco has to offer.

"Nothing quite compares to this city."

I notice that isn't quite an answer to my question, but I don't press the matter because the cab slows and pulls to the side. Jonah pays, slapping away the cash I offer, and motions me out.

If I didn't know better, I'd swear we were in the middle of a country estate. There aren't even regular city noises. Instead there are bird calls and rustling leaves and a far-off lawn mower.

I clap my hand over my mouth as I spot a sign for the Conservatory of Flowers. "Are we going there?"

"We could," Jonah says, stepping behind me and putting his hands on my shoulders to spin me in the opposite direction. "But I thought you'd appreciate Tree Fern Dell even more."

"Tree Fern Dell?" I'm intrigued. Very, very intrigued.

Jonah laughs at my expression. "Yup. It has 'leaf-sketching wood sprite haven' written all over it. It's a whole forest of giant ferns, and being in it is like hanging out at the bottom of the world's largest salad bowl."

He points the way down a paved path where lush greenery spills over from both sides, and enormous leaves, practically the size of my berth on *Sunny*, form a canopy above us. I more or less skip into the center of it. Immediately the vegetation swallows me up, and damp earth fills my nostrils. After going so long without greenery—save for the tiny bonsai tree Christian gave me—I inhale like a crazy person.

When I turn, I find Jonah right behind me. "This seems off the beaten path, even for a local. How do you know about this place?" I ask, running my fingers across the bumpy bark of a tree trunk.

He cringes. "Promise not to laugh?"

I shake my head. "I can't promise not to laugh, but I can promise not to laugh *meanly*. Does that count?" I have my phone out, Googling, so I can find out what this species of fern is called.

"I guess it'll have to. I came to see it once in high school, after I found out they shot the final scene of *Star Trek II* here. It's where Spock's coffin landed on the Genesis planet."

I look up from my screen. "You're a Trekkie?"

Jonah leans back against one of the trunks. "Mayyyybe?"

"Cool."

"Yeah?" he asks. "You a fan?"

"Sure. I mean, I prefer *Star Wars*, but that's probably just because I live with Drew."

Jonah grins and affects a shaky, high-pitched Yoda voice. "Judge not the fandoms, do I."

I grin back. "Weirdo."

"Weirdo who brought you here, don't forget. Wanna see more?" He turns and ducks under a giant hanging leaf.

"There's more?" I ask, chasing after him eagerly.

We wander the trail for a bit, and Jonah is very patient about my need to document every species with my phone. He even lets me drag him across the street to the Conservatory of Flowers, and then we hike half the park to the botanical gardens, where he covers my eyes and unveils the Helen Crocker Russell Library of Horticulture.

"Nearly thirty thousand volumes of books on all aspects of plant life," Jonah says, stepping back so he can see my face.

I gape, eyes wide. "How do you know that? People don't just know statistics like that!"

He ducks his head. "I may or may not have researched it this week when I was planning today."

Planning today? I'm blown away. I mean, I guess if I stop to think about it, obviously he had to have some kind of a road map for the day, but this goes beyond just giving passing thoughts to spots in the city he'd been to before that I might like. He *researched*? With my specific interests in mind?

He must notice how quiet I get, because he quickly adds, "Listen, I consider myself sworn and bound to convert everyone I encounter into a San Fran fanatic, and it's possible I may take extraordinary measures to assure a favorable outcome."

"Well, so far, your evil plan is working. Consider me fanatical."

"Now, now, Sprite. Don't make it too easy for me. We still have lots of ground to cover. Hey, did you bring your sketchbook?" he asks.

I pat my backpack.

"Perfect. *You* get to go inside and take all the time you want. Just so you don't have to worry about me getting bored or breathing down your neck—not that I'd do either, of course—I'm gonna hang out here and make some calls to see if any of my local gang is in town."

All the time I want in a library devoted just to plants would take us into the following year and then some, but I content myself with an hour of copying sketches from some of the first botanical books ever printed and term it heaven. When I emerge again, Jonah is sitting cross-legged on a bench, chatting on the phone. When he spots me, he holds up a finger while he says a quick good-bye, then stands.

"Was it all that you hoped for?" he teases.

"And then some. Don't mock!"

He holds up his hands in surrender. "I told you before. I don't judge the fandoms. Even when they take plant form."

I laugh, but I hope he knows how touched I am that he backed away and gave me that time in there to overdose on botany. In case he doesn't, I say, "Seriously, Jonah, that was really sweet of you to think of this and to be so patient when you could be off with your friends doing—"

He waves me quiet. "Stop. This is exactly where I want to be today. And if you want to keep exploring here, we can, but otherwise . . . *my* San Francisco awaits. Ready for it?"

"A thousand percent."

Despite blissing out all morning over everything Jonah planned for my version of the city, I'm totally ready for more exploring . . . and maybe just a little curious to see what he's into.

17

"Okay, so if there's one word to describe the tour we're about to go on, it's *random*," Jonah states.

"I'm good with random."

I follow him out of the gardens, where he hails another cab, instructing it to drop us at Seward Mini Park.

"Another park? I thought we'd moved on to your version now?" I ask. "Wait, are you a closet botany freak too?"

"Hush now. You'll see," he replies with a cryptic grin.

When Jonah has the cab pull over outside a liquor store along the way, I'm even more curious.

"Stay right here," he tells me before sliding out and popping inside.

Not much time passes before he returns and places two empty cardboard boxes on the seat between us. He begins tearing off the sides.

"Do I dare ask?"

"Nope," he says, giving me another mysterious smile.

The cab drops us on a nondescript corner, next to a tall concrete wall that blocks whatever's on the other side. Jonah finds a recycling bin for the pieces of boxes he doesn't want, then gestures for me to follow him through a gap in the wall. Immediately, I figure out what the cardboard is for.

We're at the top of a hill, facing side-by-side slides carved into the downward slope. I can't quite see where they end, only the first five feet or so, before they twist out of view. They look like waterslides, except they're entirely cement. A trio of green metal archways lines the launch point.

"Your magic carpet, m'lady," Jonah says, offering me one of the box bottoms.

"How long is this thing?" I ask, trying to peer over the edge.

"Long enough. And I want credit for passing up a perfect 'that's what she said' opportunity," he answers, and laughs when I roll my eyes at him. He drops his cardboard "sled" on the left slide and settles his butt onto it. "C'mon! Time's wasting."

When I'm situated on the right side, he holds out his hand. "When we were kids, my friends and I used to bet other teams to see which of us could keep connected the whole way down. The challenge comes when you start picking up speed; one slide's always faster than the other."

"Baby Jonah, the swindler. Or was it all just an excuse to get the girls to hold hands with you?"

"Who says they needed an excuse?" he asks with a grin.

"Now don't be a wimp. Grab on."

"A dislocated shoulder isn't exactly the San Francisco souvenir I was hoping for."

But I slide my palm against his and shriek as he uses his other hand to repeatedly push off against the concrete. My squeals soon turn to laughter as we twist and turn down the hillside. Just as my butt starts to slide off the cardboard and my fingers threaten to slip loose from Jonah's, we hit the bottom, passing under a last metal archway.

I can't stop giggling. "That was amazing."

"Right?" He drops my hand and shakes out his fingers. "I think you cut off my circulation!"

"You're the one who said we had to stay connected. I don't back down from a challenge."

Jonah laughs. "Noted. I'm not sure I'll have fine motor skills in this hand for a week or so, but hopefully Christian won't need any help hauling lines before then."

I give him a look. "Dramatic much?"

He pointedly ignores me and scopes out the playground we've landed in. "God, I loved this place as a kid. I used to beg my nanny to take me here, but most of the time she insisted it was too far."

"Your *nanny*?"

Jonah grins. "Hey, it's not like *I* hired her. I can't help my background." He steps close and uses his hands to draw an imaginary box around us. "Judgment-free zone?"

"I can handle that." I smile up at him. When he returns

it softly, I'm suddenly very aware of how little space there is between us. I suck in a breath and take a step away. "Again?" I hold my cardboard up and gesture to the staircase leading back to the top.

"Only if we can race this time," he answers.

Oh, it's on.

After the slides (which he wins every time, damn him), we take off on foot up Twentieth Street, stopping to grab slices of pizza. Our tall cups of root beer have ice in them! Normally that wouldn't merit exclamation levels of excitement, but after the last few weeks at sea, that's become a total novelty. My mattress freezer has only so much space, and none of it is dedicated to ice cube trays.

When we reach yet another park, I let Jonah drag me to the very corner, where he points. "Voilà! Our next stop."

"It's a fire hydrant."

He scoffs at my unimpressed tone. "Yes, Captain Obvious. It's a fire hydrant. But not just *any* fire hydrant."

"Well, sure, I can see that it is, in fact, a golden fire hydrant. Color me dazzled."

Jonah pretends to be offended. "It's gold because it gets painted that way every year on April eighteenth. Ever heard of the Great Earthquake of San Francisco?"

"Of course."

He examines the hydrant with a mixture of awe and respect. "Afterward, most of the city was on fire, but the water mains were damaged in the quake, meaning none of the hydrants worked. Except this one. This now-golden hydrant allowed firefighters to save most of the Mission District. Pretty cool, huh?"

What's cool is the pride in Jonah's voice as he talks about his city. I love my hometown, but there's not much to show off about it, outside of ordinary suburban neighborhoods, some farmland, and the chain restaurants in nearby Springfield.

After I pay a suitable amount of homage, as determined by Jonah, he asks, "You up for more walking?"

"Are you kidding? After being stuck treading back and forth across the same forty feet of deck for the last few weeks?"

He must take that as a challenge, because we spend nearly an hour hiking to our next destination: a hotel in Union Square. I don't care, though, because I'm soaking in everything about my surroundings, even when we're walking through parts of the city that aren't spit-shined and prettified for tourists. I like those areas; they give me a sense for what it must be like to live here.

In front of the Westin St. Francis, Jonah stops us, and I eye the deep red awnings and the doormen lining the carpeted entrance.

"Huh. Yeah, so, I'm not all that sure our relationship is at the point of 'afternoon delight,' big guy."

He snort-laughs, which should be gross, but is pretty funny actually. Why does it feel so good to make someone else laugh?

"Don't worry, I have nothing but *mostly* honorable intentions. Hey, do you have any coins on you?"

I ignore the "mostly" tease and dig in my pockets instead. "Will these work?"

"Perfect! Follow me."

We walk through an opulent lobby that is all pillars, dark wood paneling, and giant globe chandeliers, until we reach the reception desk, where Jonah asks, "Is Lillie working today?"

The clerk places a phone call and we hang in the lobby for a minute or two, until an older woman with thinning gray hair and wearing a flowered sundress appears at the far end. When she reaches us, Jonah's hug practically lifts her off her feet, and she giggles as he sets her down. Just as I suspected: serial charmer.

"Lillie, I'd like you to meet my friend Cassie. It's her first time in our fine city by the bay. How could I pass up the chance to introduce her to the only professional money launderer in the world?"

She shakes my hand as I process his words.

"I'm sorry—money launderer? Like . . ." I lower my voice to a whisper. "Like a mobster?"

Wait until Drew finds out. He and Mom were heading to Alcatraz to see where Al Capone lived about a million years ago, but *I* get to meet a real live criminal. *And* she's a woman. So cool.

Except both of them laugh.

"Not quite. Follow me," Lillie says.

We trail her through an employees-only entrance and down flights of stairs into the basement of the hotel, where she holds open the door to a small room and gestures us through. The space is hardly bigger than a closet and has black-and-white pictures of women wearing fancy hats and furs on one wall. An ancient-looking machine lines another, and a table with a handful of lamps pointed at its surface sits in a corner. On the tabletop are coins of every denomination, which appear to be . . . drying?

Jonah watches my face with that now-familiar twitch in his lips. "Lillie here washes all the change that comes through the hotel. She's the only one of her kind in existence. A literal money launderer."

Lillie inclines her head modestly. "Man before me held the job for thirty-one years, and I'm just trying to fill his shoes. It's an honor."

I can't help asking, "But why wash the money? It's the coolest job ever, don't get me wrong. I'm just curious about the reason behind it."

"Came about back in the thirties. This has always been one of the most esteemed hotels in the city. Back then, proper women wouldn't dream of being out and about without those." Lillie points to a picture on the wall and gestures to the short white gloves worn by a lady clutching her fur stole around her neck. "Our owner noticed that the ladies were dirtying theirs whenever they handled change, so he decreed that all of the coins used here at our hotel would be clean and shiny. Earned us quite the reputation too. Got to be so cab drivers around the city would know to ask 'How was your stay at the St. Francis?'

just by noting the gleam on the money a passenger paid with."

She indicates the table, where the coins are all, indeed, sparkling.

Jonah prompts, "Give her your quarters."

I hand them to Lillie, who immediately places them in the machine behind her. "These'll have to sit in this burnisher for several hours while the bird shot and Borax work their magic, then dry for a bit under the heat lamps. Something tells me you don't have that kind of time." She pauses to glance at Jonah—who shakes his head—before continuing, "Go on and grab a couple replacements."

I select two of the shiniest coins I've ever seen. "Thank you so much."

"Anything for a friend of this troublemaker," she replies, and I dart a glance at the subject of Lillie's praise. He's clearly basking in the attention.

She notices too, and says, "Stop using an old biddy to impress the ladies, would ya?"

From the corner of my eye I watch Jonah elbow Lillie lightly. "Who says I'd need your help with that, Lil? I got game when I need it. Anyway, I won't be intruding on your peace after today, because I'll be safely tucked away in Mexico."

"Still thinking you'll stay on down there?"

"Yup. Come visit. Maybe I'll hook you up with a surfing lesson, if you think you can get those creaky knees to hang ten."

Lillie doesn't return his smile. "I was hoping you would change your mind. You need a diploma, J."

Jonah crosses his arms. "Not for every job." He gestures to the coin-washing operation. "Case in point."

She puts a hand on her hip. "You know damn well I used all *three* of my degrees plenty when I worked with your father. This is great fun, yes, but it's a retirement job, not a career. Don't be an idiot, kid."

"Now you sound like Dad," Jonah says, scowling. He darts me a look, and I immediately bend over the table and resume my pretend examination of the other coins there.

Lillie says, "I'm sure he's also telling you to at least think about what you're giving up. Can you try that?"

Jonah squares his shoulders. "We should get going, Lil. Thanks for showing all this to Cassie."

Clearly the discussion part of our visit is over, and Lillie gets the message too, because after one lingering look at Jonah, she escorts us back to the lobby and hugs us both good-bye. I notice she seems reluctant to let go of Jonah.

"Good luck," she tells him. "You can always come home. Remember."

"Wanna talk about any of that?" I ask as we exit the hotel.

"Nope," he says, and his body language screams "pissed off," which is a definite departure from his usual playful vibe.

I'm not sure how to act right now—our "relationship," for lack of a better term, has been entirely based on mutual teasing and goofing around. The only time we had a real opportunity for quiet conversation—on our foggy morning sail—we both deflected when more serious topics came up, and that was just fine by me. But now, after witnessing all that, I'm strangely curious about the Jonah hiding behind those smirky grins of his. I fall quietly into step beside him.

Whether he has to force it or not, I don't know, but within a few minutes he's back to his usual smiling self as he tugs me onto a cable car in Union Square. "You're gonna love this! It's crazy fun to watch someone experience these for the first time."

We find seats, and I peer all around as we ride up the steepest hill ever, lined by immaculate buildings. Jonah pulls me off at the intersection of California Street and races us across to a different cable car, going in a crossing direction.

"Okay, no more benches for you, newbie. You've had your introduction, so now we're doing this the right way. All the way in the front, stand on the platform down here, and no closing your eyes."

We're balanced on a tiny ledge hanging off the side of the cable car, and if I were to lean over any, I'd be inches from the street. When we crest the hill it's like reaching the top of the roller coaster . . . and the downward drop awaiting us is terrifying. There's no way we're not going to hit a thousand miles an hour!

Jonah's standing close behind me, and I involuntarily lean back into him as I shriek for the second time today. Immediately, his free arm wraps around my stomach and pulls me close, and it surprises me almost as much as the fact that this car is heading down a kamikaze decline attached to the street by only a single cable. It's entirely possible he's just trying to keep me from splatting onto the pavement, but still. Even though I *was* grasping his hand in a death grip on the slides earlier, this kind of embrace is completely different, and I'd have to be dead not to notice how firm his chest is.

His breath is soft in my ear, as is his voice when he says, "I gotcha, Sprite."

When we reach the bottom, the car stops, and I exhale as Jonah releases me lightly. I step off, avoiding his eyes as I clear my throat. "Now where?"

Jonah grins easily, clearly not affected the same way I was either by the ride of terror we just endured *or* our proximity during it.

"I thought we could walk over to the ferry terminal," he says. "The indoor farmers market is there, and we can grab a snack if you're hungry. Then I want to show you the wild parrots on Telegraph Hill."

"Sure, okay. Food, then parrots. Wait, there are wild *parrots*? Your city is so cool." I pause to take in the busy streetscape and the height of the buildings we're standing beneath. "Hey, are we near where you grew up? I want the full Jonah Abrahmson's San Francisco tour."

He's quiet for a moment, and his eyes dart to the ground. "We, um . . . we were just in Nob Hill. We passed my house right near where we changed cable cars."

"We did? Why didn't you point it out?" I'm stunned, but Jonah must not think it's a big deal, because he just shrugs and continues up the sidewalk.

I follow, waiting for him to answer, but that seems to be all he's offering. "Does this have to do with all that stuff Lillie said back there at the hotel?" I ask.

"A little."

"You *sure* you don't feel like talking about it?"

He shakes his head once, like he's trying to clear it, then turns to smile at me. "Nah. Today is not about you listening to me whine. Today is all about *me* introducing *you* to the hidden depths of San Francisco."

He turns his attention to dodging a family heading toward us, and when they don't show any signs of moving either left or right, we split up to maneuver around them.

When we meet back in the middle, some crazy instinct possesses me to ask, "What if I'd rather be introduced to the hidden depths of Jonah Abrahmson?"

I went into today with every intention of keeping things fun and light between us, and we've definitely had that for most of the time. Except I got glimpses of a real person back at the St. Francis, and in a few instances earlier, and they left me curious. I think his harmless flirting is adorable, but now I'm caught off guard by how much I want to know more about him.

He stops walking and studies me with curiosity.

I scratch my neck, and speak from the heart. "There's no one else our age on this trip. Might as well become friends, right?"

He relaxes. "We're not friends?" he asks, clutching his heart and staggering backward like I've injured him. "But I showed you my fire hydrant."

It takes everything in me not to make a wiseass comment about the double entendre, but I know deflection when I see it. I stand my ground, even if it might entail opening myself up to some quid pro quo. "What I meant was, not just hanging-out, goofing-around friends, but real, actual friends."

He tips his baseball cap and wipes his forehead with his sleeve before tugging it back into place and looking down at me. When he slowly smiles, his lips show no trace of their usual amused twitch in either corner.

"You know what?" he says softly. "I think I could really use an actual friend."

Me too.

Me freaking too.

18

"**What are you** *doing*?" Jonah asks when I start a shimmy in my shoulders and move it down my body, like a boxer prepping to head into the ring.

"I'm working out my excess energy, so I'm nice and calm and ready to hear your sob story," I say, grinning.

"Oh my god, what kind of sordid tale do you think I have to tell?" He shakes his head at me and starts walking, glancing over his shoulder to make sure I'm following. A few blocks ahead is the hulking Bay Bridge, choked with midafternoon traffic, and the bay itself, visible between the low white rectangular buildings lining the waterfront.

"I dunno. I'm hoping tabloid-worthy. Or, like, juicy memoir material."

Jonah takes a noticeable breath. "You will be very disappointed, then. There have been a thousand and one memoirs with my exact plot because it's the least original in the world. In a nutshell? My dad wants me to finish my business degree so I can join him at his company and, I don't know, make widgets for the rest of my life and preside over board meetings. Have brunch at the yacht club on Saturdays and sneak in covert powwows at the Bohemian Club on Sundays. And . . . I'm not so much interested."

"Ooh, *yeah*. 'Poor little rich boy'? *Such* a trope." We're stopped at a crosswalk, and I watch the "Don't Walk" signal.

When I steal a glance at him, Jonah is grinning at me. "Am I possibly the first 'actual friend' you've tried to make? Because you kind of suck at it. I don't think you're supposed to make fun of the person opening up to you."

I shrug. "Yeah, but you're smiling, right?"

His eyes gleam. "That I am. Touché. Proceed with your convoluted brand of sympathetic understanding."

"My methods are patented, I'll have you know."

Despite my joking around, I actually do feel bad for him. Sure, it's a common-enough occurrence, but it's never happened to *him* before. I'm in no position to judge what someone has the right to be upset about. I fully understand that plenty of people weather their parents' divorce with a million times less whining than me and would consider four months of sailing a privilege, not a punishment. So there's that.

The light changes, and we cross to face an elegant building with about a hundred arches and topped by a gorgeous clock tower. A sign says "Ferry Plaza Farmers Market," and a series of blue-tented tables outside spill every variety of fruits and vegetables. I try to ignore the assault on my senses and give

Jonah my undivided attention, but I have not seen this much fresh food in weeks. There's not a can in sight!

Jonah steps closer to a table selling technicolored produce and asks—with his eyebrows and a head tilt—if I'd like an apple. I let my drool answer for me. He completes the transaction with a pigtailed worker and hands me mine before taking a bite of his own.

We resume browsing the tables, and I ask, "Can you please tell me what exactly covert powwows at the Bohemian Club are? Those could totally be tabloid-worthy, right? Given that I don't think I've ever heard the word 'covert' outside of spy movies."

Jonah swallows his second bite. "Without a doubt. It's a secret society my dad belongs to, along with a whole bunch of other captains of industry."

I choke on the piece of apple I'm chewing. Maybe not so clichéd after all. This doesn't sound garden variety. "Secret society? For real?"

Jonah looks alarmed as I punctuate my questions with coughs. He whacks my back twice before I wave him off. When I recover he says, "I can walk you by their 'clubhouse' later, if you want. It's actually a very proper building, and there's this cool plaque of an owl with the words 'Weaving spiders come not here.' I think the club itself used to mean something different back when Mark Twain and Jack London were members."

He moves us past a tent selling butchered meats before continuing. "But now it's all businessmen who plot to take over the world. They have this private forest in Sonoma where they go for two weeks every summer. My dad's pretty close-lipped about it, but they have this ceremony called the Cremation of Care where they burn away their 'burdens.'" He takes a last bite of apple and wipes his mouth with the back of his hand.

"Should you be telling me this stuff?" Translation: *Tell me more, tell me more!*

Jonah's eyes grow wide and he tugs me inside the Ferry Plaza building, pulling me into a corner behind the doorway. He steps close to shield me, darting glances around suspiciously. "You're right—we can't trust anyone! We should split up and meet back at the safe house!"

I laugh and push his chest until he falters a step. I like that he's opening up to me *and* we're keeping things goofy too. It's . . . nice.

"Pretty sure I'm not spilling any state secrets," he says, resuming our walking exploration. There are more permanent market stands in here, displaying pottery and artisanal soaps and flowers. "That part's all on the internet. There are more sinister rumors too, like that they've orchestrated influential campaigns. A few past presidents are current members."

"Oooh, very *Manchurian Candidate*." I toss my apple core in a can we pass.

Jonah glances over at me in surprise. "You know that movie?"

I grin. "Thank my uncle. His hobby is conspiracy theories. He'd probably have you locked in his basement right now, a vial of truth serum in his hand, if he heard you talking about this stuff."

Jonah's expression falls somewhere between amused and concerned. "Remind me not to meet your uncle in a dark alleyway."

I finger a hand-knit shawl in the opening of one of the shops. "I don't think conspiracy theorists do dark alleyways. Anyway, he lives in Minnesota with six cats and an ugly sweater collection, so you're probably not in any real danger. Okay, more secret-club stuff, please."

Jonah grabs a free sample of a soft pretzel bite offered on a tray outside one of the stands. He hands it to me and takes another for himself before saying, "That's all I got on the subject."

I pout and he chuckles. "Don't worry, I have plenty more about my dad, if you want. For fun times, I could tell you about his reaction when I changed majors halfway through last year."

"From what to what?"

Jonah winces slightly. "Business to philosophy."

"I can see why that might not have gone over well with a captain of industry."

"Yup. The guy's pretty much all work, all the time. Seriously, nothing in this world baffles my father more than the concept of adult coloring books." Jonah grins. "I'm sure you can also imagine, then, how he now feels about having a college dropout for a son."

We approach a coffee stall, and I ask, "Am I gonna need caffeine for this?"

He doesn't answer, just immediately pulls me into the line. I insist on paying, and when we've gotten our drinks, Jonah leads us outside again. We grab seats on long backless benches in the sun.

The air is pungent with now-familiar fishy smells, and I can't tell if it's the seafood stalls of the market or the bay beside us. Maybe both. Above, seagulls circle low and loud, waiting for any spoils. I dip my nose into my coffee cup and inhale deeply to chase the smell away. After being on land all day, I'm nowhere near ready to acknowledge any sights or smells that remind me my current life is on the water.

"So why philosophy?" I ask as we settle in.

I catch Jonah midsip with my question. He makes a face before pulling out three sugar packets and dumping them into his cup. I like him so much more for obviously having a raging sweet tooth that rivals mine. It's starting to worry me a little, all the reasons I can find to like him.

"I took a seminar in it. The irony is that I ended up there because my Environmental Econ class didn't have enough students enrolled to run it, and philosophy had the only opening that fit my schedule. I told my dad I was just gonna take fifteen credit hours instead, because what use would I ever have for a course like that? But no. No son of his would carry a regular course load when there was overachieving to be accomplished."

"Well, then he has only himself to blame."

"Truth." Jonah grins. "The first few assigned readings were like hieroglyphics to me, but then, I don't know, some of the stuff just started to click. . . . I can't really explain it. Most of these guys we were reading lived centuries ago, but the stuff they wrote about is so universal, even today, that it makes me think they had to be onto something, you know?"

I cringe. "I'm really sorry—I'd love to nod along, but I don't know the first thing about philosophy."

"I'll bet you do and you just don't term it that. It's all around us—I'll start pointing it out when I see examples." He looks at me with an expression I can't place before saying, "Can I just say, I totally love that you aren't afraid to admit there are things you aren't an expert in. That's really unusual in my circles."

I blow across the top of my coffee to cool it down more. "Oh, there's no limit to the things I don't know. It sometimes amazes me that I get through a day without totally humiliating myself."

Jonah laughs. "Don't sell yourself short there, Sprite. At least you have the good sense to befriend me. That alone should earn you Mensa status."

"I'll check into that," I say dryly.

"Lemme know what they say," he replies. "So, anyway, when Uncle Chris called to ask if I knew anyone from the yacht club who was trustworthy and might want to crew for him, it just seemed like the universe was dropping a Plan B in my lap."

"Okay, stop me if I ask anything too personal, but I'm confused. Wouldn't your dad rather you get a degree in philosophy versus none at all? Why did you feel like you had to drop out altogether?"

Jonah sighs. "He would, but that would have meant three more years of listening to him bitch about it or make nonstop threats to stop payment on my tuition if I didn't switch back to business. I've been working my butt off at marinas and as a camp counselor since I was fourteen, specifically so I wouldn't always have to rely on his money, but those savings would barely make a dent into costs at Cornell."

I remember how my mom threatened me with my college expenses a few weeks ago and how pissed off it made me. It's not like she or Dad owe me help with tuition or anything, but it's always been something they've offered, and I've been making my college picks based on having that assistance. I'm guessing it was the same with Jonah. I totally understand why he'd rather give his dad a giant F-U than let his father use that money to bully him.

"Were you guys close before this?"

"Me and my dad? Not particularly. I mean, I think he likes the idea of having someone to carry on the family name and someone to show off around the yacht club, especially if I was winning that weekend's regatta."

Wow. He doesn't even sound upset, just matter-of-fact. But to me, it sounds so sad. How could his dad not appreciate how sweet and funny his own son is? Impulsively, I reach for

Jonah's hand, and though I clearly surprise him, he recovers quickly. He gives me a small smile and squeezes my fingers before releasing them.

"What about your mom?" I ask. "Is she around to run interference between you two?"

"She's around. But not for interference. My mom would sooner wear off-the-rack than cross Dad. I don't really know how to describe my parents. Neither is overly warm and fuzzy. To be honest, I didn't see all that much of them growing up. Mostly I was with a nanny. So I guess they don't really know me all that well."

I'm not sure what to say to that either. I may have my fair share of issues with my mom, but I've never had to doubt whether either of my parents *knows me*. Or whether they appreciate me for who I am, not what I can do for their social status. I'm sure my mother would have loved if I'd taken ballet along with her friends' daughters instead of spending all my time digging in the dirt and potting flowers, but she never pushed her agenda on me. She kept me supplied with aprons and gardening gloves and trowels. Once, she and my dad ordered an entire dump truck of dirt when I was desperate to convert a third of our backyard into a vegetable plot. And my dad helped me with my French homework almost every night of sophomore year, never giving me a hard time for struggling with it or making me feel stupid for not catching on faster. They haven't been perfect parents, but the one thing I never wondered about was whether they actually loved me. I mean,

I guess I've probably *said* that about my mother this past year, but deep down I never truly questioned it. Just her methods of showing it, maybe.

"I'm so sorry," I mumble.

"No need. It is what it is—and it's only one small part of my life." His mischievous smile is firmly in place again. "Hey, do you think we've had enough actual-friend bonding, because I think I may have just realized what this day needs!"

I can only blink at him when he turns the grin's full wattage directly at me.

Here's the thing. If you put an extremely attractive boy in front of me, I'm going to at least notice. But a cute charmer is easy enough to resist.

Except the Jonah I'm spending the day with is going from "all flash" to "lots of substance" pretty damn fast, and it's throwing me for a loop. I wasn't planning for our hangouts to be anything more than a diversion, but I'm suddenly feeling a little . . . invested.

Invested is not exactly what I'd expected from today. But then again, neither is this version of Jonah.

I gather a quick breath before any of my conflicted emotions can play out across my face for him to see. "When we get back to the docks, I will punch your time card to signify completion of one entire actual-friend bonding session." I squint up at him. "Although I thought we'd already established this day needs parrots next."

"Another time. This is better. Unless—oh man, I just talked your ear off and all you told me about yourself is that you have a cat-lady uncle. I'm an ass. I'm sorry. Do you want a turn on the psychiatrist's couch? I insist on an equal opportunity, true-blue friendship."

God no. It's bad enough I'm feeling invested after hearing a little of his story. If I let down my defenses and loop him into my own saga, what then?

I lean down for my coffee cup on the ground. "That is very, very sweet of you, but you just told me there is something better than a pack of wild parrots, and I need to see this for myself."

Jonah's expression turns serious. "You sure? Joking aside, I'm happy to listen whenever."

I nod and avoid his eyes. "Thanks. I'll take you up on it sometime."

I stand, waiting for Jonah to do the same, and we turn toward the street. As we walk, he says, "Hey, so, I appreciate your not running away screaming when I unloaded on you."

I bump his hip. "Judgment-free zone, remember?"

He makes a "Hmm" noise in his throat, and I can feel his eyes studying me. But when I glance over at him a second later, his expression shifts quickly and he grins as he says, "Just so you know, Sprite, a grouping of parrots is not a pack. It's a pandemonium."

I gape at him. "A pandemonium of parrots? Aside from being the best band name ever, that is just plain awesome on every level. How do you even *know* that? And remind me. *Why* aren't we seeing them?"

He winks. "Fancy private school education. And because my idea is better than a pandemonium of parrots."

"Now I'm extra curious. Wait. Do we have to get back on that death trap of a cable car?"

"Oh no, I have an entirely different death trap in mind for us."

I raise my eyebrows, but he's tight-lipped.

We cross the street and fall into step with a crowd of pedestrians on the sidewalk. I try my best to take in the honking and the jackhammer and the snippets of conversation from people on their cell phones. I will miss this tomorrow when we're back to listening to the clanging of halyards against the mast or occasional splashes as birds dive-bomb for lunch.

Jonah breaks into my thoughts. "Hey, speaking of hilarious animal terms, did you know a grouping of hedgehogs is called a prickle?"

I bump my hip against his again. "You are so weird."

He bumps back. "Judgment-free zone, Sprite! Judgment-free zone . . ."

19

It turns out *death trap* is the exact proper term for the GoCar Jonah and I rent. GoCar, not go-kart, although it might as well be. The little yellow vehicle is small enough, and looks like one too, with no roof and only a U-shaped metal frame to lean back against. There aren't even any doors, just a scooped-out opening. It has two wheels in the front, but only one in the center of the back. How this thing is even legal for street driving, I'll never know.

"I thought you were supposed to leave your heart in San Francisco, not your spleen!" I yell as we careen around a curve on Lombard Street, the twisty, turny road I know from movies set here.

"Quit your moaning. You know you love it, Sprite," he calls back.

He's right. My stomach is in my throat the whole time, and I think that's exactly what Jonah intended when he suggested it. It's the perfect antidote to our serious conversation back at the farmers market; the carefree spirit of exploring comes right back.

We zip by AT&T Park and over to the Presidio, and then we take the car across the Golden Gate Bridge and down into Sausalito, where Jonah shows me the driveway leading to his summer house on the bay. He doesn't seem to want to linger there, and after our talk, I totally understand why. My guess is his parents don't even know Jonah is in the city.

I hate that this day has to end, but eventually it's time to turn the GoCar in. We make one more pit stop back at Ghirardelli's so he can stock up on tiny chocolate squares. Judging from the size of the bag he drags back to the marina, he'll have enough to see him through an entire lifetime in Mexico.

I spend the last few minutes of our walk up Pier 39 having a very colorful internal debate with myself over whether or not I want Jonah to ask me to hang out with him and his friends later. I know he has plans, because he mentioned them after his phone call at the botanical gardens, and I'm really not looking forward to a quiet boat with just my mother and brother for company. Not after how exhilarating today's been.

Except some time away from Jonah would let me get a handle on the strange ways I've been reacting to him today and shut it down once and for all. I might be willing to admit that maybe there's more to him than I first assumed, and that it's possible he might not be quite the player I made him out to be, but that doesn't mean there aren't other very valid reasons to keep him at arm's length.

For one, there's still the matter of our forced proximity. If anything were to happen with Jonah and then it didn't "take," we'd still have to bump knees at cozy cabin meals for the next three months. It's bad enough being trapped on a boat with one person I want to get distance from, but *two*?

Okay, and if it *did* work out, against all odds, that's equally bad because anything we might have would come with an automatic expiration date. And then we'd have the lengths of two entire countries between us. My parents couldn't even make things work under the same roof, which also doesn't exactly give me much hope for relationships in general.

Definite lose-lose situation.

Or, what about this? Maybe this entire internal debate I'm having with myself is completely beside the point. Maybe Jonah only wants friendship from me. Despite all his flirty innuendos, he's been perfectly platonic all day, aside from that one instance on the cable car, which could very easily be explained away. When I took his hand after he opened up about his parents at the farmers market, he was quick to drop it after one small squeeze.

See, now, *this* is exactly the boy drama I didn't want and don't need!

I'm startled by Jonah's baseball cap settling on my head. "Earth to Cassie? Sorry if I'm interrupting a good daydream, but you're off in la-la land. I've said your name twice. But if the fantasy is about me, please carry on and also narrate as you do, 'kay? Thanks."

I laugh to cover how *not* that far off base he is. We reach the gate to the marina, and Jonah slips the hook free and slides it open. "Ladies first."

"I thought it was brains before beauty," I say.

"Oh, well, in that case." He moves to pass by, but I shove him out of the way and step through ahead of him.

"I did say brains first," I tell him, brushing off my palms.

"No, *you said* brains before beauty. But since you have both in equally staggering quantities, I figured I'd do the gentlemanly thing."

I roll my eyes. "You're so full of it."

"Admit you love it." He grins and resumes walking.

Sunny-Side Up is halfway along the dock and I can already make out the black hull, so I'm surprised when Jonah slows his pace. I stop and turn to face him.

"Hey," he says, stepping forward so he's inches away. "It turns out seeing my city through your eyes was pretty awesome. Thanks for that."

He moves slightly closer, and when his hand accidentally brushes mine, I jolt involuntarily.

"Yeah. Really g-great," I stammer.

My body and my brain need some time to get on the same page here, because one is this close to betraying the other right now.

When he shifts nearer yet, I stumble back a step.

Jonah's eyes flash confusion, and he looks away briefly before returning them to my face. His smile is tentative as he reaches up and swipes the baseball cap from my head. "Just— just trying to grab this before you absconded with it. I know you're San Fran's number one fan after today, but the Giants are more of an acquired taste. These guys you have to earn the hard way."

I force a casual grin and nod. He tucks both hands in his pockets and turns to leave, but then spins back. "Hey, any chance you'd want to head out again later? I'm meeting up with a group of friends from high school, so probably not much sightseeing on the agenda, but . . . they're cool. Might be fun?"

After my big internal pep talk about why it would be good to get some space to better clamp down on my attraction to him, it turns out that I'm a monster fraud, even to myself, because the "Sure!" leaves my mouth faster than Drew can take out a Star Destroyer in his favorite video game.

Jonah's eyes crinkle at the edges as he smiles, for real this time. "Great. I'll swing by in a couple hours. Say, eightish?"

I nod.

"Okay, perfect. *Bytes*' slip is the next dock over, so . . ." He lifts his chin in the direction he's indicating. "See you in a bit."

I nod again and watch him as he walks away. Then I turn and deliver a stern lecture to the jumping beans throwing a party in my stomach. *Not cool, traitorous body. Not cool at all.*

"Hey, stranger," my mother says when I descend the steps. "Thanks for all those texts."

"Oh *crap*," I say. "Sorry."

"You know, you say I need to treat you like an adult, but how am I supposed to do that when you act like a child?"

"Mom, I—"

"No, Cassie. I'm not interested in whatever excuse you're cooking up. You give no indication at all that you spare a thought for me, and whether I might be worried about your safety and well-being. *Adults* take responsibility and follow through on their promises."

The jumping beans in my belly lie down and play dead, but my blood boils. What she's saying *might* not be totally off base, but it's nearly impossible to process her words when most of what I hear is the tone she uses to deliver them.

And, yes, maybe I did forget to text, but if only she knew how *many* thoughts I spare on her—and how miserable and conflicted they make me. Is it so wrong to have wanted just one day's respite from them?

Still, I'm not up for getting into it, so I murmur what I consider a very contrite "I'm sorry."

"Too late for that now, Cass. You're grounded tonight" is all she says.

Grounded? She can't *ground* me. Well, I mean, technically she can, but oh god, what am I supposed to tell Jonah? The guy's twenty years old and completely on his own in the world and there is *nothing* more babyish-sounding than,

"Oh, hey, I can't hang out tonight after all. My mommy grounded me."

"I have plans!" I say. "This isn't fair!"

"Sorry you feel that way. I beg to differ."

I gape at her, then brush past and into my berth where I nearly knock over Drew.

"Hey," he says with a sympathetic cringe. No conversation goes unheard around here.

As if to demonstrate how well he's aware of this, he holds up his cell phone, where he's typed, She's just in a mood because she heard back on that phone interview she had yesterday.

If I weren't so angry I might feel bad for her, but now *I'm* the one paying the price. I grimace, and Drew and I exchange looks of understanding. He pockets his phone.

"Searching for something?" I ask, dropping my backpack on the floor.

"Charger," he answers. "Still plugged into your laptop?"

I swing open one of my cubbies and point it out. "What'd you guys get up to today, Roo?"

In other words, *please distract me before I'm tempted to go all Lizzie Borden on our mother.*

"Dude, you missed out on Alcatraz," he says. "They had this audio tour where you could hear from real inmates and prison guards. The cells are way smaller than this boat. I'm talking totally claustrophobic.

"Oh, and Mom and me took a Segway tour of Fisherman's

Wharf and then Christian took us to this digital arts center place that was whatever, but outside there was this fountain with a Yoda statue in the center. It was pretty cool. I took pictures. Oh man, and guess what else we found? One of those booths that does the photo strips! You know, like at that arcade near Nana's? Here, check out the faces Mom and I made. We should totally go back there, the three of us. Hang on, lemme find the shots I took of Yoda—"

He takes his phone back out and begins scrolling through, leaving me to stare at the photo strip. In the bottom one Mom's making the only silly face she knows, thumbs hooked in the corners of her mouth and pointer fingers pushing up her eyelids. Drew wiggles bunny ears behind her head.

It would be obvious to anyone how happy and easy with each other they are, and as much as I want to protect my brother from all the ugliness, I wish so hard I could tell him what she's really like.

I wouldn't have to be alone in feeling this way.

Drew turns his phone around, and I hand him back the strip and exclaim appropriately at the images he shows me, but as soon as he bounds off to check out a commotion above—which sounds a lot like a sea lion might have landed in someone's boat—I flop down on my bed and close my eyes. It's been a roller coaster of a day, emotion-wise, and I need for my world to stop spinning long enough for me to catch my breath.

I accidentally fall asleep, and when I wake the sun is

definitely lower in the sky. Crap! It's 7:37. Jonah's supposed to be by in twenty minutes and I have to intercept him before my mother tells him exactly why I won't be hanging out with him tonight.

Damn. Damn, damn, damn. I don't have his cell. We never got around to exchanging numbers because at sea we use the radio to communicate, and at dock, we've usually been within easy shouting distance.

Being grounded means I can't even walk over to *Reality Bytes* to talk to him in private. Instead I camp out in the stern of our boat, waiting for the first sign of him striding up the dock. When he appears, I have to fight back a groan. The universe is pure evil, because he looks good. Really, really good. He's very obviously fresh from a shower: his hair is still damp and he's wearing a lightweight button-down shirt that clings to him in a few patches. He must have put it on before drying off completely. Even if I've mostly managed to convince myself platonic friendship is where it's at, I can still pause to pay homage to the guy's genetic gifts.

I hop onto the dock, racing to meet him a few slips away, before he gets within earshot of Mom and Drew. The last thing I need is them eavesdropping.

"Hey. You look great," Jonah says.

I glance down at the same outfit I had on earlier. "I—I didn't change."

Wow. So much for thinking any attraction might possibly be mutual. Clearly he didn't even pay enough attention to me today to remember what I was wearing for the seven-plus hours we spent together.

"I know. I just didn't want to make you feel bad about it when I clearly got all fancied up," he says, adding a totally endearing one-shouldered shrug.

I grin back at him, but then let it fade as I shift my eyes to the wooden dock. "Um, so it turns out I can't make it tonight after all. Sorry. I, uh, probably should have checked with my mom first because she made late dinner reservations for the three of us, like a family thing, I guess, and . . ."

I trail off after delivering the lamest excuse ever.

"Oh." Jonah looks over my shoulder, then says, "Right. Yeah. No, I totally get it. Of course, you should spend time with them. Nothing more important than family."

And now I feel a thousand times worse because we both know perfectly well he doesn't exactly have one to speak of at the moment. Or at least not one that he'd want to grab dinner with. Which I've basically rubbed in his face without meaning to.

"I'm sorry. I—"

He interrupts. "No! Look, I completely understand. We're only here for one night and you already ditched your mom and brother all day, so it makes perfect sense they'd want you along for a nice dinner out. Where are you guys headed?"

Oh crap. I definitely didn't think this through enough to research restaurant names.

"Um, I'm not sure exactly." I pretend to be very absorbed

with watching the man a few slips down hose off his deck, so I can avoid Jonah's eyes.

"Too bad my friend Chet isn't around. He does this dead-on impression of the vice president you could use to score reservations anywhere in town. Kills with the girls."

I shift my eyes back to him, squinting. "Wouldn't the jig be up when a twentysomething kid showed up to claim the table, as opposed to a slew of Secret Service agents and an old white dude?"

"See, you identified the fatal flaw in his plan far faster than poor Chet."

I relax a little. At least we're joking around like normal, and he doesn't ever need to realize I'm a totally lame high school kid who gets grounded for forgetting to register her location with her mother at regular intervals.

"What about you? Any party tricks of your own?" I tease.

He gives me an exaggerated wink. "Wouldn't you like to know? Guess it's your loss you're not coming out tonight."

I roll my eyes. "Something tells me you'll get over it. There must be at least a few former conquests who aren't immune to the Jonah Abrahmson brand of charm. I'm sure you could scrounge one or two of them up for a night on the town, couldn't you?"

The evil, not-on-board-with-logic part of me hopes he'll dispute this, but he just grins and says, "Aw, now, you're not jealous, are you, Sprite?"

I force a laugh and then pause when Jonah gives a casual

wave to someone behind me. Turning my neck, I spot my mother climbing down to the dock. She walks up to us with a paper grocery bag in her hand.

"Cassie. Should you be out here?" she asks, her voice holding a note of warning. I send her silent pleas with my eyes, begging her not to say anything overt about my punishment. Miracle of miracles, she continues walking toward the pier without waiting for my reply.

A few feet away, she turns back to us, lifting the bag in her hand slightly. "Hey, Jonah, have you guys figured out where the trash area is? I want to get rid of the remains from tonight's dinner before it attracts any hungry sea lions. Cass, you were sleeping, but we got you lo mein—it's keeping warm in the oven."

My eyes go wide, just as Jonah's cloud. He looks at me, his confusion written all over his face. As I watch, his expression turns to something harder to interpret. I open my mouth, but he doesn't give me a chance to speak.

Instead he spins and says, "I can show you where the trash is, Mrs. McClure," while jogging a few steps to catch up with her. I stare after them their entire walk down the dock, but he never once glances back.

Damn it! The only reason I lied, instead of confessing my grounding, was so Jonah wouldn't see me as some immature kid unworthy of spending time with. I loved today, and I wanted a whole series of days just like it, the entire way between here and Mexico.

And now? He sees me as a liar. Or, even worse, what if he thinks I decided I didn't want to hang out with him because of everything he told me about himself today?

Nice going, Cass. The one person you actually want to spend time with on this trip and you just ruined it.

20

As quickly as we sailed into San Francisco, that's how fast we leave it behind the next morning. If we had to get sidelined for days by a weather system, why couldn't it be *there*, instead of in tiny anchorages that have zero amenities or signs of modern life.

The weather is the very opposite of my mood—blue skies and puffy clouds offering the perfect summery backdrop as we sail under the Golden Gate Bridge, all three of us craning our necks to take it in. I snap my daily "minus" picture for Dad—the bridge fading into the distance while we leave the city for good. We're headed south to Half Moon Bay. Another day, another port of call.

At least checking them off the tally feels like progress.

And I'm more eager than ever to see them pass by, especially after the disaster I made of things with Jonah last night. The sooner I can retreat to the safety and comfort of Pleasant Hill, the happier I'll be. Tara and Jess in person make a much better sounding board than they do via group text.

Not that I didn't resort to that five seconds after Jonah walked off with my mother. Their take:

Tara: Just come clean about the grounding and tell him that's why you lied about dinner.

Jess: Cosigned

Me: Meaning he'll think I'm an immature high school kid. Who wants to hang out with one of those when you're twenty and on your own?

Tara: Right. I see your point.

Me: Advice?

Tara: Basically you're totally screwed.

Jess: Cosigned

Me: So happy I turned to you guys in my hour of need.

Jess: Can I ask something?

Me: . . .

Jess: Is this about not having someone to hang out with the rest of the trip? Or is this about not having *Jonah* to hang out with?

Tara: Ooh, good one. This is why we voted you president of E.A.T. Me.

Jess: YOU REMEMBERED! ♥♥♥

Tara: ⌒☡ 👄

Jess: Just for that, when I get off work I'm bringing you the expired Milk Duds from the box office display case.

Tara: Um . . . thanks? Is anyone else noticing Cassie is suspiciously quiet?

Jess: Suspiciously

Me: He really opened up to me and I feel like I betrayed that by lying to him. What if he thinks I was rejecting him after everything he told me about his family? You guys, I would hate if I hurt him.

Tara: Oh. My. God.

Me: What?

Tara: You *like* him!

Jess: Cosigned

Me: I like him as a FRIEND!

Tara: Uh-huh. Sure. Screwed.

Jess: Cosigned

Me: NOT HELPFUL!

Jess: Fine. I say you put on your big girl panties and apologize. If you don't, you actually *are* being the immature high school kid.

Me: Crap, you're so right.

Jess: Madame President's got your back, Rush Coordinator (that's your new position. No need to thank me. I already know the depths of my awesome).

Me: I love you guys

Tara: All for one and one for all

Jess: Cosigned

I smile, rereading our conversation again now, snuggled under blankets in the cockpit. I *should* be working on my apology to Jonah, but my brain is still on my friends. When I'm texting with them, I feel like I'm right there in Pleasant Hill, but as soon as I pick my head up and look around, I'm surrounded by this whole other world.

The weird thing is, this one is starting to feel like the more familiar one and my *real*, regular life seems a million miles away, instead of only a couple of hundred. How is it that I could hop in a car and be in Pleasant Hill in under ten hours, when it's taken us this long to sail here? I know from past experience that "vacation time" stretches like saltwater taffy until you can't remember what day of the week it is anymore, but even accounting for that phenomenon, it feels like an entire lifetime ago that I was sleeping in my own room, with dust bunnies and my old stuffed animal collection under my bed . . . instead of a freezer.

We're only heading into our fourth week at sail, but already the rocking under my feet and the constant droplets of spray in my hair feel more normal to me than the sensations of being on dry land.

Even my muscle memory has been betraying my loyalties to home. Back there, it used to be my job to lock up at night, since I was typically the last one in. I could noiselessly slide the dead bolt, flick off the porch light, and turn down the thermostat with my eyes already closed in anticipation of the sleep that awaited.

Now my brain has somehow perfectly recorded the steps from my berth to the bathroom in the middle of the night, the location of all light switches in the cabin, which drawer to open for the cutting board, and which button to hit on the

VHF radio to turn off the computer voice that broadcasts the marine weather forecast on a loop.

Like it or not, I'm living at sea, and it already feels less like something new and different and more like our normal way of life. I guess it's sort of a relief not to be fighting the idea every second of the day, but it also scares me that I already feel so removed from my friends' lives—and they definitely wouldn't recognize mine. That took less than a month. Yes, Tara, Jess, and I are keeping in touch just fine, but what about after four months? What will it be like to go back?

My mood, still recovering from the rapid swings it took yesterday, is part melancholy, part unsettled, and the vastness of the seascape makes me feel hemmed in and restless.

When Drew complains of a headache after lunch, Mom sends him down to the cabin with orders to stay there resting. I'm tempted to say the same, so I can retreat below too, but I know if I stay up here to help if needed, Drew will actually let himself relax.

I'm less than thrilled to be stuck alone with my mother, but I snuggle deeper under my blankets and watch birds dive off our stern and try to work out what to say to Jonah when I see him. If this were last year, I'd be asking Mom's advice, and knowing she's five feet away but still not accessible to me in that way sucks big-time.

She catches me looking at her and her eyebrows rise. I turn away, but she obviously thinks I was giving her an opening because she asks, "Did you guys have a good time yesterday?

You never told me everything you did."

Because you were too busy grounding me.

I give her a carefully abbreviated version of our sight-seeing.

She has sunglasses obscuring her eyes, but I can feel her studying me carefully. "You covered a ton of territory for one day."

"I guess. It's a really cool city."

"And Jonah? Is he a 'really cool' tour guide?" she asks, her voice teasing.

Why not just come out and ask what you want to know, Mom? It's obvious what you're hinting at. "I know you don't like him, but he's actually really nice."

My mother steals a glance at the instruments dash, then takes a seat on the bench next to me. "Okay."

I raise my eyebrows. "That doesn't sound like an 'okay' the way you said it."

"I *do* think he's nice. I just think he's sailing away, and that it's going to catch up with him sooner or later."

"Sailing away?"

"Yeah. Dropping out of school and taking off for Mexico is sailing away, in my opinion. Like running away, only by water."

"Except you don't know the whole story."

She lifts her hand and drops it to her side in a *What can I say?* gesture. "I know what Christian's told me."

"*Christian* is taking off for Mexico and you don't seem to find any fault in him."

199

Now that I've had time to think about it, I've realized which part about Drew's recounting of yesterday has been tugging at me. It was the tidbit he so casually dropped in, that Christian took them to see the Yoda statue. Which therefore meant Christian spent the day—or at least part of it—with Mom.

"That's different and you know it," she says. "Christian isn't sailing *away* from anything. He's sailing *to* something. Retiring there has been his dream for a long time, and he's worked hard to achieve it."

"You don't think Jonah is sailing *to* anything? How do you know he doesn't have plans once he gets there?"

She slides her sunglasses onto her head. "I think Jonah's plans very conveniently fell into place when Christian needed someone to crew for him."

"Wow, I guess you and Christian have had lots of time to talk over Jonah's private issues. That's so great for you both."

"Honey, do you have a problem with me talking to Christian? And don't think I didn't notice your comment a few minutes ago about my not finding any fault in him. What's up with *that*?"

I shake my head. "I don't have any issue with you *talking* to Christian. I have an issue with you talking to Christian about someone's personal stuff behind his back because that's disrespectful. I have a problem with what you might have said about me in return."

She sighs and takes a sip from her water bottle. I'm careful not to look at her because hot tears are beginning to prickle behind my eyelids and I don't want to give her the satisfaction of seeing them. I used to be able to have regular conversations with my mother, ones that weren't laced with sarcasm and accusations, and the fact that this is our new default makes my heart hurt. So does even *thinking* about her with another man who's not my dad, even though I know full well she's already "been there, done that."

"I have an issue with you maybe more than talking with Christian." I speak softly, my face turned away.

Her bottle clangs on the deck. "Cassie, please! That's not even a remote possibility." She sounds genuinely shocked, but I've been well-schooled in the many ways Mom can deceive, and let's be honest, if she was hot to trot with a wedding ring on her finger, what would hold her back now? I subtly wipe my eyes before turning to her with a raised eyebrow.

"No?" I challenge.

She holds my gaze. "God no! I'm not ready for that with anyone, and I don't even want to guess when I will be. The divorce is barely finalized, for Pete's sake."

I so badly want to call her out on her righteous indignation right now. So. Very. Badly. But that's a can of worms I refuse to open. Not here and not now. Instead I say softly, "If you say so."

"*I say so!*" she exclaims. "Geez, Cassandra!"

Okay, okay, I get it. Nothing is going on with her and Christian. At least for now. Obviously that makes me happy, but I'm taken aback at how deep my sense of relief is. I exhale a long breath.

We're both quiet after that, and the water slapping against the boat becomes a soothing rhythm. Mom's eyes are closed and her face is tipped to the sun when I ask, "Which one are we?"

One of her eyes opens and studies me. "Which one are we what?"

"Are we sailing to or sailing away?"

Mom's silent for so long I wonder if maybe she's fallen asleep. I'm just about to get up and grab my laptop when she speaks. "Neither, I guess. I think we're sailing in."

I can't contain my bark of a laugh. "Sailing *in*? What does that even mean?"

She sits up and levels her gaze at me. "It means I don't think we're necessarily running *from* anything, but I also don't think we're running *to* anything, since we won't be staying once we drop the boat."

She pops up halfway to glance at the depth meter before sitting back down. "I think in our instance it's more of a 'the journey is the destination' thing. At least that's what I *hope* this trip can be for us."

At the rate we're going, we'd have to sail to Tahiti and back to make any progress in our relationship.

I'm quiet again. After a few minutes, I stand. "I'm gonna check on Drew."

My mother's lips turn down, but she doesn't say anything

else until I'm halfway into the cabin, when she speaks to my back. "Good talk, Cass! How about we schedule fifteen or sixteen hundred more of those."

I continue below without comment.

21

I still don't have Jonah's cell phone number, and when it becomes evident after anchoring in Half Moon Bay that we'll all be doing our own thing for the night, I have no choice but to suck it up and try to reach him on the VHF.

With anyone else tuned to the same channel able to listen in, it's quite possible this is going to be the most public rejection ever. At least Mom and Drew are up above, trading the depth meter for the anchor light and covering the sails for the night. I sigh and grab the transmitter.

"Sunny-Side Up *to* Reality Bytes. Reality Bytes, *do you copy? Over.*"

"*Copy,* plantita. *What's up? Over.*"

Great. It's Christian. Why did I think the universe would make this easy on me?

"*Um, could I please speak with Jonah? Over.*"

There's a long wait, and then Jonah's voice echoes through our cabin. "*Hey.*" There's a pause and then, "*Over.*"

None of those three syllables give me much to go on as far as determining whether he's written me off entirely or not, but they sound flat. Crap.

"Hey. Um, would you possibly want to ride ashore with me? I read there's a really good ice-cream place. My treat? Over."

His reply is quick. *"I used to have regattas here, and the closest ice-cream shop is in the town of Half Moon Bay. Over."*

"Right. Isn't that where we are? Over."

From *Tide Drifter*, Abigail very helpfully chimes in with, *"We're in the* bay *named Half Moon, but the town is nine miles south. Probably more like eight if you're measuring nautically. Over."* She clearly forgets to take her finger off the transmitter because next I hear Amy in the background yelling, "Leave those two be, Abby. You'll understand when you're older."

This is not my life.

Screw it. Desperate times, desperate measures and all that . . .

"Thank you, Abigail. Jonah, can I interest you in a trip ashore with me to sit on some rocks and indulge in a dessert of whatever is nearby, *most likely slimy seaweed soaked in salt water and sea lion droppings? Over."*

This time the smile in Jonah's voice is unmistakable. *"Why didn't you start with that offer, Sprite? Pick me up in five. Over and out."*

I exhale and do a small happy dance.

Fingers crossed.

"Watch out for pelicans! They're absolutely everywhere. Over."

"Abigail, give me the transmitter. Sorry, Cassie! Over and out."

I'm laughing as I turn down the radio and grab my sweat-shirt.

But when I pick Jonah up minutes later, he's subdued again and my mood shifts to match his. The dinghy's motor is loud, so the only conversation we have is him asking if I'd prefer him to steer us ashore. Soon enough, though, we're settled on a narrow strip of sand, and my time of reckoning is here.

I draw my knees to my chest and tuck my chin on them. "I owe you an apology for last night. I'm really, really sorry."

"Accepted."

I lift my head and face him. *"What?"*

"Accepted." He shrugs. "I don't need to know more, I just needed to know you were sorry."

"So you don't want to hear my reason for lying?" I'm totally thrown off-kilter by his response.

"Actually, I think I already know it. Or at least I've narrowed it down to two plausible things."

He draws little circles in the sand with his finger.

Eventually I say, "Are you going to tell me them?"

Jonah peeks at me, then goes back to his sand art. "Yup. When I replayed our day in my head, I realized something. You, my actual friend, played your cards very close to your vest yesterday. Somehow you did an intake of my entire family history without telling me anything overly personal about yourself. Impressive feat."

I didn't—I wasn't—that wasn't intentional. More or less. But I don't speak because I want to hear what he adds next.

"I then drew my highly unscientific conclusion, which is: you realized that sooner or later these Ivy League smarts I possess would kick into gear and I'd recognize your crafty evasive techniques and call you out on them. And maybe you suspected our outing with my friends would involve alcohol, which is widely proven to loosen tongues, thus making you even more likely to spill secrets. So you figured you'd ditch me before that could happen."

His delivery is hilarious and his assumptions so, so off base. But I'm mostly relieved he doesn't think I was running scared from the things he told me about himself, which was my biggest worry all day. I couldn't stand the thought of him thinking I was passing judgment on him or his family. I open my mouth to rebut his accusation, but he holds out a hand to stop me.

"Being a responsible detective, I do have an alternate hypothesis."

I bite down on my smile before dropping my chin back onto my knees. "I wouldn't expect anything less from an Ivy Leaguer such as yourself."

"Back on the dock, before. I mean, not last night, but earlier. When I was saying good-bye after our day . . ."

I cup a handful of sand and let it fall through my fingers but avoid his eyes. I hope the moon isn't bright enough for him to read my embarrassment, because I'm pretty sure I know exactly what he's referring to.

"Right," he says lightly. "Well, I thought perhaps you, um, misinterpreted what I meant to do when I was reaching for my hat. I thought maybe you assumed I was going to, uh, kiss you." He rushes on before I can react. "And maybe you were too polite to come right out and tell me, 'Hey, Jonah, possibly no one's had the courage to mention this to you before, but you actually smell like the inside of a grizzly bear that's been dead for three days and you should probably get that taken care of before you put the moves on anyone, but since I'm too much of a lady to say that to your face, I'll just avoid any one-on-one time with you from here on out.'"

By the time he finishes I'm laughing, half at his words and half because I'm grateful he's turning it into a joke instead of making it some incredibly awkward thing.

"You've been next to my allergic-to-the-idea-of-deodorant brother, right? If anyone smells like a three-days-dead grizzly bear . . ."

"Insides," he says.

"What?"

He slides a mound of sand over my bare toes. "I said the *insides* of a three-days-dead grizzly bear."

"And I so appreciate the extra layer of graphic detail. Thank you for that." My head is still tucked into my knees, but I turn my face to smile at him.

He holds my stare. "Sprite?"

"Hmm?" I'm scared for what he's going to say next,

especially because of how serious his expression turns.

"I need you to know something."

"Okay," I whisper.

His eyes are locked on mine, and somehow they're gentle and hard at the same time. Earnest, maybe?

He exhales and says, "If one or both of those hypotheses are even close to the truth, I need you to know that it's fine. You don't ever have to spill your guts to me if you don't want to. And I know I joke around and make suggestive teasing comments, but those are just to make you laugh. I want this actual-friends thing to work . . . even if it stays a little lopsided on the give-and-take gut-spilling part."

I have to look away. Does he have *any* idea that when he says things like that, looking at me the way he is, it's almost impossible for me not to fall sideways—right into his arms?

Instead I replay all the reminders of why I should shut up and say thank you and let our platonic friendship resume: drama, expiration date, potential for heartache in a year where I've had more than my share of it.

"Thank you," I whisper.

His smile is soft and he shakes his head slightly. "Not necessary."

We hold eyes for a long moment and I have to force myself to look away.

Jonah stands and brushes sand from his legs. "I feel like maybe this moment needs a mood-breaker. Do you know any filthy limericks?"

I laugh and take his outstretched hand, letting him pull me to a stand. "You mean, like, 'There once was a man from Nantucket'?"

"Ah. An oldie but a goodie. Go on, then."

"Except I don't really know the rest of it."

He laughs and begins walking toward the jetty that juts far into the bay to offer a buffer to our anchorage. I follow.

It feels like everything is set back to normal, but I really do hate that he thinks our friendship is one-sided. How crappy is that?

I didn't want to talk about my family yesterday when he offered to listen, but it was because I didn't want to ruin such a great day by digging around in that muck. Okay, if I'm being honest with myself, it's also because I knew it would be way easier to slam a lid on my attraction to him if I stayed guarded. But that's not really fair of me. If I want him as my "actual friend," I need to be one right back.

I kick at a pebble as we walk. "Jonah?"

He looks down at me. "Sprite?"

"My parents split up at the beginning of the year and it's totally messed with my head."

He reaches for my hand, and we walk in silence for a little bit before he says, "I'm sorry." He takes a deep breath and adds, "Don't be mad, but Drew kind of already told me about the divorce thing. I mean, he didn't say a word about you in relation to it, though."

I'm so stunned I nearly slip on the rocks. "What? When?"

Jonah raises a shoulder. "This morning, before we left San Fran. I stopped by your slip to see if you maybe wanted to talk about last night over a run, but Drew said you were dead to the world and went with me instead."

"What? What time was this? I didn't even sleep in this morning!" Except now that I think about it, I did a little, because I'd been up so late tossing and turning over my guilt at the expression on Jonah's face when he realized I'd lied to him.

"Um, pretty early. I'm kind of an up-at-dawn type."

"Drew didn't even mention anything."

Jonah makes a noncommittal "mmm" sound in the back of his throat. He's quiet for a second. "I *am* really sorry about your parents splitting up. I mean, in my parents' case, that might actually be a blessing for everyone concerned, but to hear Drew talk about how close your family was, it sounds like a totally different situation." He still has my hand in his and now he squeezes it.

"What did Drew say about us?"

Jonah grins. "Not *that* much. He was having a tough time keeping his breath on the hills."

If they were anything like the one we rode down on a cable car yesterday, who could blame him?

"He said he thinks your mom's kind of a badass for handling this trip on her own. I gotta agree on that one."

My laugh is as much of a bark as a sea lion's. Jonah turns his head to stare at me before uttering a low whistle. "Ah. Got it."

"Got what?" I hate how defensive my voice sounds in my ears.

"I take it you're not Team Elise. Now that I say that, I'm piecing together moments from the last few weeks."

I drop my eyes to the rocks. "My mother isn't that badass, trust me. She kind of hijacked me from my life."

"Ouch."

"Yeah, well, *parents*, right?"

Jonah shakes his head. "Amen to that."

We walk in silence for a little bit, until he says, "I'm trying to keep quiet over here, to give you space for anything else you want to confide."

I smile. "What if I said that's about all the gut spilling I can handle for tonight?"

I feel a million pounds lighter for having confessed the little I did to him. There's so much more, obviously, but small doses are perfect for my comfort zone right now.

"Then I would say, no problem. And, since it appears you don't actually know any filthy limericks to conclusion, I would suggest a rousing game of Would You Rather instead."

I love that Jonah knows exactly when and how to change the mood. I *really* was not giving him enough credit before yesterday.

But he doesn't need to know that. Instead I say, "You're seriously weird."

"No. What's weird is this question. Okay, would you rather . . . eat a thirty-pound block of cheese in one sitting *or* . . . have a metal pin in your jaw for one month that constantly picks up radio stations?"

"*What?*"

"Answer fast, Sprite. These are gonna keep coming."

22

I grin like an idiot at Dad's email:

> Lassie,
>
> See, I told you if you'd just stop bugging us about the homeschooling thing, we'd take it under consideration. Only took five years . . .
>
> Happy first day of school from someone who refuses to admit he is anywhere near old enough to have a daughter starting her senior year in high school. I should have held you to that promise you made when you were three, that you'd stay my little girl forever!
>
> Hugs and kisses,
> Dad

Ha! I can't believe he even remembers the start of seventh grade, when I begged my parents for months to let me homeschool. Tara and Jess weren't in any of my classes that year, and Kelsey Jacobi had made torturing me her pet project. I endured backhanded compliments in the locker room about my being "super lucky not to need a bra yet, because it's just *so* uncomfortable to have all the constant attention from the boys," and more "innocent" offers at the bathroom sinks to "tweeze just a tiny bit here and there, unless you're married to the idea of a unibrow." I swear, why are girls always one another's worst enemies?

Of course, both my parents laughed off the idea and claimed learning good social skills was as important to my future as learning the stuff inside the textbooks, so being isolated at home was therefore "not in my best interests."

Oh, how times have changed. Now it's not concerning to anyone but me that I'm cut off from all my peers and getting my education from an on-screen woman who may or may not be an android. Her monotone voice droning on and on about the roots of a polynomial makes Siri on my phone sound like the Tasmanian Devil on speed.

This is not the senior year I ever pictured. But at least school is something different to do. With a projected ten hours under sail, today's journey from Half Moon Bay to Santa Cruz is one of our longest segments of the past three weeks, so even though it's a Saturday, there is no time like the present to knock out a few online class recordings. I have *plenty* of time on my hands.

I attempt it, I do. But by hour seven, I've had all the studying I can take and I'm about ready to climb the walls. I twitch with relief when the radio bursts to life.

"Reality Bytes *to* Sunny-Side Up. Sunny-Side Up, *do you copy? Over.*"

I spring into action at the sound of Jonah's voice and am across the cabin in two-point-three seconds. Finally, a distraction other than Drew's incessant recitation of anchoring and mooring regulations. As opposed to throwing himself into any studying of the school variety, he's decided he wants to get his captain's license and has been reviewing documents online to prep for an exam. I can't even . . .

"*This is* Sunny-Side Up. *I copy. Over.*"

"*Hey, Sprite. Got iTunes loaded on your laptop? Over.*"

Drew and Mom are doing their usual sailing stuff, so it's just me down here to interpret what nautical information could be gleaned from iTunes. "*Uh, yeah. Over.*"

"*Okay, follow my instructions precisely. Wait, you're not needed to help sail right now, are you? Over.*"

I snort, although who knows what that ends up sounding like on his end. "*No! Never! Over.*"

"*We're gonna have to work on that, you know. You can't go home after months at sea not knowing how to raise a sail. Over.*"

That's debatable, as far as I'm concerned. I choose to ignore him. His next words are, "*Follow my instructions. Open iTunes. Type in* The Lost Boys. *Over.*"

I do as he says, still not sure what he could need from this. "*Okay, I've got it. Over.*"

"*Good. Rent it. Pop pretend popcorn because I know you*

don't have a microwave on board, and I doubt you bought any *Jiffy Pop* to make on the stove top. Over."

"Wait, rent it? Why? Over."

The laugh comes again. *"So we can watch it together. Obviously. Over."*

"But I don't—"

He doesn't wait for me to finish my thought or say "over." Instead, he continues, *"We're three hours from anchoring in the town where this movie was filmed and it will make it way more fun to explore the amusement park later, because after seeing this you're gonna be looking over your shoulder the whole time. Over."*

I guess we're watching a movie "together."

We chat for a little while as the movie loads, and then we both push play at the same time. The plot is total eighties cheese. Two teens are forced to leave their home when their mom gets a divorce (oh, how I can relate) and they land in the fictional town of Santa Clara, California, which, according to the self-proclaimed vampire hunters who own the comic book store on the boardwalk, is home to a local gang of hard-partying, hot teens who moonlight as Cold Ones. And the grandfather they move in with is into taxidermy.

I kind of adore it.

I also kind of adore watching a movie this way. Skype would be far more private, but who's to say nearby boaters don't need a little eighties pop culture education. Besides, this is definitely more unique.

Near the end, Mom comes below for some water. "Oh my

god, I used to *love* that movie when I was in high school. I had the biggest crush on Corey Haim. Or, wait, is that one Corey Feldman? I could never keep the Coreys straight. Whichever one died from a drug overdose . . . he was the one I liked."

"Nice."

"Well, I didn't like him *because of* the drugs, or anything. I liked him because my fifteen-year-old self thought he was cute."

I squint a little at the screen and, yeah, I can see it.

Mom watches over my shoulder. "Jason Patric was in this too? I forgot how many hotties this had!"

The receiver crackles and Jonah says, *"Did you catch that part with the noodles turning into maggots? I couldn't look at Chinese takeout containers for the longest time after I first saw this. Over."*

Mom's eyebrows rise. "*This* is why the VHF's been going crazy?"

I keep my eyes glued on the screen as I speak into the radio. *"Sorry, I missed that because my mom was running through a list of which cast members' posters she used to have over her bed. Over."*

Mom makes a face at me as Jonah's voice sounds through the cabin. *"I hope you're referring to Edward Herrmann, Mrs. McClure. Over."*

Mom snatches the transmitter out of my hand. *"It's Elise, remember? And that man is old enough to be my father. I was referring to Corey Haim! Over."*

"Okay, that makes sense. Total druggie though, right? Over."

I laugh and Mom sighs. *"You two should cut the guy some slack, he was a troubled child actor."* She shakes her head and I see the smile she's biting back. *"Over."*

To me she says, "I don't know why *you're* laughing. You get Lindsay Lohan. We had Corey Haim. Why do you think I never let you try out for that car dealership commercial when you were eight?"

I pause the movie. "Mom, they were auditioning for a kid to play a crash test dummy. I hardly think that would have led to a life of booze and slamming my Mercedes into restaurants."

My mother dips two fingers into her water glass and flicks them at me.

I ignore that. "Laine Medley bought an entire Lego village with the money she made off that commercial. Although, come to think of it, she did go rogue last summer. Do you think she could have been at"—I lower my voice to a whisper—*"rehab?"*

Mom rolls her eyes. "You know perfectly well she was a volunteer for the Special Olympics."

"Such a shame. She had so much potential before that run-in with showbiz."

She grins and flings three more successive water sprays at me (completely ineffectual since I'm used to enduring the same from the ocean every time I step on deck) before turning to the steps.

Behind her back, I grin too. Maybe it's just my relief at having things with Jonah resolved that's mellowing me out right now, but I don't think Mom and I could have shared a moment like that a few months ago. As angry as I am at her, part of me likes knowing some of how we used to be is still there, underneath everything else. It doesn't change my feelings in any huge way, but . . . maybe I need to hold on to those glimpses of better times too. Process them along with everything else.

I pick up the transmitter. *"Okay, don't kill me, but I had to pause for a few minutes there. Tell me your time stamp so I can catch up. Over."*

"I'll rewind to you," Jonah replies. I tell him which scene, and in the silence that follows, I hear a distinct crunching.

I squint, trying to decipher the noise. *"Wait, how do you have popcorn? Over."*

"Duh. Because I'm an experienced seaman and I knew to pack Jiffy Pop. Now stop talking, you're ruining the part with the impaling. Over."

"Um, did you just use the words seaman *and* impaling *in the same breath? Over."*

"You are fantastic, Sprite. Now shush with your dirty mind. Just watch." It's quiet, and then there's a whispered, *"Over."*

An hour after the movie ends, we're motoring into the harbor next to where it was filmed. It's actually the real-life town of Santa Cruz, but everything about the pier ahead of us looks the same as its movie version, from the roller coaster to the boardwalk. Although I can't imagine how the filmmakers managed to capture any dialogue over the constant barking of what has to be a thousand sea lions hanging out under the pier.

They almost put San Francisco's numbers to shame.

"We can go ashore, right?" I ask Mom. We got such an ass-crack of dawn start this morning that it's only late afternoon, and I'm itching to get off this boat as soon as possible.

"Bag up your laundry for me first. Miranda and I have a girls' night in at a Laundromat planned. Otherwise, as soon as we secure this mooring, you're both free to head over, so long as you stick together and you let Drew captain *Minecraft*." Mom smiles at me. "And watch out for any cute guys on motorcycles who might actually be vampires."

"Gross," says Drew, before asking me, "Wanna check it out?"

"Obviously. Jonah wants in too. Hey, think there's funnel cake?"

Santa Cruz is everything I would picture if asked to imagine a quintessential California beach town. There are kayakers all around us in the harbor and, in the distance, along a wide swath of beach, surfers swoop through cresting waves. Seagulls circle overhead, ready to pounce on any wayward boardwalk food, and carnival music and occasional screams from the rides at the edge of the pier float out across the water and mingle with the sea lion racket. The white wooden roller coaster lords over the scene, postcard-ready. I can practically taste the cotton candy and smell the sunscreen.

We swing by the yacht for Jonah, and then Drew steers the dinghy around some playful sea otters and toward the public landing along the pier, where we "park." No matter how many times I've done it now, I still need a moment to get my land legs back whenever I come ashore after more than a few hours at sea. Jonah takes my elbow to steady me.

"Happens to me too," he says, grinning.

Drew, on the other hand, must have been a merchant marine in a past life, because he seems perfectly comfortable maneuvering back and forth between land and water. I'm a proud big sister, watching how expertly he secures the dinghy.

By unspoken agreement, we all head straight for the roller coaster. In under five minutes we're buckled into aqua-blue cars, Drew and me in the first row and Jonah directly behind us. I was all bravado when I insisted the front was the only place to ride, but I have to admit I'm a little fluttery as the car enters a tunnel, takes a few shallow dips, and emerges at the base of a giant hill. I love the big thrill rides, but usually not until I get to the middle parts.

Click. Click. Click. The car ticks off each section of track as we climb the first hill with excruciating slowness. I peer over the side at the wooden slats. How old *is* this coaster anyway? Didn't I read somewhere that salt water rots wood at a much faster rate?

"Is anyone else nervous?" I ask.

"Nope. This entirely beats stuffy lecture halls and the quiet room at the library," Jonah says, leaning forward to speak into the gap between where Drew and I sit.

I force my eyes away from the beach, which is growing more distant by the second, and turn my head to his.

"You spent your Saturday nights on campus at the quiet room in the library?" I ask, disbelief in my voice.

"Ri-*ight*. It's Saturday—I'm losing track of days out here. Well, no, in that case I'd probably be bombed and passed out in my dorm."

"Impressively mature," I say cheerfully as Drew laughs.

Jonah replies, "Yeah, yeah. Just wait until it's your turn. I'll be waiting by the phone when you call to beg forgiveness for your snide remarks. Unless you'd prefer to radio instead."

"Depends. Will your tropical beach hut in Mexico have a landline?"

Below us, the people strolling the beach are the size of minifigs, and the wooden structure groans underneath our car. Jonah ignores my dig and says, "C'mon, this is a pretty amazing way to spend your night, no? Admit you're having fun. Right, Drew?"

Drew gives a thumbs-up, and Jonah leans back as we finally reach the top. We crest the hill and stop, poised, for only a breath. I screw my eyes shut and lift my arms into the sky just as my butt rises off the seat.

I let go.

We rocket toward the bottom, and tears, caused by the rush of wind, leak from the corners of my eyes.

"Okaaaaaaay, thissssssss issssss funnnnnnnnn!" I scream, grabbing on to my brother and laughing the whole way into the next curve.

23

Three nights later, I wake up to voices in the cabin and immediately reach for my phone to check the time: 4:33 a.m.

What the—

Oh.

It's 4:33 a.m. *on Drew's birthday.*

I know just what the voices are.

Ever since I can remember, Mom and Dad would tell each of us the story of our birth at exactly the moment it happened however many years before that. Luckily for me, I was born at 8:52 p.m. Drew was not as blessed in the time department.

Despite the insanely early hour, they would always wake me up too, and I'd crawl under the covers with Drew and half listen, half doze while my parents sat on the edge of his bed and took turns. Just like with my version, they each had their assigned portions, and there have been enough years by now for them to fine-tune their lines; it's a well-oiled accounting. It's also completely cheesy, really, but it's tradition, and I'm positive Drew is as sentimental about it as I am.

I do quick calculations. It's 7:33 p.m. in Hong Kong and it's a Tuesday, which means Dad is teaching his night course. He hates teaching at night (Dad is a total morning person and by dinnertime he's got one eye closed), and I'm certain he's especially pissed about tonight's class, since it means he can't even Skype in for Drew. I have no idea if he'd suck it up and tell the birth story with Mom for Drew's benefit, but I guess it's a moot point.

It's all on her now.

I creep to the door and press my ear against it. Usually it's impossible *not* to hear every little sound in the cabin, but at first all I can make out are murmurings. I slow my breathing and strain my ears.

". . . trying to come up with a list of everything I ate that day, to tell the anesthesiologist," Mom's saying. "And I hear the nurse on the phone with the doctor at home. She's asking how long it's been since my water broke and how far apart my contractions are. . . ." Mom pauses, and I whisper Dad's interrupting line under my breath: "Okay, so get this now!"

Mom rushes over it. ". . . Because the doctor's in the middle of showing her family all the pictures she took on the trip to Egypt she'd just gotten back from, and she doesn't want to abandon that until she absolutely has to."

My eyes begin to well. Here's where Dad always takes over and says, "Do you know how torturous it is to look at someone else's vacation pictures? For weeks after that I would walk to the mailbox expecting to find a thank-you card from that doctor's kids for saving them that night."

Mom recounts Dad's lines nearly verbatim, and I swallow over the lump in my throat. I wish I could hear Drew, but he's silent as she continues.

Mom reaches the ending. "Then, right as the surgeon lifted you from my belly, you peed all over her. We knew right then and there that you, my son, were a true pisser!"

She gets Dad's line just right again, and now I'm actively crying. Drew murmurs something that's impossible to make out because his newly deep voice is so low, and then it's quiet again.

I turn back to my bed but, of course, a floorboard creaks as I do.

"Cass?" my mom calls softly.

I ignore it and ease under the covers. Tears are still streaming down my cheeks. I can't even imagine how I'm going to hold it together on my birthday next month. It's shocking how I can be feeling slightly better about things with Mom and then something like this comes along and—whammo! Back to square one.

There's no chance I'm falling asleep after that.

I'm claustrophobic. I can't breathe. I need to run and scream and be alone and I can't do any of those things on this stupid boat. Although maybe I *can* make a small jailbreak, just for a little while.

I wait at least a half hour in the quiet, until I'm sure both Mom and Drew have gone back to sleep, and then I slip into my bathing suit and creep up the steps. At the top, I have to unlock the doors that barricade us in at night and keep us safe from anyone who might try to board while we sleep at anchor. I do it as silently as possible, then slide them back into place behind me after I slip outside. With them closed, Mom shouldn't have any reason to suspect I'm not sound asleep in my berth.

The coast of Capitola is off the port side. Despite the fact that we're steadily working our way toward warm Southern California, we are most decidedly not there yet. Meaning: it's chilly this morning, and it's definitely going to be even colder in the water.

But I don't care one bit. My frustration is charging me to the point where I doubt I'll even feel the temperature.

My plan is to swim the few hundred yards to the farthest boat in the harbor and back, as many times as I need to. I'll have to weave among the dozens of boats moored here in the harbor, but they'll also provide safety if I get tired or start to cramp or anything.

I dangle from the platform, then ease myself into the water, and HOLY HELL, is it freezing! There's a reason surfers wear wetsuits in these parts. I force myself to duck all the way under before I lose my nerve. When I surface, I lick salty water from my lips and pedal my legs to try to keep them from turning into blocks of ice. So much for anger-fueled oblivion.

Hoping "inhospitable" will turn into "invigorating" once I get going, I do my best swimmer's crawl toward an anchored catamaran bobbing nearby and then cut around its side. Despite the freezing water, it feels good to slice through the glassy surface, leaving ripples in my wake. I try not to get creeped out thinking about the abundance of sea life just beneath me.

Before long I've passed by ten or so boats, keeping the lights of the pier in sight when I lift my head. Circulation comes back to my toes and fingers as I pick up speed. This is good. I don't even think; I just move. Exactly what I need right now.

I reach the outer anchorage, circle around a motorboat, and tread water until I'm convinced I've distinguished the mast light of *Sunny-Side Up* from all the others surrounding it. I aim and resume my strokes.

And then it hits. Out of nowhere.

The way my night went from peaceful to heart wrenching in an instant is just one further reminder—no matter how much I allow myself to relax and let down my guard, there's always the potential, in the space of a single breath, for everything to go black. And I'm not just talking about my parents' divorce, which I'm not naive enough to think won't get easier to deal with as time goes on. I'm talking about all of life. In every moment of light, darkness is always lurking in the shadows, just waiting to pull the rug out from under you and steal your innocent happy away. At any second. It happened before, and it's only a matter of time until it happens again.

All the emotions I held inside when Mom was telling Drew his birth story press down on my chest. All the tears I wouldn't let myself cry, for fear they'd hear me, flood my throat. I have to do a backstroke because I can't breathe through them with my face in the water.

I'm losing it. I reach a sailboat and grab on to its platform with one hand. The occupants are probably sleeping, and even if they were moving about, I'd be hard to spot unless they leaned over the stern to peer below, but I still struggle to contain my crying so I won't give them reason to investigate.

When I compose myself enough, I slip off and aim for the next mooring, then the next, sobbing in the open water and choking on tears while I rest at each boat. This is not what I had in mind for my swim.

Then again, I guess a complete breakdown is long overdue.

I have my head in the water, aimed at a motorboat, when something brushes against my leg. *Eeek!* I pull my knees in and dart my head around. *Please don't be a shark, please don't be a shark, please don't—*

It's Beatriz.

Her usually fluffy fur is plastered against her as she paddles closer to plant a slobbery kiss on my face.

"Hey, mutt! You scared the hell out of me! What are you doing out here in the dark, girl?"

She swims off, turning her head to make sure I'm following. I take a few deep breaths to calm myself and give chase. When I round the front of the motorboat, I spot her again, now holding a tennis ball between her teeth and bobbing her way over to a yacht. Christian's yacht.

Where Jonah stands bundled on the platform, urging her on.

Crap.

He hasn't noticed me yet, but when he does . . . Well, he wanted opened-up Cassie. He's about to get her in a big way, splayed and gutted.

Beatriz reaches him and scrambles aboard, dropping the ball at his feet and shaking off her fur. Jonah jumps out of the way just in time to avoid getting showered, and despite my mental breakdown, I almost manage a smile as I execute a sidestroke in their direction. The distraction has forced me far enough out of my own head to allow me to regain some control, thank god.

Before Jonah can throw the ball again, Beatriz splashes back in and heads right to me. Jonah puts a hand over his eyes to shield them from the anchor light and tracks our movements until we're close enough for him to make out who I am.

He drops his arm and rushes to the ladder, where he stands on the top step.

"Sprite, what are you—are you crazy? The sun's not even up yet! And you must be an icicle!"

He helps me out and waits for Beatriz to follow. This time we both get covered in dog spray when she shakes. He jumps into the cockpit and tosses down a towel.

"Wrap up and follow me."

I trail slowly behind him. "Where's Christian?" I whisper, suspecting the answer.

"Sleeping, you nut. You do know what time it is, right?"

"I know. What are you doing awake?"

He glances at me over his shoulder as he pauses in front of a door. Despite having spent a lot of time aboard *Reality Bytes*, I've never been in this part of the yacht. "I told you, I'm always up crazy early. It's both a blessing and a curse."

He pushes the door open and stands aside for me to enter. I swallow when I realize it's his room. I look around to distract myself from the awkwardness of being alone with him in here.

His berth is at least twice the size of mine, though it's hard to tell exactly, because every inch of it is a mess. He's clearly made himself at home. Laundry piles fill every corner and the bed is a jumble of blankets. The metal-framed backpack he was wearing when we met in the woods leans against a wall, and books are propped open on every surface. It looks like he's reading at least five at once.

"Sorry," he says, his arm sweeping over the area. "I, uh— wasn't expecting company."

"S'okay," I mumble, suddenly overly conscious of the fact that I'm only wearing a bathing suit and a thin towel.

"Okay, let's find you something dry to put on, stat." He pulls open a drawer and rifles through it, handing me a sweatshirt and flannel pajama pants, alongside a pair of folded striped boxer shorts. Oh god, am I supposed to wear his underwear? But if I don't, then I'm going commando in his pants and . . . this is the very definition of *dilemma*. Seriously, if you were to look it up, there'd be a picture of this moment.

"I—" My skin is already crime-scene red from being in frigid water, but now it splotches even more.

Luckily Jonah already has one hand on the door. "I'm gonna get Beatriz some fresh water and give you privacy to change. I'll be back with coffee, okay?"

I murmur a thanks and wait for his footsteps to fade before quickly shucking my damp suit, wrapping it in the towel, and putting on his clothes. They smell like Jonah—fresh air and sunshine and fabric softener. It's light-years away from grizzly bear, dead or otherwise.

I stand stiffly in his room because it feels too intimate to sit on his unmade bed, but inside I'm a mess of activity. The unexpectedness of happening upon Beatriz and him shocked me sober, but now, in the quiet, the emotions start to creep back. It's not the deep, gulping, suffocating feeling from before, but there is evidently still a slew of residual tears that need an outlet. They slide down my face and I turn to the wall and dab at them with a corner of the bundled towel.

When Jonah taps lightly on the door a few minutes later, I'm no closer to getting them under control. *Damn it!*

"Come in," I call, still facing the wall and sucking in breaths to calm myself.

"I have coffee—wow, you're shaking, Sprite." I hear him set the mugs down. He grabs a blanket from his bed and settles it gently on my shoulders, wrapping the edges around my front. My heart seizes briefly at the sweetness of his gesture.

Three, two, one . . . I count to myself in a last-ditch effort at composure, then force a smile before turning around.

"Thanks." I think I manage an easy tone, but he takes a step back and cocks his head.

"Not shaking," he says, studying me closely. "Crying. Why are you crying, Cassie?"

The fact that he sounds so concerned and that he uses my name instead of teasing me with Sprite unleashes a steady stream of fresh tears down my cheeks, making a response pointless.

I half expect him to bolt for the door. He's a twenty-year-old guy and some girl he barely knows is having a meltdown in his bedroom. But he doesn't. He walks forward and tugs the edges of the blanket tighter, bundling me like a sad little burrito. Then he takes another step in and wraps his arms tightly around me.

"Hey. Whatever it is, it's gonna be okay. Hear me?" he whispers near my ear.

I nod, because that's all I can manage with the size of the lump in my throat. Although I'm suddenly having a hard time deciphering if the lump is being caused by my tears or by the new feelings that rushed in when his arms came around me. Those particular ones are burrowing deeper at his responses and his sympathy and the way he's holding me so sweetly and—

How it is possible to have insane romantic thoughts about a guy in the same instant that my head is so completely messed up over everything else? Why are emotions just the absolute worst?

He continues to hold me, rubbing his hand up and down my arms gently, while I fight to get myself under control. Eventually, I'm able to wind down to just some lingering sniffles and he pulls his head back to ask, "Do you want to sit?"

I nod again and he shuffles us to his bed before settling me on its edge, still wrapped in his blanket. He joins me, scooting back and leaning his torso against the headboard, maintaining a perfectly respectable distance.

I'm way too embarrassed to look at him, but he doesn't push the issue. Instead he asks, "So that swim; was that actually your attempt at a swift getaway? Because I gotta warn you, without a mermaid tail you're not getting too far in these parts. And you know what happened to the last guy who tried to escape our caravan."

Now I do turn to stare at him with wide eyes. "They found Tommy?"

He makes a face. "Well, no, actually. But in my fantasies, he's turning on a spit over hot flames for stealing from Uncle Chris."

I try to laugh over a sniffle and end up hiccuping instead, which makes *him* laugh.

"Yes, I was attempting a prison break," I answer.

"From . . . a bad dream? I'm trying to picture what else could have been going on over there at four in the morning."

I give him an abbreviated version of the birthday ritual and his forehead wrinkles. "I'm sorry, I don't—are you upset because you were missing your dad during it?"

I nod, then shake my head. "Yes. No. It's my mom. I just couldn't take it . . . her . . . anymore. She acts so matter-of-fact that life without my dad is our new normal now and I had to . . . had to—"

I can't help it—I start to cry again. "Sorry," I manage.

Jonah moves closer and puts his hand on my knee. "No. Hey." I take a shuddering breath and turn my face toward his. His eyes are soft and concerned. "It kind of—it kind of seems like you're keeping a lot in. Maybe letting go like this is a good thing."

He speaks the words gently, but they have the opposite effect. They slap me back to reality, to where I can see how I'm acting. This is not cool. This is *not* how I cope. I might sulk or get annoyed or act passive aggressively, but I *don't* fall apart. I stiffen my shoulders. Screw this sadness. What I need is to get angry. What I need is to remember all the reasons to *be* angry.

"I hate her," I spit, and Jonah's eyes widen. My tears evaporate, and I embrace the surge of this new emotion gratefully. Anger I can handle. It's not confusing at all, unlike my feelings about my mother or for the boy sitting next to me right now. Anger and I have only been intimately acquainted for about six or seven months now, but we're already old friends.

"Okay," Jonah says. His simple acceptance is too easy. It's sweet that he's in my camp with so little persuasion, but I need him to understand *why* I'm angry. *Why* I hate her.

I think I need to tell him. Everything.

Well, I need to tell *someone*. . . .

I can't believe I'm considering unloading on him when I haven't even told my best friends in the world. But Jonah hasn't known my mother his whole life the way my friends have. He doesn't even know *me* that well, nor will he probably want to after I unburden myself on him like a freak. In some ways, it feels more removed from reality this way. Safer.

Before I can second-guess myself, I say it:

"My mom cheated on my dad."

I have never—literally never—uttered those words out loud, and they suck the breath out of me.

Jonah flinches, but he doesn't take his eyes from mine. "God, Cassie, I'm so sorry. Was it—was it a long-term thing, or—"

I shake my head. "I don't know. I don't know any details and I don't think I want to."

"Right, yeah. No, I get that. And why you're so upset with her."

I shake my head again, vehemently this time. "I'm not upset with her. I *hate* her."

I wish that were true. I wish *like hell* that were true, because all of this would be so much easier if it were.

Jonah nods. "Okay. I mean, I'm not trying to say I understand it all because I've never been in that particular situation, but I can imagine how I might feel."

I stare at him for a long pause.

"Do you *always* say and do the exact perfect thing?"

He blinks. "Um . . . what?"

I huff in frustration. "It's just, you're always so self-assured and in control of your emotions and, like, even when you talk about your parents, you're so levelheaded about things, and I was just wondering if you're always that way or if you have, like, maybe one or two flaws. It kind of makes me feel like a basket case compared to you, just so you know."

Jonah's silent for a couple of beats, then he hangs his head with a rueful laugh. "Yeah, okay, I guess I can see that I come across that way. Probably because I was literally *groomed* to be like this." His shoulders rise with a silent laugh and he closes his eyes and breathes deeply. "If you knew what my schools were like—those pressure cooker, elite private school clichés exist for a reason. You show even the slightest sign of weakness and—" Jonah slices a finger across his neck and I manage a small smile. "Confidence—or maybe I should call it bravado—is currency in those places."

I give him a tiny smile through my drying tears. "You must have been very rich, then."

"Very," he answers, with a small head shake that seems sad. "But, trust me, I have plenty of flaws."

"Besides not being able to snap your fingers?"

"Hey, I said that was a defect, not a flaw!"

I smile again, then duck my head to wipe my nose with the back of my hand. "Well. You should try dropping the bravado and being completely exposed sometime. It's freaking awesome, lemme tell ya. You get to feel like a total idiot *and* look like a total mess."

"Sprite." He waits for me to steal a peek at him before saying, "You don't look like a total mess, and I don't think you're an idiot at all. Seriously. At all."

I shrug.

There's a long silence after that while I study the thread pattern on his quilt, and then, finally, Jonah says, "Thanks for . . ."

I glance up at him, confused, as he trails off and his hands flutter to his sides. After a second he continues, "Uh, just . . . I know you probably didn't plan to wind up here or anything, but I—it means a lot that you trusted me enough to confide in me. Really."

Teasing Jonah is gone. His expression is intent, and the weight of his words settles in my chest. I nod slowly and lower my chin.

"And I swear I'll take everything to my grave."

I whip my head up, my eyes wild. "Oh god, you have to. I'm the only person who knows about the cheating, outside of my parents, and they have no clue I do. No one else knows. Like, *no one*. Drew would—I can't let Drew find out."

Jonah leans back and makes an X on his chest with his

finger. "Cross my heart and hope to die."

He stares at me without smiling until I relax a little, believing in his sincerity. I'm fairly certain I can trust him with this secret.

The quiet descends again, and to cover any awkwardness, I pick up a framed picture from amid the clutter on his nightstand. It's a shot of him and an older man leaning over the railing of a boat. The man's smile is more restrained, but Jonah's laughing at the person taking the photo.

"Your dad?"

Jonah nods. "Last summer."

I nod too, before replacing it and moving my gaze to the wall above, where a sheet of notebook paper is taped. The handwriting is hard to make out, so I have to stand and move in front of it to read:

Something to do
Someone to love
Something to hope for

"What's this? Grocery list?" I ask.

"Don't poke fun, Sprite. That there is the official formula for happiness, according to author George Washington Burnap, although I've taken it upon myself to use Alexander Chalmers's version."

I study the words more closely before declaring, "I like it. I'm having a really hard time trusting in the idea of a happiness that lasts right now, but if it exists, this seems like as good a formula as any."

Jonah's smile is bittersweet. "It exists, Cass. I've seen it."

I shrug and turn my eyes to the small porthole, where the lightening sky above the waterline reminds me that, although it's still early, people will be up and about soon. Jonah must have the same train of thought because he says, "I'm guessing no one knows about your little outing and there'll be hell to pay if they wake up and find you missing. Yes?"

I nod. I didn't even leave a note this time.

"C'mon, I'll drop you back."

It's still quiet in the harbor, and I don't want to announce my return by pulling up with the Zodiac's engine roaring, so I help Jonah paddle us over instead.

"It is a very good thing I'd already roped you into being my friend," I say, glancing up just in time to see something pass across Jonah's face before he relaxes it into a smile.

"Yeah, why's that?" he asks.

I pick up a piece of hair that the dried salt has clumped into something resembling a rat's tail and let it fall. "Between this and my outfit, I'm afraid I'd never have been able to hitch-hike a ride back on my own."

Jonah leans in. "I don't know. I think you look pretty cute in my pajamas. At least I don't have to wonder whether you have that purple polka-dotted thong on today."

I blink rapidly.

He snickers at my obvious shock, and I'm ridiculously

grateful that we're mere feet away from *Sunny-Side Up*. The second we touch the platform, I slip off the boat before he can tease me about my flushed cheeks. When I'm safely in the cockpit, I lean over and mouth "thank you" alongside my small wave.

He grins and salutes before turning his attention to paddling.

All is quiet on the boat as I slip into my berth. I change out of Jonah's clothes before I have to answer any questions about them, but I can't resist a last inhale of his sweatshirt. *Not exactly the best way to stifle feelings, Cass.* I climb under the covers and stare at my bonsai tree's delicate branches, waiting to drift back to sleep and thinking about Jonah's happiness formula.

Something to do: that one's a bit outside my control at the moment, although I at least have *something*, even if it's not my first choice in activities.

Someone to love: Drew. Dad. Tara. Jess. Do I count my mother if I won't allow myself to show it? I can't objectively answer that at the moment.

Something to hope for.

I picture Jonah's genuine concern when we talked this morning and remember the comfort of his arms around me as he held me. I take a deep breath and finally admit it to myself: I think I want Jonah to be my something to hope for.

It's not practical. It has an expiration date. I've said goodbye to too many things and people I care about this year, and

I'm not sure I can handle another one. Keeping things light and platonic between us was supposed to have been the one thing under my control this trip.

But I'm pretty sure my heart might be laughing at me for believing I had any real say in the matter.

24

When I wake a few hours later, the sun is bright and the cabin is thankfully empty. I grab coffee and drink deeply before preparing to head above. I'm determined not to let my mother guess I overheard them this morning. Except there's no one on the deck, and I peer over the side to check on the dinghy. It's gone, but Drew is crouched on the platform, casting a fishing rod into the water.

"Hey, Cass, I caught a goddamn mako shark!" he yells when he glances up and spots me.

Did he say shark? I start to back away, but he looks so eager that I force myself to stop. It *is* his birthday, after all.

"I'm not touching a shark," I insist, climbing down to join him. "I don't want to go pissing off any of its brothers and sisters who might seek me out as a revengeful snack." I lean over and give him a quick hug. "Speaking of brothers, happy birthday to my favorite one."

Drew snorts. "I'm your *only* one."

I grin and shrug. He rolls his eyes and holds up a slimy body. "Check it. Makos are *not* terrifying."

He's right. It's definitely more fishlike than Jaws-like. This guy wouldn't even merit a cameo on Shark Week. Nevertheless, he's still icky.

"Mom got me a fishing license and gear for my birthday! Oh, and a book to identify my catches. I'm thinking we should go ashore later and buy one of those hibachi grills that screw onto the railing, like Amy and Miranda have, so we can cook this guy up."

"Where *is* Mom?" I ask.

"Grocery run," he answers.

We're hanging here in Capitola for several days because Christian has relatives nearby he wants to spend time with on the way down, since he doesn't know how frequently he'll be back and forth once he settles in Mexico. These delays, Mom explained calmly when we anchored here, are the kinds of concessions you make when you're traveling as a caravan. And, on day twenty-four of our trip, we're back on schedule, so there's no case to be made for pushing on.

At least Drew's enjoying himself. "Hey, if we find a grill, I can barbecue. You don't have to eat the shark. I'll try to catch a tuna next, or maybe some salmon."

He's so earnest, it's sweet. How is he fifteen now, when at times he still looks about six? I almost hate to burst his bubble. "I don't think barbecue tuna is a thing."

"You don't know that for sure. Dad's gonna Skype as soon

as he wakes up, so I'll get advice from him. I'll bet he has something that would work."

"Go for it, Roo."

He sticks his tongue out at me. I'm positive both of us are thinking about how much it sucks that Dad isn't here for this birthday, but neither of us says a word. I even make sure Drew doesn't see me snap the picture of him fishing that I send to Dad later with a "today's good one" caption.

I spend the rest of the day calling Drew "The Grillmaster" every chance I get and blasting annoying show tunes at top volume while I hose off the deck.

It's the least a sister can do.

I also spend a fair amount of time trying *not* to think about how many butterflies take flight in my stomach every time I picture Jonah. Now that I've admitted to myself that I like him, he's occupying half of my brain space, and I spend twice as long getting ready as I ever have for a simple dinner with everyone.

When we all gather on *Tide Drifter*, I try my best to not let on about my shifting feelings. Suggestive flirting aside, I don't even know if he would want anything more than what we have. What if that thing on the dock in San Fran really *was* him reaching for his hat? What if I make a move and he shoots me down?

Drew's mako—the only thing he caught, despite several more hours of trying—is not on the menu. It's hanging out on ice in Christian's freezer (mostly because his freezer has space for things like slimy, icky fish, and partly because no way was I sleeping with a shark underneath me. I don't care how un-Jaws-like *or* dead the thing is).

Instead, Amy made her signature bacon carbonara dish since Drew went crazy over it the last time she cooked it. And when Mom snuck off earlier, it turns out she was actually using the full-sized oven on Christian's yacht to bake Dad's great-aunt Mariel's upside-down pineapple cake, Drew's absolute favorite. I definitely thought boat living would make keeping that tradition impossible, but Mom managed.

I can tell by Drew's constant chatter and grins that he's having a good birthday, in spite of it being the first one without Dad around, and even though it might physically pain me to do it, I have to give my mother some credit for pulling it off.

In fact, everyone is relaxed and laughing, and I try to let myself get swept up in the prevailing mood. Jonah had a questioning look for me when we first arrived, but I shrugged and smiled, and he seemed reassured that I was doing better than I was when he dropped me at *Sunny*'s platform this morning. We've caught eyes a few times since, but it's all been very normal between us. Thank god.

Next to me, Drew squeezes his eyes shut and collects his breath before blowing out his candles. I wonder what he wishes for. I wonder what *I* will when it's my turn next month.

I picture me, Dad, Mom, and Drew at the little metal café table in the center of my garden, a year ago tonight, eating this same cake. My Prairie Harvest roses were in full bloom and scenting our party, and a floppy branch from my hydrangeas was tickling my leg. Are they in bloom now? Is anyone remembering to deadhead the roses? Tara's last spy mission had encouraging results, but still.

Even a week ago my wish would have been a no-brainer—to go straight home, no passing Go, no collecting $200. Except now . . .

A hand waves in front of my face.

"Earth to Cassie," Jonah says.

"Huh?" I snap out of it and return to the cramped quarters of *Tide Drifter*, where everyone is looking at me.

"Are you up for it?" Jonah asks.

"Up for it?" I repeat blankly.

"Wow, you *were* gone." He gestures to my brother, who holds up a Frisbee. "Drew just opened his present from Abigail and Grace. It has LED lights in it, so we can play at night. We were thinking about heading to the beach after cake. You in?"

Abigail bounces onto my lap, forcing an "oomph" from me. "Please, Cassie? I'm *really* good at Frisbee and you can be on my team."

I laugh at her upturned face and obvious excitement. How do you say no to that, even if I wanted to, which I definitely don't.

"Yes!" I say, tweaking her nose and releasing her.

Jonah slides a piece of cake onto a paper plate and holds my eyes as he passes it to me. "Cool." His accompanying smile is soft and hesitant. I know he's probably thinking back on our talk this morning and wondering about my emotional state, but the intimacy of his expression tickles my insides.

I glance down quickly before my *outsides* give me away.

When we've sufficiently stuffed ourselves with upside-down pineapples, we leave the adults drinking their wine, and all us kids load into the Zodiac. Drew begs to captain and Jonah concedes him birthday privileges.

"Know which movie was inspired by *this* place, Sprite?" Jonah asks as we motor toward the shore. "Here's a hint. Caw! Caw!"

"Caw! Caw!" Abigail and Grace jump right in, which makes me laugh.

"Um, *Dumbo*?" I yell over the motor and the incessant crow noises.

Jonah shakes his head. "What kind of a guess is that? No, it's *The Birds*. Hitchcock was visiting this town and heard about a real-life version of a mass attack that took place here."

"That movie was based on real events?" I shudder. I've never seen it, but I know the premise, and being pecked to death is not something I want to contemplate, especially on a day when I've already been three feet away from a shark.

"Yup. They figured out only a few years ago that the seabirds were all infected by some toxin produced by red algae."

"Cool!" Drew pipes in.

"See, botany can be interesting." I can't help a little gloating.

Jonah smiles at us, then tells Drew, "Hey, watch out for the surf up ahead. It's high tide and there are some decent breakers on this stretch."

I dart a glance at Jonah. "That doesn't sound comforting."

"Don't worry," he says. "Drew's already a pro with this thing."

He reaches across the dinghy and takes my hand. I try to pretend his simple act, meant to be soothing, doesn't send my heartbeat into the stratosphere. But I think I might gasp a little because his eyes snap to my face and he studies me for a second, his head slightly cocked.

His palm against mine is warm, despite the cold breeze off the ocean and the dropping temperatures now that the sun has set. He adjusts his thumb, and it sends tingles along my arm. Since when have I been a girl who gets tingles? I didn't have them when we held hands in Half Moon Bay—was all this chemistry right under the surface, just waiting for me to surrender to the idea of us? Or is it nerves, thinking about what I might try to initiate?

I look up to find Jonah's eyes still on me, perplexed. *Damn. He can tell I'm acting weird.* I give him a small smile and glance away.

Abigail, who has finally gotten bored with making crow noises, spots our clasped hands and giggles. She starts singing at the top of her little lungs, "Cassie and Jonah, sittin' in a tree."

Grace abandons her usual shyness to jump right in for the

duet on the K-I-S-S-I-N-G line.

Jonah subtly untangles our fingers and I feign unnatural interest in the approaching shoreline, rimmed with pastel-colored houses and storefronts. Unfortunately, that doesn't deter the girls. By the time Drew expertly surfs our dinghy over a cresting wave that we ride straight onto the beach, Jonah and I have first found love, then marriage, and are now the proud owners of a baby carriage. I laugh louder than anyone else in the boat, to cover my embarrassment, but am grateful when we scrape ground.

Capitola's action is centered around a beachfront bar and some touristy shops. Aside from the dusky outlines of a few stray walkers, when we land we have most of the stretch of sand to ourselves. The upper beach is lit by spillover from the stores and restaurants, but the night is cloudy and moonless, so the packed sand down by the water is heavily shadowed, which should make using the lighted Frisbee more fun.

Jonah hops out first and offers his hand again, this time to help me from the dinghy. I shake my head and jam my fingers into the pockets of my rolled-up khakis. "Are you kidding?" I jerk my chin at Abigail and Grace, scrambling over the sides like little monkeys. "They see me take that now and they'll put triplets in our baby carriage."

Flirty Jonah appears as he grins wickedly and places his palms on either side of my waist, lifting me easily out of the boat. He sets me down at the water's edge with a cute little smirk. "Triplets could be fun."

Before I can form a smart-ass answer, he turns to the others. "Okay, girls, who's the best Frisbee catcher on this beach?" he asks, ducking down to scoop Grace up and tossing her over his shoulder as she squeals happily.

We start with a fairly civilized game of Frisbee, gently floating the lighted disk to one another to accommodate the younger participants, but things devolve pretty quickly once Grace and Abigail lose interest and begin collecting seaweed to weave bracelets with. (I'm skeptical, but apparently they saw some YouTube DIY video and are determined.) Once it's just Drew, Jonah, and me, we switch to Keep Away, with Jonah in the center.

"Drew, go high!" I scream, but as I stretch my hand up to snag the disk, Jonah's chest is in my face.

His arms wave all around mine to block me and he easily snatches the Frisbee away, grinning evilly. "Your turn in the center."

I give him my most threatening look and step into place. As soon as Jonah releases the Frisbee, I lunge for Drew. He ducks me and catches the disk, winging it to Jonah before I can even pivot. The sand is unforgiving on my calves as I attempt to race back and forth between them, ignoring their taunts.

On a high floater from Drew, the Frisbee hangs in the air for an entire lifetime and I line up right in front of Jonah, jumping as high as I can to block him. Unfortunately for both of us, I land off-balance and tumble against him, knocking us to the ground. We're a tangled mess of legs and arms sprawled on the sand.

"Are you okay?" Drew calls in the distance, but we're both laughing too hard to answer. After a few seconds, my giggling slows and I pick my head up. I startle at how close Jonah's face is to mine; he must realize the same because his eyes widen and his laugh catches in his throat.

It feels like it happens in slow motion when his gaze drifts down to my lips. I suck in a breath and freeze. Is he *possibly* on the same wavelength here?

His eyes flick back to mine and crinkle in confusion.

"Seriously, guys—are you okay?" Drew yells again from across the stretch of sand.

Another long heartbeat passes where we're like deer in headlights, and then Jonah takes a deep breath and answers, "Yup!"

He keeps his eyes locked on mine as he pushes up and onto his feet. He pulls me to standing and moves behind me to brush sand off my back. I'm still having a hard time restarting my heart, especially because it feels like his hand lingers a beat or two longer than necessary on the bare shoulder I exposed when my T-shirt was tugged aside by the fall. Jonah takes the fabric between two fingers and settles the collar gently up into place and, I swear, I have to fight off a whimper.

I swallow thickly and avoid his gaze as he hands me the Frisbee.

"I'll take a turn being 'it,'" he says, clearing his throat.

It doesn't take long for me to land in the center again, and Drew and Jonah find way too much pleasure in making it impossible for me to grab the Frisbee by keeping all the action well above my head. Stupid tall boys and their stupid height. I'm huffing and puffing when Jonah finally steps right beside me.

"This what you want, Sprite?" he teases softly, advancing another deliberate step with the Frisbee dangling loosely off his pinkie at hip level. "Come and get it."

I look at the sky and feign curiosity at something I see there. Jonah lifts his head to peer up and I take advantage of his being distracted to snatch the Frisbee. I spin, but he realizes what I've done and grabs me around the waist from behind. He pulls me against him as I squirm and fight to keep the Frisbee in my grip. He bends back slightly, lifting me off the ground, with my legs kicking out in front of me.

Jonah's laugh tickles low and warm in my ear and my body reacts. I instantly forget about the Frisbee, all my focus on the fact that I'm wrapped tightly in his arms. Again.

He must sense the shift in my attention, because he stills too. He easily snatches the Frisbee from my fingers and sends it flying hard and far. It sails well beyond Drew's reach, past where Abigail and Grace have their heads bent to the sand, engrossed in their seaweed search. My brother trots off after it and the darkness swallows him.

Jonah takes his time sliding me back to the ground, and

his arms stay loosely around my waist even after my feet are planted in the sand. I turn halfway against his chest and sneak a peek up at him. His eyes find mine, soft and searching, and my heart slams into my rib cage.

The breeze pulls pieces of my hair out of my ponytail and against my face, and Jonah moves his hand from my waist to my cheek, where he separates the strands and tucks them behind my ear. He doesn't break eye contact.

"Hey," he says in a husky voice, and now my heart stutters. *How* am I getting so lucky that he seems to feel this chemistry too? Not a lot's been going my way this year and I'm not sure I can let myself have faith it will again, but the way he's looking at me . . .

"Hey," I answer. My voice trips over the simple syllable and his eyes widen.

The Frisbee comes flying at us. Jonah gives an irritated huff and plucks it from the sky. He barely has time to spin it in his fingers before he hauls off and sends it far and wide again, this time to the opposite corner of the beach.

I hear the distant sounds of Drew's protests, but they barely register because I'm too focused on Jonah. He studies the sand, saying softly, "Remember this morning when you said I should try being completely exposed and vulnerable sometime?"

He's looking down, not at me, but I nod anyway, because I don't trust my voice.

He drags his eyes back to mine. "This is me, exposed." He takes a deep breath, then says, "I like you. A lot. You're so . . .

real, and I feel like I can be that way with you too. But at the same time, we're barely ever *not* laughing. And you call me on my crap like nobody's business, which I love." He stops and breathes again and continues before I can react. "I'm getting all these mixed signals from you, and I honestly have *no* idea how you feel . . . although I guess if I did, that would negate the whole exposed/vulnerable thing . . . so, um, I'm just gonna say this. I don't want to be your friend, Cass. Or . . . at least . . . I don't want to be *just* your friend."

Holy. Crap. I want to play every bit of what he just said on a loop in my brain, over and over, until the words all sink in and I can let myself believe this is happening.

Jonah glances up, then smoothly sidesteps and snatches the lighted Frisbee out of the sky. I hadn't even noticed it coming. He whips it back, and turns to focus on me again.

"Look, I know you're going through all this stuff, and I don't want to be the guy who takes advantage of someone whose head might be in a weird place right now, so if you—"

"Jonah." My heart is in my throat.

He stops speaking but continues to stares at me. "What?"

"You're still doing it."

His forehead furrows. "Doing what?"

I cross my hand to my opposite shoulder and squeeze, trying to hold in my thumping heart. "You're all exposed and vulnerable and yet you're *still* saying and doing the exact perfect things. How is that possible?"

He looks adorably bewildered. "It's . . . a curse?" He blinks at me. "And that wasn't really a response from you, though. I have more to say, if it would help plead my case, because—"

"Could we just skip ahead to the part where you kiss me?" I ask, biting my lip and giving him a shy smile.

He exhales the deepest breath ever and his gaze darts to my mouth. "*God yes*. I thought you'd never cut me off, Sprite. Who *knows* how much more embarrassing I would have gotten if you'd let me ramble on."

I could seriously take flight right now, there are so many winged creatures flapping around my insides, and at the same time I'm so giddy I might just start laughing hysterically, which will probably not lend itself to a stellar first kiss.

He takes a step toward me at exactly the moment when a trail of light whizzes by my peripheral vision. The hard plastic Frisbee slams into the side of Jonah's head and he jumps back, his eyes wide with pain.

"Heads up!" yells Drew.

"Oh god, are you okay?" I ask, and he nods, cupping his ear.

"Oh man, I'm sorry! I couldn't see that you weren't watching for it," Drew calls, sounding closer than I would have expected. I see Abigail and Grace running behind my brother on their little legs, and it slowly begins to sink in.

Jonah and I are not going to be getting a private, moonlit, romantic first kiss right now.

Still rubbing his ear, Jonah bursts out laughing when he sees my face as I reconcile this fact. "Sorry. This laughter is just relief that this frustrates you as much as it does me."

"More," I say, but that's all I have time for before Drew is in front of us.

He bends over and puts his hands on his knees, catching his breath, before saying, "The girls claim they're tired. Should we continue this another time?"

Jonah gives me an innocent look. "What do you say, Sprite? Should we continue this another time?"

I kick a bit of sand at his calves and reply, "Preferably *very soon*."

He smiles down at me. "Completely agree."

Drew looks between us, confused. Then he shrugs. "Hey, can I captain back?"

"Still your birthday, right?" Jonah asks.

All I can think about the entire ride to the boats is kissing Jonah. I'm 99.9999 percent sure he has the same thing on his mind, because the quarter inch or less of air between our bodies on the dinghy bench is practically crackling. It's like those science catalog toy spheres where the electricity inside connects to the warmth of the palm you place on the glass and creates sparks wherever you move your hand.

I'm ready to jump out of my skin.

I don't understand how everyone around us doesn't sense the crazy energy, but Drew seems totally chill, eyes focused ahead as he steers toward *Tide Drifter*'s anchor light, and Abigail and Grace are yawning up a storm. I tap my fingers restlessly on my leg until Jonah settles his hand over them and shoots me a knowing smile. A second later his thumb slips under my palm and begins moving in small circles against it, and—I'm gonna just say it—if those sweet monsters become alert and start singing preschool rhymes at us right now, I promise I will drop them overboard without a second thought.

"Who's tying us on?" Drew asks as we approach the platform.

Jonah gives my hand a reluctant squeeze before withdrawing his. "I got it," he says, hopping off and grabbing the rope Drew holds up.

Amy and Miranda come out and take the sleepy girls from us.

"Your mom headed back to your boat already," Miranda tells us.

I was holding out hope that Mom and Drew could ride in *Minecraft* and somehow, some way, Jonah and I could subtly finagle some private time, but so much for that idea. Jonah gives me a halfhearted shrug and lets Drew steer us over to *Sunny*.

He secures us and offers me his hand. I accidentally-on-purpose lean into him more than necessary as I exit and his arm comes around my waist to "steady me." He pulls me close and whispers in my ear, "This is gonna happen."

Before I can ask what "this" is—the kiss? Us?—he releases me to offer Drew a hand, then hops back inside the Zodiac.

Drew tosses Jonah the rope, then turns to me. "Oh, hey, Cass. I forgot." He raises his elbow and stuffs his armpit in my face. "Check it out. I remembered deodorant. Well, Jonah texted me a reminder, but that's still progress, right?"

"That's great, Roo," I say with a sigh. I can hear Jonah laughing as he starts the outboard engine.

Yup. Just *exactly* where I saw this night headed a little bit ago.

25

I wake up the next morning in the middle of a dream about being in Pleasant Hill and, in a sleepy haze, in the pitch black, I forget I'm not in my own bedroom. When I reach for my lamp with its polka-dotted shade and instead encounter a wooden cubby, I jolt back to reality.

For a second I'm upset, until I remember Jonah, and then I'm just plain confused at how much I suddenly don't want this trip to ever end. For most of the time up until now I've wanted to be back home, but nothing's black and white anymore. It's like how I always used to think the ocean was blue, but the more time I spend surrounded by it, the more I see the greens, the grays, the purples, and the whites.

Only one thing is crystal clear. I still, pretty desperately, want Jonah to kiss me. I'm a thousand percent *un*conflicted on that one.

When I poke my head out of the cabin, I'm greeted with a wall of white fog as murky as the insides of my brain. I'm guessing we're not going anywhere today.

"Isn't supposed to clear at all," Mom confirms. "Might even rain later. We're hanging tight until tomorrow. Christian and Jonah went to the harbormaster's office to try to get some better charts for maneuvering out of here, in case it doesn't lift by then either."

I sigh and retreat to the cabin like a turtle headed back inside its shell. I email Dad and spend some time grooming my bonsai tree. How long does a trip to the harbormaster take? What excuse can I find to get Jonah alone today? I can't come up with any more ways to kill time, so I land on schoolwork. I attempt a rough draft of a paper, but my head isn't in it. It's on replaying every word Jonah said on the beach last night. When I hear his voice, just after lunch, I'm convinced I've conjured it in my imagination.

Except that it's really him.

I throw on a Windbreaker and tug a brush through my hair before racing above deck. He smiles when he sees me, but it's overly casual. No hint of the charged looks he was giving me last night, which I guess is good, because my mother is watching closely.

"I don't know," she's saying to him, leaning against the bench and crossing her arms. "It's pretty gross out there."

"What's up?" I ask.

"Jonah was just dropped off to see if you wanted to grab some lunch with him."

Jonah nods. "Cabin fever. Christian's had his fill of his

relatives, so he's on board, and the man is unnaturally obsessed with opera. That's okay most of the time, but some days . . ."

He lifts his hand as if to say "have some pity, ladies!" and my mother laughs. I force myself to keep quiet and watch instead, curious about how this will play out. I'm worried if I attract any attention to myself, she'll be able to read every emotion I'm sure I must be wearing on my sleeve right now.

Her nose scrunches as she peers over Jonah's shoulder at the wall of fog between us and the shoreline. "I don't think it's a great idea today. I know you're a pro with the dinghy, but there are a lot of boats anchored out here to navigate around, and landing ashore in this fog could be tricky. You're completely welcome to hang out here with us as long as you'd like."

Better than nothing, in my opinion, but the idea of hours in a confined space with Jonah and two of my family members as chaperones presents its own set of dilemmas.

Jonah glances at me and smiles confidently. I narrow my eyes.

"How about a compromise, Mrs. McClure—"

Mom interrupts. "For the hundredth time, Jonah, please call me Elise. Mrs. McClure is my mother-in-law."

Was her mother-in-law, she means, but I don't correct her. For once the divorce reminder doesn't even bother me; I'm too interested in what he's about to suggest.

My mother tilts her head. "I'm all ears."

Jonah points to the dinghy. "What if Cass and I were to

get in, but not actually *go* anywhere?"

Mom's forehead creases, along with mine.

Jonah elaborates, "We were interrupted last night in the middle of a conversation, only it's kind of a personal topic and I'd rather we keep it one on one, if that's okay?"

He seems to be carefully avoiding my eyes as he says this, and I stifle a smile. *Conversation.* Mmm-hmm.

"And you think the rope is long enough to afford you that privacy?" my mother asks, but her eyes are twinkling and I know she's just teasing him now. She has no reason to say no, unless she suspects what we really want the time alone for.

It's kind of a perfect plan, really. Even just twenty feet out from *Sunny-Side Up*'s stern, we'll be almost impossible to hear. Ordinarily, sound travels easily across water and we'd have to be a whole lot farther from the boat not to be overheard. But the fog smothers everything. It's almost creepy how quiet the busy harbor has become, compared to the last few days here. It's like at home, when we wake up to a blanket of snow and the whole world is hushed.

We'll also be completely invisible. We'll basically be wrapped in a cocoon out there.

"I'll grab my shoes," I say before she can consider any longer.

Three minutes later, Jonah has tugged the dinghy in and lined it up against the back of *Sunny-Side Up*. The tingles hit hard when he grabs my elbow to help me board. I don't know how I feel about being the girl who gets tingles from a guy's touch, but the sensation itself is pretty great.

"Send up a flare when you need snacks," Mom calls, though I know she still doesn't suspect we might be doing something that would work up an appetite. Not that I would ever get all that carried away with my mother right at the other end of a hardly that long rope. But a kiss or two? Oh yeah. I am *definitely* plotting those.

Unlike Christian's fancy Zodiac, *Minecraft* is heavy-duty canvas and inflatable, almost like a white-water raft. In the back there's a small motor that raises or lowers into the water as needed. And spanning its center is a hard plastic bench. Usually when we ride ashore, we distribute our weight, with me in the middle and Drew and Mom perched on the sides, which are wide enough to act as seats.

Instead, Jonah and I sit next to each other on the floor, wedged between the bow and the center bench, and use the sides of the dinghy as our backrest. From above—like in the cockpit where my mother is sitting—it looks perfectly practical for an intimate talk, but I'm digging the forced proximity.

"Hey," Jonah whispers. We're still very much in both eye- and earshot of my mother.

"Hey," I answer, and we share a secret smile. God, this feels good. His hand fumbles for mine, down by our hips, and he threads our fingers together. Even that small act makes me happy enough to squirm like a puppy.

While we wait for the fog to wrap itself around us and

for the outline of *Sunny* to fade, I say, "Thank you for saving me just now" and nudge his shoulder with mine. "I was trying to write a paper on *Wuthering Heights* and it was not going well."

"Poor baby," he teases. "I remember reading that in sixth grade. Good book. Even though Austen is way better than either of the Brontë sisters."

"I'm sorry, *sixth* grade?"

"Fancy private schools, remember, Sprite?"

"Geez, what were you reading when you hit senior year? *War and Peace*?"

"Nah."

I exhale. "Thank god. You'd give me a complex."

"*War and Peace* was junior year. Senior year was *Atlas Shrugged*."

I shake my head. "You will be the best-educated burrito-stand worker in all the land."

"Surf shack!" he protests. "Well . . . maybe burritos. I do love burritos. . . ."

How we're talking about this when all I want is his lips on mine is beyond me. I check on our progress. Still way too close for comfort and we're barely drifting. Where's a good ocean breeze when you need one?

I sigh. "This could take a while."

His breath is warm in my ear as he murmurs, "But 'something to hope for' is one of the essential criteria for happiness, remember?"

My pulse jumps and my breath is shaky as I exhale. "Distract me with some of your deep philosophical musings."

Jonah laughs and turns to face the sky. "Okay, musings, let's see. How about 'Your attitude, not your aptitude, will determine your altitude.'"

I pretend to gag. "I'm extremely sure that exact quote is on a poster in my guidance counselor's office, right next to the framed print of the kitty dangling from a tree branch that reads 'Hang in There.'"

"Damn. Well, now you're totally onto me. I tour the country dropping in on unsuspecting guidance counselors to steal platitudes from their walls, all in an effort to sound deep and philosophical." I snort and he grins before continuing. "Although I *do* also have a Quote of the Day tear-off calendar next to my bedside."

I snort. "Ah, well. I missed that in your room yesterday, but it explains so very much. Does it offer a daily vocabulary word too?"

"Nope. Yoga pose."

I burst out laughing. "I can't picture you in downward dog!"

He raises an eyebrow. "Can't you now?"

I give thanks to the sunburn gods that my cheeks got enough of a tinge helping Drew fish yesterday to hide my blush. To cover, I ask, "So, do you have any personal philosophies that don't come from my guidance counselor or fortune cookies, or do you always plagiarize from the pros?"

His expression grows more serious. "Okay, ready? It might sound ridiculously cheesy, so you can't laugh."

"I already told you, I can't make that promise. When people say I can't laugh, it makes me super punchy and way more prone to giggles."

"Interesting. Does that opposite-effect thing work on you for other stuff? Sprite, whatever you do, do not tickle me right now."

I grin and very deliberately dance my fingers across a strip of skin under the edge of his T-shirt. He stills and sucks in a breath. After a second he exhales carefully. I get a crazy thrill, knowing my touch affects him like that.

He recovers quickly though, and his grin grows wicked. "Sprite, whatever you do, do not—"

I slap my palm over his mouth. "Watch it, mister. My mother is only one tug on this rope away."

He scoots up a little to check on our progress and groans. "We're drifting sideways now. I think we're actually moving closer to your boat."

I roll my eyes. "Of course, because the universe hates me."

Jonah gasps. "Blasphemist!"

I roll my eyes and he grins.

"Okay, philosophy time," he says. "Ready? The Jonah Abrahmson Mission Statement: 'And love, I think, is no parenthesis.'"

"I hate to burst your bubble, but that is *not* a Jonah-ism. That's an e. e. cummings–ism."

He lets loose with a low whistle. "I'm impressed. Girl knows her poetry. You must be getting *something* from your lowly public school education."

That warrants a punch.

In response he takes his hand out of mine and drapes his arm over my shoulder, tugging on my sleeve until I bend my elbow and give him my left hand instead. Then he reaches across his torso to take my other one too.

"There. I feel much safer from your abuse now," he says.

I move our entangled hands to whack him in the bicep and he yelps in protest.

"Actually, Sprite, much as it pains me to point this out to you, you are incorrect. e. e. cummings wrote 'for life's not a paragraph / And *death* i think is no parenthesis.' Which *I* interpret as meaning that death is final so you should live wholly in the moment, experiencing everything to its fullest. Not a bad life motto. I just thought it needed a little tweaking."

I scoff. "You thought *e. e. cummings* needed editing? Egotistical much?"

He makes a face at me. "Okay, true confession time. It was a total screw-up on my part. Unless you believe, as James Joyce said, that a man's mistakes are his 'portals of discovery.'"

"Less impressive quoting, more 'Jonah screws up,' please," I order.

His sigh is exaggerated. "Fine. Okay, so we were studying the e. e. cummings poem in English and I forgot to bring home my textbook. I was grounded, for something I can't even remember now—so don't bother asking."

He steals a glance at me and laughs at my opened mouth. I'd been about to do exactly that. I'm also comforted by the fact that he's known his share of grounding. That'll help when I get around to telling him the real reason I lied in San Francisco.

"Anyway, my dad had my laptop and my phone and I wasn't speaking to him, so I couldn't ask for them back, even to do homework," he continues.

"Been there, done that."

"I was convinced I remembered enough to write an essay about it, except it turns out, I didn't. According to *my* memory, the last line read 'and love, I think, is no parenthesis.' So I wrote this whole paper on how e. e. cummings was trying to tell everyone that love is the main event, not a parenthetical part of something else. Basically, love isn't some aside to the meaning of life—it *is* the meaning of life."

He exhales and sounds embarrassed when he says, "Okay, so I know this isn't groundbreaking stuff and a million people have said something like that before me, but sometimes the simplest ideas are the ones we need to hear again and again in a hundred different ways, right?"

"Definitely," I agree. "It's perfect."

He lights up at my words and I get Champagne bubbles in my belly. Jonah around everyone else is all casual and jokes, and I love that he lets me see this other side of him. I want him to talk and talk until I know everything there is to know about him. Except I also want him to shut up and kiss me, so there's that.

Luckily/unluckily for me, he jumps right back in. "Writing that paper was probably the beginning of me landing here, because it forced me to think about things like that in respect to my own life. I mean, I was Drew's age, so it's not like I did anything about it. But it's probably the biggest reason I *do* subscribe to Napoléon's belief that 'there is no such thing as accident; it is fate misnamed.'"

"You know you're not impressing me with all this name-dropping, right, Ivy League?"

He makes a face. "Who, me? How do you know that wasn't yesterday's tear-off calendar quote?"

"Puh-leaze," I reply, and this time he tickles *my* waist.

I squirm against him and ask, "So that paper set everything in motion, so to speak?"

"Yup. That and Environmental Economics being under-enrolled. Happy accidents."

I try to think whether I have any happy accidents like that. Maybe I do and I just don't have enough of the big picture to see the effects of them yet. I mean, the divorce definitely set a ton of things in motion, but I don't know if I'll ever be able to bring myself to think of it alongside the word *happy*.

Except that I wouldn't be here right now without it. On the other hand, I also wouldn't be apart from my dad, and my mom and I wouldn't be at each other constantly. I would still trust in a world where good things happened to people who tried hard to be decent, and I wouldn't be constantly on guard for the next aftershock to hit. I wouldn't know pain like I've known this year.

So no, not such a "happy" accident, even if one or two of the ripple effects have been not so terrible.

I realize I've gone quiet and so has Jonah, waiting patiently.

"Sorry," I murmur. "I went into my head a little there."

"S'okay. Maybe I can help bring you back here. . . . Did you feel the rope pull taut just now? We're finally all the way out."

I peek and he's right. I can't see *Sunny* at all. Just like that, the bad mood that threatened with my last line of thought blows right over. Jonah's eyes hold mine. The expression in them makes my mood shift yet again as all the charged energy from last night comes rushing back. Minutes ago we were having a true philosophical discussion, but just now my brain would have to slug itself through waist-high drifts to reach any thoughts beyond how close we're sitting and the delicious weight of his arm across my shoulders.

He asks, "So, did any of your guidance counselors ever have that one poster that says, 'There Comes a Time for Less Talking, More Doing'?" The pad of his thumb is tracing the same circles on my knee that he was making in my palm last night, and I'm not sure I can take much more.

I *need* him to kiss me. Badly.

My head shake is slow and deliberate and my voice is

barely there as I say, "I don't think so, but I'm liking the senti-ment. I could go for less—" I break off as Jonah's face moves closer, his eyes on my mouth. He brushes his lips against mine, his touch so feather-soft I'm not sure they're actually there. Oh god, this *is* happening. Finally.

"Sorry, what was that?" he murmurs against my mouth.

Mmm. Lips are definitely there.

Want. More.

I tip my chin to get closer to them, but he withdraws. "You could what?" he asks again, ducking his head into the crook of my neck and teasing me with his soft breath.

"I could definitely . . ." I gasp as his lips press against my jaw.

"Continue," he urges, his mouth now trailing to the dip in my shoulder.

"Go for . . . ," I manage.

His nose nudges aside my hair and his lips move, whisper-light, to my earlobe. Okay, so college boys are in a whole other category.

"I'm listening," he says softly, and his voice hums in my ear. I shiver and feel his smile against my cheek.

"Go for less . . . ," I say, and my words are choppy and breathless. Jonah turns his face so our lips are lined up, and he looks into my eyes. He quirks his eyebrows in an amused question, and I know just what will happen the minute I get the last word out.

Bring it.

I wind my fingers into the curls at the back of his head.

"Less talking," I state firmly, and tug his hair to bring his lips to mine, but he's already beaten me there. His mouth captures mine gently, then with more heat as my lips open under his. He runs his hand up my back and his fingers cradle the base of my head while his palm lightly cups my face.

I sigh and press against him, not caring one tiny bit that this perfect kiss is happening in the well of *Minecraft*.

26

Who was it who wanted this trip to hurry up and end? Not me, right?

This new version of Cassie is a whole lot less upset than I expected to be that today *should* have been the start of my road trip with Tara and Jess.

This new version of Cassie isn't the least bit annoyed that it's the middle of August—day thirty-six of our trip, to be exact—and we've been docked in Port San Luis for *seven days*, awaiting a clear weather forecast to tackle Point Conception. It's the peninsula that divides central California from Southern California, and it's apparently known for super-crazy ocean conditions, like waves that come from all directions at once and wind that goes from zero to a million knots in seconds.

Christian says the only thing to do with Point Conception is to hold out for perfect conditions and then race like hell around it. I'm perfectly fine with that. Both from the "not dying" and from the "more chances to hang out with Jonah" perspective.

It took us four days to sail here, overnighting in San Simeon and Morro Bay along the way. When you add the seven we've spent here, it's been eleven days of sneaking toe-curling kisses.

Jonah and I are not *exactly* hiding things from my mother . . . except that we more or less are. I figure I'll have a whole lot more freedom to hang out with Jonah if everyone thinks we're just becoming better friends because he's the only other person my age out here. Mom made it clear early on that she didn't approve of Jonah's "grotty yachty" status, and I'd prefer to skip the lectures, thanks very much. To be honest, I don't think she's letting herself see what's in front of her face, because I suspect she's just relieved that I'm in a *much* better mood these days and we've been fighting way less as a result.

Luckily, turns out stolen kisses are the best kind of kisses. Who knew?

Er, except when they're stolen kisses in Bubblegum Alley. Those are still amazing . . . but messy.

I was very skeptical that there existed an entire wall—nope, make that an entire *alley*—in the center of San Luis Obispo where the bricks from top to bottom on either side are lined with wads of used chewing gum placed there by decades of visitors, but Jonah assured me that not only was this an actual thing, but that we would be leaving our own behind, since it's the thing to do.

Of course, he insisted on trying to extract *my* piece of gum from my mouth himself. With his tongue. It might sound gross, but if you knew the things this boy can do with his tongue, you would have let him too. You also would have let him push you up against the wall when the kissing got a bit intense. You probably *also* wouldn't even have minded having to hide in your berth that night using tweezers to remove bits of someone else's Bubble Yum from your ponytail.

Let's just say Dad got a much more PG-rated photo of the gum wall. . . .

We've been kissing in all sorts of other spots too. When it became apparent that we were going to be lying in wait in Port San Luis for more than a few days, Christian rented a car so we could all explore the area, but mostly he's just handed the keys over to Jonah.

Usually we have Drew (who we did tell) along, and sometimes a couple of the others. Jonah actually ran a shuttle service when everyone, adults included, wanted to visit Hearst Castle. And we took Grace and Abigail to a story time at the library, which was a slice of normal childhood they'd never experienced before.

Happily, every once in a while it *is* just us, like today, when we're using the car to run errands. These are my favorite times because it feels so normal, and I can forget for a few minutes that we're living on a boat on the Pacific Ocean and that, in another month, things will get even more foreign because then when we venture ashore, we'll be shopping for supplies in Spanish.

But not today. Today there are In-N-Out burgers and a slow drive back to the harbor.

"See?" I push my phone under Jonah's face.

Jonah, being the responsible guy that he is, waits until we stop at a red light to take it from my hand. "What am I looking at right now? And why is Tara making a sad face?"

"According to Jess, *that* is a six-hundred-pound cement statue of Kurt Cobain with a single tear trickling down his face, in Aberdeen, Washington."

Jonah mouths "Wow," then passes my phone back. "Are you bummed you're not hitting the road with them?"

"Honestly? Yeah. A lot. We'd been talking about it for months. It sucks to miss out."

Jonah reaches across to squeeze my hand and I smile my thanks. I add, "Not that hitting it with you isn't a decent alternative."

Jonah's eyebrow raises. "Are you gifting me a 'That's what she said,' Sprite, or was that just dumb luck?"

"Eww. I meant the road and you know it."

I'm quiet for a second, studying the barren mountain range out my window. The terrain is all packed dirt and clumps of scrubby bushes, so different from the lush rainforest of Oregon. "'Hitting the road' is the weirdest expression though, don't you think?" I ask. "I picture someone out there with a baseball bat smacking the pavement."

Jonah laughs. "It does sound pretty violent."

"Which is weird, because most expressions having to do with things on land are very positive. As opposed to sailing ones, which are all negative," I say, sneaking a fry from the bag resting on the console between us.

Jonah smacks my hand. "Those are for Uncle Chris. I *told* you to order yourself the large!"

I stick my tongue out at him and snatch another when he returns his eyes to the road. Without turning his head, his hand snakes across and grabs it from my fingers. He glances at me, then pops it into his mouth.

When he finishes chewing, he says, "Okay, now what are you on about, Sprite? Sailing expressions are negative?"

"It's true!"

"So what do I get if I name a whole ton of positive ones?" he asks.

"What, like a bet? Okay, I'm down with that. I challenge you to come up with one positive sailing saying to cancel out each of my negative ones. You really think you got this?"

He glances at me. "Without breaking a sweat. Though I do need to know what's in it for me."

I peek in my purse. "I have . . . four dollars, one tube of sunscreen, and the sea lion Christmas ornament I bought yesterday. Take your pick."

Jonah says, "I would never take Gus."

I stare at him in confusion and he shrugs. "I named your sea lion."

I turn the tiny plastic animal over in my hand as he asks, "What else do you have there? Sunscreen and four bucks? Neither interests me. What, oh what, could a little wood sprite have to offer that I might want?" I groan and his eyes go comically wide. "What? I don't know why *your* thoughts went to the gutter. Maybe I have something perfectly innocent in mind, which I do, but I'm not telling you until after I win. You can do the same."

"Okay, fine," I concede. "I'll come up with the negative ones, you go positive, and we'll see who's the last woman standing. I'll start: 'weather the storm.'"

"I don't think you know the definition of negative, my friend. It's a good thing to weather a storm. It means you came out the other side."

"The connotation is bad. No one wants to *have to* weather a storm. If you hear that phrase it's someone trying to feed you a line, because you're miserable and in the middle of something."

Jonah rests his hand on the gear shift between us. "Hmm. I'm gonna give that to you, but I'd like the judges to note that it's under protest. Okay. Positive one: 'smooth sailing.'"

I narrow my eyes and take a sip of my soda. "Fine. You got lucky, mister. My turn again. 'Has the wind knocked out of his sails.'"

"Which never made sense to me," Jonah says. "How do you knock wind? You knock heads, wood, knees. But air?"

"Doesn't matter, because it's a negative one and I'm winning."

Jonah makes a turn and the harbor comes into sight. "Pfft. Whatever. Hold on. Lemme think . . ."

I sneak another fry and gloat. "Can't find one, can you? Whereas I could go on and on with the negative ones. 'Unanchored,' 'at the mercy of the winds,' 'dead in the water,' 'between the devil and the deep blue sea'!"

He holds up his hand. "You are scraping the bottom of the barrel with these, Sprite. Which, by the way, is a sailing expression."

I stare at him. "What does scraping the bottom of the barrel have to do with sailing?"

"Food was stored in them during ocean crossings and when they were getting low, the cook would have to scrape the sides and bottom to get every last morsel. So is 'bite the bullet.' They used to give sailors bullets to bite down on when they had to do surgeries at sea, before anesthesia was a thing."

"Proving my point. All sailing expressions have bad connotations."

Jonah pulls into a parking spot near where *Minecraft* is tied up and waiting. "I refuse to concede this."

"Now, land ones, on the other hand . . ."

He turns off the engine and faces me, tucking a hand under his chin as he waits for me to illuminate him.

No problem there. "All good ones. 'She's so grounded'—compliment. 'On solid ground'—implies security."

"That's not fair. I *know* there are more good sailing ones." He's quiet for a second and then exclaims, "Ha! Got one! 'A safe harbor in the storm.'"

I gather the empty fast food wrappers from the floor, to let him know we can move on because this contest is all sewn up. "Which really just means you've come in from sailing and gotten close enough to the awesome that is *land* to be protected again. Admit that I'm right. Land rules."

"Says the wood sprite." He scratches his cheek. "Okay, okay. Prepare to surrender. Ready?"

I crumple the trash in my hand and humor him. "Dazzle me."

He pronounces proudly, "'Mother, mother ocean, I have heard you call.'"

I laugh in his face. "That is *not* an expression, Abrahmson! That's a Jimmy Buffett lyric! Soo doesn't count."

He hangs his head, and I say, "I'll just go on then. 'Putting down roots'—generally considered a good thing."

"Depends who you ask. On the other hand, 'footloose and fancy-free' sounds pretty darn positive *and* is a sailing term. Bottom of the sail is called the foot, and if it's not attached to the boom, it's footloose and causes the boat to sail all over the place." He puts his own drink up to his lips and slowly takes a sip, looking all cocky and confident. Then he pulls the straw away and shakes the clearly empty cup; only a few ice cubes rattle.

"And *that's* a good thing?" I ask, offering him my soda.

His face falls. "I mean, I guess not when it's happening on your boat, but the expression . . ."

I snort. "Face it, the cliché writers had it out for sailing."

Jonah extracts the crumpled wrappers from my hand and

stuffs them inside his cup. He steps out and tosses the trash into a nearby can before circling to open my door and propping an elbow on the roof to lean in over me. "First of all, there is no such thing as cliché writers. What do you think, people with Rasputin beards sit at desks coining sayings for the masses?"

I grab the bag of fries and my drink and gently push him away so I can join him on the asphalt. "Sore loser. You're a sore loser. What's the second of all?"

"Hmm?" He steps close, backing me against the car.

"You said 'first of all,' which generally implies a 'second of all' to follow."

"Oh. Second of all . . ." He leans into me. "Second of all . . . this."

His lips find mine, and I may have been talking about being on solid ground a minute ago—I may actually be *standing* on solid ground—but I practically float away. When we finally break apart, I murmur, "What was the topic again?"

He steps back. "I thought of another one while we were kissing."

"Your brain cells worked during *that* kiss?"

He offers a bemused smile. "Windfalls. Nautical term, commonly referencing a stroke of luck, but used to mean 'when a rush of wind speeds up a vessel's progress.'" His arms cage me in place. "Used in a sentence: 'Meeting you was a real windfall, Sprite.'"

"Okay, that was so sweet I'm awarding you the win."

Although I'm kind of feeling like a big fat winner myself right now.

Jonah does a victory dance in the lot, then returns with an especially wicked grin. "This is excellent. As mentioned, I have my prize all picked out."

I brace myself. He picks a piece of nonexistent lint off my shoulder and says, ever so casually, "From here on out, I'd like you to refer to me, in all instances, as Pirate Sexytimes."

My eyes go wide and I slump a little. "Oh. My. God! You *did* read my texts that day I dropped my phone!" I duck out from under his arms and put both hands on my hips. "I can't believe you would do that!"

He shrugs, and his eyes dance. "Are you sure you didn't mean to say 'I can't believe you would do that, Pirate Sexytimes'?"

"Are you going to be impossible about this now?"

He tucks a finger into my belt loop and tugs me close. "Are you *sure* you didn't mean to ask, 'Are you going to be impossible about this, Pirate Sexytimes?'"

27

Batten down the hatches—another negative boat cliché to rub in Jonah's face. It's also what we need to do in preparation for today's sail.

Just the name Gale Alley sounded scary enough to convince me things were going to be far worse than they actually were. Point Conception, however, does not sound nearly as ominous.

And yet.

The way everyone shares war stories about it in the marina and the way we had to sit at dock for so long, waiting for perfect conditions, and the way even Christian looks wary when he discusses our strategy for rounding it with the rest of our caravan . . . I get the message loud and clear. Big Bad Wolf stuff.

"Okay, so we're sure we don't want to go wide, right?" Mom asks. The group of adults (which includes Jonah, in this instance) is huddled around nautical charts in the cabin of

Reality Bytes. Drew and I let ourselves get roped into playing Chutes and Ladders with Abigail and Grace, while I keep one ear on the other conversation.

"We'd have to go out at least forty miles to avoid the compression zone around the mountains," Christian answers. "Even then, that stretch of channel between San Miguel and the Point can be a beast if we hit bad conditions. I think we're better tucking into the countercurrent near the shore, like we discussed. We'll just go like hell and send prayers to the gods of calm seas."

I don't pretend to understand half of what he said there. How is it that my fate is about to be decided by "prayers to the gods"?

"Forecast is saying light five- to fifteen-knot winds, but those usually double on the Point itself, so let's be prepared for twenty-five to thirty and steep waves, okay? Keep the rain gear and harnesses prepped," Miranda says.

God, the mood in here is so tense.

It stays that way as we return to our respective boats. Drew hangs behind to sail with Christian, and Jonah joins us, but this is no "fun date at sea," even if we weren't trying to keep things between us on the down low. This is all business.

I head to the cabin and make plenty of sandwiches and fill thermoses with coffee, zipping everything into a soft-sided cooler and bringing it above to set inside a bench. I sit and watch Jonah and my mother run through a pre-sail checklist.

"Sprite, come help," Jonah says, gesturing me over.

I shake my head, and he leaves Mom's side by the mast to crouch in front of me. I glance at my mother, because his position is borderline intimate, but she's busy winding the long ends of a rope in loops between her elbow and hand.

"I don't sail, remember," I tell him.

"Got some news to break to you. Since you've refused to address me as Pirate Sexytimes, I've devised a new prize."

I steal a peek at my mother and lower my voice. "I thought that makeout session last night was your prize!"

He offers a regretful smile and a smirk. "Nope. That was just bonus for a job well done."

I can't hold in my laugh. "You're a nut."

"I am most definitely a nut. Know what else I am?"

I lean back and wait.

"A truly excellent sailing instructor. I spent five summers teaching classes for kids at my yacht club. I figure you can't be *that* much worse than the little boy I found swinging upside down from the mast after getting tangled in the halyard."

I cross my arms. "You're going to be impossible today if I don't agree to this, aren't you?"

He rocks back on his heels and smiles. "That would be affirmative.'"

I gulp. It doesn't seem like the ideal scenario for a learn-to-sail experience, but I guess I *could* use a distraction, and if it gets too intense, I can always bail.

"Fine." I stand and wipe my palms on my thighs. "But I'm not promising to like it. Where do you want me?"

In response, Jonah arches an eyebrow suggestively, and the corners of his lips twitch. I ignore both and brush past, trying not to let him see my shoulders shake with laughter. He catches up and points me toward the bow of the boat. When we pass my mother, she glances at us, but doesn't comment.

"Okay," Jonah says, once we're standing in the very front. "We're going to sail downwind to start, so we need to unfurl the jib."

"English, please."

He puts a hand on his hip and points to the sail closest to us. "We're gonna put this thing up, so it will fill with the wind coming from behind us and carry us faster toward our destination."

"Cool."

He reaches around me to grab a rope and puts it in my hand.

"Pull," he orders.

"The rope?" I ask.

"The *line*. On a boat, ropes are referred to as lines."

"Whatever." I pout but do as he says, and the sail starts to unroll. When it's fully extended, Jonah nods in satisfaction.

"Not too bad, right?"

I make a face and he laughs. "Okay, I'm gonna help your mom hoist the mainsail. You take notes."

I trail him back to the cockpit, where he demonstrates how to wrap the halyard (another rope—no, *line*!) several times around what he calls the "winch drum" and then pulls the remainder through as my mother feeds it to him from her spot at the mast. When it's free, my job is to coil it for storing. Jonah shows me the difference between finishing off the halyard in a way where we can quickly yank it apart if we need to lower the sail in an emergency and tying the knots around the coiled dock ropes, which we won't use again until we stop for the night. It actually isn't all *that* complicated. But then again, we are still at dock.

Soon enough, though, everyone radios their state of readiness and we cast off and head for open sea. I still have an anchor in my belly over what might be ahead for us.

All is supposed to be calm until we reach the Point, so once we're under way, Mom—who, so far, has resisted any comments whatsoever on my sailing tutelage—goes below to answer some emails and get out her rain gear in anticipation of the larger waves that await.

I stand next to Jonah at the wheel as he tells me, "Okay, sailing is really just a matter of feeling the wind. We're gonna start with a beam reach, which means we'll position our heading so the wind is blowing straight across us—sideways." I watch the flag at the top of our mast for wind direction while he maneuvers us.

"Okay, now steer right for a minute or two and watch the sails. Then try it with the wheel to the left. You'll be able to see how the sails respond to different wind positions. Eventually, we want to find that sweet spot where they're not luffing." He steals a glance at me. "Flapping. Sorry, I'm trying to speak

English. Nautical has its own language."

"What's that all about? Why can't we call starboard 'right' and lines 'ropes'?" I ask, following his instructions and studying the sails as I do so.

"Obviously because then we wouldn't sound nearly as snooty. I thought that was clear."

I laugh. "Okay, okay. Proceed."

"That's pretty much it. It's really just about filling your sails with enough wind to get you where you want to go. It's not rocket science."

"That's *it*?"

He shrugs. "More or less."

Somehow it always seemed more involved. I'm maybe a little embarrassed I've been so actively avoiding it.

Jonah shows me how to trim the sails for optimal speed and then leans close to whisper in my ear. "Don't look now, but you're sailing, Sprite."

I'm sailing.

Huh.

We're moving fast—really fast—skimming along the tops of the small whitecaps as if we're the boss of them—and *I did that*. There's a world of difference between riding in the back-seat of a car and the exhilaration that hits the first time you pull out of the driveway in the driver's seat, with the windows down and the radio blaring. This might be even better because there are no speeding tickets or stoplights out here.

I breathe in the crisp wind and let it fill my lungs and puff out my chest. The coastline off our port side winks in the sun, looking small and insignificant from this angle.

"Do you think it's weird we don't have to file a flight plan with anyone before we leave?" I ask Jonah.

"A flight plan?"

I grin. "Yeah. The thing that lets air traffic control know you're up there, so if you don't land where you say you're going to, they can worry. I mean, even when you're out for a day hike, you're supposed to let the park ranger know which trail you're taking, so they can send search parties if you don't come back. But, like, we could just take off for China right now and no one would know or care. Couldn't we?"

He tilts his head. "I guess so. I never thought about it like that."

"Well. It's not a very comforting thought, is it?"

"Where's your spirit of adventure, Sprite?"

"Oh, it's here. It would like to stay here and not in a watery grave, is all." I pause. "Are you the least bit afraid for Point Conception?"

To his credit, he doesn't laugh off my question. He considers for a moment and then says, "Hard to figure out which parts are fear and which parts are exhilaration."

"Meaning . . ."

"Meaning, sure I'm scared. But I'm more scared of not trying stuff and living a totally boring, mundane life. Besides, if you're telling me you want to be a botanist, you must have some of that adventure bug in you too. That's not typically a desk job, at least I don't think."

He . . . might be right. Do I? Could I?

"'The greatest life is one spent choosing curiosity over fear,'" Jonah quotes.

"Another of your philosophers?"

"Author. Elizabeth Gilbert. She wrote that *Eat, Pray, Love* memoir. Did you read it?"

I shake my head. "Nope. But I like that you're an equal-opportunity quoter when it comes to gender."

Jonah raises his hands in mock surrender. "Hey, I'm all about the brain, not the reproductive parts it shares a body with."

I roll my eyes and sneak a quick peck.

As we approach Point Arguello, about ten nautical miles before Point Conception, the wind speeds increase, and between the two points they ramp up again. The seas go from calm to confused and the wind gusts reach as high as thirty knots, which is serious stuff. The waves are the biggest I've seen this trip and a couple even crash onto the deck, wetting our feet as we move around the cockpit. That, coupled with the spray from breaking crests, has me grateful I put my rain gear on.

But otherwise, it seems . . . manageable. We all have jobs to concentrate on and we're working in unison. I'm way less out of my element than I thought I would be, even when Jonah and Mom decide to reef the mainsail (don't ask me why they can't call it what it is: lowering the big sail partway and attaching it in a different way) and I'm assigned to gather the dropping luff (plainly put, the sail we're lowering) while Jonah stands at the mast and secures something called a tack cringle into a tack horn. (*Why*, nautical terms, *why?*)

I follow all instructions both Mom and Jonah give me, and I have to admit, it feels good to help beyond just offering moral support. I like being part of things and getting treated like an equal. And Jonah's right, it *is* more exhilarating than scary, particularly with a task to focus on.

"There's the tip of the point," Mom finally yells, pointing off our port side. "Get ready to say hello to Southern California!"

I've been told that SoCal is the promised land for sailors. The water temperatures jump from the fifties into the mid-seventies, and the sea turns from rough and gray to glassy and aquamarine. I like the sound of all that.

Jonah whoops and barrels down the stairs. A few seconds later the Beach Boys singing "Catch a Wave" blares over the remaining wind. He returns to the cockpit with three sodas and we wait for the moment we round the bend to toast with them.

As soon as we've sipped, my mom grabs the cans and puts them aside before tugging me into her arms.

"We did it!" she yells, swinging me around. For once, I don't fight to break free. I laugh and let her dance me across the cockpit. When we bump into Jonah, he catches me and she releases me into his arms. I nearly forget and kiss him, but I stop myself just in time.

It's dramatic how quickly the conditions return to calm, flat waters on this side of the peninsula. Jonah heads down to the cabin to check on the others via radio, and Mom and I slump side by side onto one of the benches. The adrenaline finally starts to wear off and we're companionably quiet for a few moments, listening to the garbled voices from the radio downstairs.

That is, until she asks, "So when are you going to tell me about you and Jonah?"

Oh crap. I am so not in the mood for an argument right now. I sigh heavily. "Look, I know you don't—"

Mom interrupts me with a hand on my knee and a smile. "Relax, Cass. I can admit when I'm wrong."

She—what?

"It was amazing watching him teach you to sail today. And I'm not blind to how much happier you've been the last couple of weeks."

She steals a glance at me, then adds, "I think maybe Jonah's good for you."

"God, Mom, he's not a multivitamin."

She laughs, further blowing my mind. "I know that. But he *is* a nice kid."

I listen to make sure Jonah's still on the radio before saying, "What about the whole grotty-yachty thing?"

Mom winces. "I may have been projecting a personal experience there. Jonah's been nothing but respectful and helpful, and like I said, I love seeing you like this. I may be old enough to be your mother, but—"

"Mom, you *are* my mother."

"Exactly," she says, grinning. "But that doesn't mean I'm too ancient to remember what a vacation fling feels like."

I smile tightly and pick at my cuticles. It's not as though Jonah and I have labeled what we're doing, but I hate how dismissive "fling" sounds when she says it out loud. Below us the radio noises end and the music resumes, cycling through the starts of several songs as Jonah searches for one he wants to play.

"Oh . . . ," Mom says softly when I don't respond. "Maybe *not* just a vacation fling?"

I shrug. Jonah and I are so new that I don't have any expectations about our future, per se, but I don't exactly enjoy thinking about what's going to happen when we reach Land's End. I'm sure my mother will relish lecturing me on how impractical even the thought of anything long-term would be.

She shocks me again by saying, "Well, you can't fight feelings, right?"

Is she talking about me and Jonah or her and Mr. Whatever His Name Might Be? The reminder of her mystery guy sets me on edge, but before I can get worked up, she follows with, "Also, you never know what the future holds. You both have a lot of flexibility in what comes next for you, so maybe you'll be one of those lucky couples who finds a way to make things work."

I—can't believe my mom and I are talking like this again.

If this were last summer it wouldn't even be noteworthy, but now?

I glance at her and her eyes are soft. "I just want you to be happy, honey. I know you don't believe that, but it's true."

Where was that attitude when she was considering this trip in the first place? Although I can't deny that, at the moment, I *am* happy to be here. And I'm kind of beyond words that my mom is being, well, the way she used to be. The only ones I can think of are "Thanks, Mom."

I whisper them just as Jonah returns. In reply, she squeezes my knee.

She stands and moves to the opposite bench, gesturing at Jonah to take the seat next to me. When he sits, I snuggle against him, much to his surprise.

Mom puts the binoculars to her eyes and pretends to be very absorbed in studying the coastline, but I can see the smile dancing on her lips.

For the first time in a long time, it doesn't annoy me.

28

I'm reveling in my newfound sailing abilities. To be honest, I'm totally pissed at myself for not trying it sooner. It's possible I could have screwed myself a little with my own idiotic stubbornness, but I'm determined to make up for lost time now.

Case in point, I'm currently helping Drew get the boat ready for our midmorning departure for Catalina Island. It will be another overnight, and once again, we're planning to swap deckhands so Jonah can sail with us. Not because we're expecting any conditions, but because Drew adores everything about helping to sail Christian's yacht and, well, I love everything about the idea of a quiet night with Jonah by my side. Mom too, but I conveniently forget to include her in any of my daydreams. I'm hoping she's feeling extra sleepy tonight, and I have an evil plan to promote lots of wine drinking on her part to help ensure this.

I work with Drew to check the deck for any gear that could

come loose under sail and to identify possible snag points for our lines. When I finally climb down into the cabin to declare us nearly prepped, I find Mom staring off into space, her computer open on the table.

"Cass," she says quietly. "We need to talk."

I bypass her and turn into my berth, calling behind me, "Okay, but first lemme just email a paper to my teacher before we get under way, so I'm free to help with—"

"Cassie," my mother interrupts, appearing in my doorway. "Honey, I got some news today."

I'm swiping aside some laundry and leaning across my bed for my laptop, but when the tone of her voice finally penetrates, I freeze, fingers clenched around a folded T-shirt. "What news?"

An acrid taste fills my mouth as I wait.

"It's about the family subletting our house. They've been spending the last few weeks seeing every home on the market in Pleasant Hill and, well, it turns out they want ours."

I turn to face her. "I don't get it."

She puts a hand on my knee. "I guess they've really settled in and our house has everything they have on their wish list. They've made Dad and me an offer. A very, *very* generous offer."

My breathing is shaky. "But it's not for sale!"

"I know, sweetheart, I know. It's an unexpected development. And under ordinary circumstances, it probably wouldn't be anything I'd consider, but other than that one disastrous phone interview, the résumés I've been sending out since we left haven't yielded even a single nibble, and the money we'd make on this sale would end our financial woes for a good long time. The housing market is hot right now, and we've owned so long we've built up a lot of equity in that place. With you off to college next year and, well, with Dad gone too, maybe it makes sense to downsize. It'd be crazy for us to not at least consider it, Cass."

"So what, they'd just . . . stay? What about our stuff? Where do we go when we get back?"

I *thought* things were genuinely getting better between us, I really did—but now my old familiar anger rushes right back in, like it had only been taking a quick commercial break.

"We'd have to work all those details out, Cass. I know this is a lot to process," Mom says. "But I wanted to keep you in the loop. I'll be telling Drew as soon as he's done up there, and I also emailed Dad. He obviously has a say in this too."

But clearly *I* don't. Keeping me "in the loop" is light-years away from that. I never seem to have a say. Which shouldn't *keep* surprising me, but goddamn it, I'm so tired of having the ground drop out from under me.

It's my fault. I let my defenses down, dared to relax and be happy . . . and she struck again, out of the blue.

I'm not hanging around to hear her hollow reassurances. I jump up and push past her, climbing the stairs two at a time. I don't answer Drew when he calls to me from the bow of the boat; he'll be "in the loop" himself soon enough, though I can't count on him to be in my camp when nothing else has seemed to faze him like it has me.

It's only when I have the dinghy untied from the platform and the engine started that I let the tears flow. I zoom off with no particular destination in mind, just *away*.

There's a lump in my throat as I picture my house, with its cheerful yellow siding and the black window boxes I fill every year with trailing ivy and annuals to match the season. The handprints I made as a three-year-old are in the concrete by the basement steps, and my first hamster, Sir Alfred Buckminster Wellington, is buried in my second-grade *High School Musical* lunch box by the back fence. I learned to roller-skate, bike, play hopscotch, and shoot with a hockey stick in that driveway. I snuck my first and only cigarette, with Tara and Jess, on the flat roof over the garage, back when we coveted a training bra above all other possible possessions.

Every root I put down, I put down *there*. Both literally, in the garden I love with all my heart, and figuratively.

The last place that really represented all that my family once was—that held all of our best memories—is going to have strangers living in it when I get home. What will we do, tiptoe around them to pack up the rest of our things? Like we're intruding on *their* space? I imagine a perfect, happy family unit waving to us from the brick front path as we pull away from the curb, reminding us of all that we're not anymore.

Once again, my future blurs and shifts.

Is this how it's always going to be from now on? *Don't get comfortable, Cass. Don't let your guard down because the hits, well, they just keep coming.*

I don't trust that I'll be able to land the dinghy on shore, given the size of the breakers hitting the beach, so after circling the anchorage area once, I do the next best thing and steer to *Reality Bytes.* At first all I can think about is finding Jonah and letting him wrap me up in his arms, but it's Beatriz waiting to greet me when I dock. I climb aboard, sink onto the deck, and bury my face in her fur.

"What would a bad day be for you, hmm, Bea? No kibbles in your bits? No seagulls to chase on the beach? You ever had anyone sell your doghouse out from under you?"

"Sprite?" Jonah crosses the deck, an expression of concern on his face as he takes in my tear-streaked cheeks. He slides down next to me and puts his hand over mine on Beatriz's fur. "What's going on?"

"Where's Christian?" I ask, not wanting anyone else to see me like this.

"Ashore grabbing a couple last-minute supplies he forgot. What happened?"

When I fill him in, he tugs me close. I keep one hand on Beatriz and turn my head into his warm chest; his sunshine-and-fabric-softener smell is familiar now, and comforting. As distracted as I am by thoughts of home, it doesn't escape me that being back there in any form means not being with him, and my mood nosedives even more. Why does everything have to be either-or? Why does everything have to end? Why can't anything just stay like it is?

Jonah wipes a few of my tears away, sighing deeply as he does. He waits for me to drag my eyes to his before saying. "You know how you told me last week that it's easier to get some distance from the divorce out here, because it doesn't feel like real life?"

I drop my eyes and nod.

"Maybe it'll be that way in a new place once you get home," Jonah says.

"It won't be home; it'll just be a house, and a constant reminder of all that I lost will be right across town."

He sighs again and is quiet, stroking my hair. After a minute he says, "Maybe you can find a way to take home with you." He rummages in the pockets of his shorts and pulls out two Ghirardelli chocolates, unwrapping one and passing it to me before turning his attention to his own. "Case in point?"

I hand mine back. "It's not that easy. That house, the garden behind it—those have been my safety nets my whole life. Even after everything that happened, that was still the one place I felt most *me*. Can you take *safe* with you?"

Jonah folds and refolds the wrapper in his hand before saying, "I feel like, maybe . . . I don't know, you have to make yourself the safe place. No one can ever take *you* away from you, right?"

Even if I believed him, I wouldn't have the first clue how to do that—make me the safe place.

I resume scratching Beatriz. She rolls and squirms closer to offer me full access to her belly and I can't help but crack a small smile at her antics.

Jonah seizes on it. "Maybe it could end up being a good thing. Like this trip turned out to be?"

I sniffle and wipe my cheeks with my sleeve. "Maybe. I guess." I'm quiet before adding, "But I'd still feel like . . . It's just . . . the divorce was only the first instance, but since then, it's *everything* coming at me without warning . . ." I collect a ragged breath before continuing. "I don't want to always be wondering what's waiting around the corner to knock me over. I just want to feel like nothing can get to me."

Jonah traces a circle in my palm and speaks softly. "To really feel that way, you'd probably have to be an agoraphobic, shut up in your house."

I pull my hand from his and stand, needing to breathe and move. I pace for a few seconds before leaning my stomach into the railing. Beatriz rolls and scrambles to her feet next to me and I rest a hand on her head, stroking her silken ears.

"Plenty of bad things can happen to agoraphobics," I say. "Home invasions, grease fires, carbon monoxide poisoning. You could get a stupid splinter that gets infected because you won't leave to go to a hospital and then you contract gangrene."

Jonah rises and steps next to me. "You're basically proving your own point. No one ever knows what's coming next. Look, lots of those unexpected things are gonna be crappy, but some of them are gonna be unbelievably *amazing*."

He grabs my face in his hands and says, "Like this." The kiss he plants on me is really, really *not* safe. It leaves me breathless, and I can tell that's just what he intended by the satisfied look he gives me when he releases me.

"You've just gotta let go of the stuff you can't control," he says.

I'm still wobbly from his kiss, but also annoyed that he's boiling my biggest fears down to such simplistic terms. "What, so you think I should just accept the unknown? Let the current carry me wherever?" If I wanted to hit low, I could point out that it's basically what he's doing with his life right now. But I'm not willing to go there. Instead I ask, "Doesn't that basically make me a sitting duck?"

He shrugs. "Not if you're smart about it. You can still take precautions to help tame the unexpected. Check the deck for snag points, get your routine checkups, wear seat belts in the car—but, beyond that, I don't think you can lock yourself away and let the what-ifs keep you from living your life. It's just a matter of doing it with the expectation that it's all subject to change."

Beatriz nudges my hand with her wet nose and I resume petting her absentmindedly. "I'm not so good with 'subject to change.'"

He's smiling softly when I glance up. "You didn't expect to meet the devastatingly handsome Pirate Sexytimes in the woods, and that's a change that hasn't been terrible, right?"

Despite myself, I snicker. "You really need to let the Pirate Sexytimes thing go."

He laughs, then sobers. "How about I let go if you let go."

"If I let go of what?"

"No. Just *let go*. Stop fighting to keep things the way they were, and embrace the future, with all its unknowns, good and bad. Instead of looking back at what you once had, move forward to what you could have instead."

The lump in my throat grows to epic proportions and I can't force out any words, even if I knew how to answer him. *Is* all of this me holding on to the past too tight?

"If I let go, isn't that like saying the things that are the most important to me aren't worth fighting for? My family, my home?"

Jonah watches me for a second from the corner of his eye, then drops one of his hands to mine and squeezes. "I don't think those are the things you're fighting for, Cass. I think it's what those things represent. Safety, comfort, a place where you can be yourself, people who will love you unconditionally. You can still have all those things—they just might come in a different package. Your family doesn't look the same now, but they're still the same people and they still love you just as much."

Even though he says "they," I know he's talking about my mother. "She's *not* the same person, though. The Mom I knew wouldn't make all these huge decisions on a whim like this."

"Unless she's trying to move on. Maybe it's hard for her

to be in that house, with everything it represents. Maybe she's trying to put her past behind her every bit as much as you're trying to hold on to it."

"It *should* be hard for her to be there. She *should* have to live with the consequences of what she did."

Jonah's quiet, and we both study the harbor below. Then he asks, "Wanna know what I think about your mom?"

I nod.

"I think she's just as scared as you are."

I bring my head up to stare at him. "What?"

"I think *you* scare her more than anything else. The way you've been shutting her out. Maybe taking drastic measures and making you all come on this trip was her way of trying to show you that she'll do whatever it takes to be close to you again, and she's scared it wasn't enough to prove to you how much she cares about that. About you."

"The problem is that she cares about herself more. If she cared about me, she wouldn't have cheated. She would've fought more to save her marriage after my dad found out. She wouldn't have ruined my life at the worst possible time."

"Cass, really? Don't you think maybe that's kind of harsh? Maybe she had her reasons for doing what she did, when she did. You've never asked her."

I came here to be *comforted*, not to argue with Jonah, but now my anger is directed at him. "Are you seriously suggesting there's ever a good reason to cheat? I can't believe you'd defend her!"

Jonah winces. "I'm not. I'm just trying to help you look at the situation from every angle." He drops his hand to his side and studies the water again. "You push her away out of fear and she pulls you closer out of fear. You're both doing opposite things, but for the same reason, when if you'd both just stop and *listen* to each other . . ."

I know he's trying to be helpful, but his matter-of-fact tone pisses me off. Of course that seems like the obvious solution to him. He's not in this. When you're in it, it's impossible to set aside all the *feelings* that color everything and just have a rational, dispassionate conversation. I hate that he doesn't get that.

He clearly doesn't pick up on my frustration because he keeps right on going. "I think you're scared to hear her side of things, because if you do and she makes any sense at all, then you might have to stop being mad at her."

My jaw drops. "Why wouldn't I want that? You think I *like* being pissed off at her all the time?"

"Because if you forgive her and make peace with the fact that the situation—the divorce happening, you being on this trip, your house maybe getting sold—is what it is, then you have to acknowledge that things are never, ever going back to what they were. You have to accept things as they are."

I *hate* that he's all calm and logical and "oh, let me just mansplain all your hidden motivations and fears to you, Cassie, and then you'll be magically fixed." I don't *want* him to be logical. I don't want him to confront me and push me on this issue with my mom. Why can't he just say, "You know what, Cassie, it totally sucks that you might lose your house on top of everything that's already happened and you can vent to me all you want, and I will sit back and listen and then distract you from it all with crazy-good kisses?" He wants to talk about acceptance, but how about just accepting *me*, the way I am? Why does he think he has to fix me? Maybe I should be grateful he's trying to help, but instead it pisses me off. Especially when he has *no room to talk*.

"You should turn the mirror around. You're not exactly an expert on the subject—I don't see you having nightly heart-to-hearts with your dad." My tone is sharper than I intended and I wince when his eyes flash pain.

"Sorry," I say, shaking my head. "I probably shouldn't be human-ing in my current state of mind."

He grimaces. "No, it's—um, I was gonna tell you when I saw you later, but then later became *now* and it didn't seem like the right time."

I cock my head as he runs a hand through his hair.

"I actually did call my dad. The other night. We talked." His words are simple and clear and drama-free and I suck in a breath.

"You *did*?"

"Yeah. It went okay. He probably still thinks of me as his deadbeat son, but at least he listened a little more than before and he didn't raise his voice until the very end of our conversation. So that's progress, right?"

He shrugs and ventures a small smile and I know I should

be happy for him. Instead, I'm ashamed that my first thought is *traitor*. Why does he get to make headway with his dad when any I'd made with my mom just went up in flames? Why can't he be on the "parents suck" train with me, in solidarity, when I need him there more than ever?

Despite how horrible my internal thoughts are, I try to school my expression into something positive and supportive.

"That's great," I say. "Seriously. I'm really glad for you guys."

"Yeah, well. Baby steps."

"But you took them. That required a lot of guts."

I hate that I'm *saying* the right things, but inside I feel completely abandoned and alone in my misery. I like Jonah—a lot. I should *want* him to be happy. But what if he and his dad continue to get closer, right as this crack between my mom and me grows into a canyon? What if he stops being sympathetic to the things I'm going through? What if we stop understanding each other? What if the thing that bonded us to begin with becomes the thing that pushes us apart?

"What made you decide to call him?" I ask in a small voice.

He looks uncomfortable. "Actually . . . your mom. We, uh, had a conversation about it the other night when we were cleaning up after dinner. You guys were timing Abigail climb the mast and your mom was asking me about stuff with school and I mentioned him and . . . we had a good talk. She said some stuff that got me thinking."

Now I'm fighting back angry tears. I thought his opening

up and being vulnerable and talking about his family stuff was because of something only I brought out in him. He said he liked me because he could be real around me, like that was different and new for him. But after five minutes alone with my mother, he's spilling all his secrets? He's not allowed to bond with *her*. What else is she going to take away from me?

"So, what? She gave you advice, and now you're on her side?" I ask.

"What? No!" He puts a hand on my arm, but I shake it away. "It's not like that. I'm not taking sides here."

It's the last straw. I lose it. "You *should* be taking sides, Jonah! You should be taking *my* side! That's what you do when you're someone's . . ." I fumble for the right word. The things we've said to each other are definitely things you don't say to someone you're only casually dating, but we've never labeled anything, and now, with him talking to my mom the way he did, I'm doubting whether what I thought we had was really so special after all.

I wave my arm in frustration. "When you're someone's actual friend!" I finally spit out, taking in his helpless expression before stomping away with Beatriz at my heels. Halfway down the deck, I pivot. "You should stay here for the sail today. I'd rather have Drew for company."

When I reach *Minecraft*, I add over my shoulder, "And thanks so much for adhering to our judgment-free zone, you ass!"

My chest aches and burns at the same time as my emotions

war it out to see which horrible one gets to take center stage first. This morning I woke up feeling like a boss, with the whole learning-to-sail thing, conquering Point Conception, and the talk with my mom about Jonah. I was actually looking forward to today. It finally felt like I'd had a win, even if it was a small one.

One step forward, one million steps back.

How is it that, in such a tiny span of time, I went from a win to so many losses?

Like any chance of working things out with my mother.

My home.

Maybe even Jonah?

Hope.

29

There is nothing "sunny-side up" about me when I pull beside the cheery italic script and tie on to the platform. I don't see Drew, but the shower's running as I descend the cabin stairs. My mother's in the kitchen and I brush past her without a word. When she follows me into my berth, I stand with my back to her, running my fingers absently along the branches of my bonsai tree.

"Did you hear from Dad?" I ask, my voice tight and cold.

Behind me, she exhales. "I did. I had to wake him up, but we talked. He thinks we should accept the offer."

I drop my chin to my chest and close my eyes briefly. Then my anger takes hold. "Accept it. *Accept it*." I chew the words and spit them out. "Obviously you'll accept it. Because everyone but me finds it oh so easy to simply accept things and move on. You. Dad. Drew. Jonah. Everyone just shrugs and says 'Oh well, that's life. What's next?'"

"Cassie, that's not true. We all have our own ways of dealing with things. We're *all* working hard to adjust to everything that's happened this year."

I whip around. "Really? Because it sure doesn't seem like that. Dad left without a fight. Drew's perfectly happy to be here. You're . . . I don't even know what you are."

Mom takes a step toward me and I stop her with a brusque head shake.

Her hands flutter to her sides. "I'm struggling with this in my own way, Cass. I'm sorry if I haven't been better about expressing that—I guess I was just trying so hard to make everything seem okay to you guys that I didn't think I could show my pain. But if you think I'm not hurting too . . ."

The last thing I need right now is her sob story. Not after everything else. "I'd like to be alone, please."

Mom opens her mouth and then closes it. "If you'd just—"

I throw up my hands. "*Stop* trying to reason with me. Why does everyone think I need to be reasoned with today?"

Mom's eyes narrow and she studies me closely. "Did something happen with Jonah?"

"You mean the guy you told me you couldn't respect because he was running away from his life, but are now trying to make your new bestie? That Jonah?"

My berth is tiny and the walls are always closing in, but never more so than they are now. The air between us is hot with our breath and it's stifling.

"My bestie? Cass, I have absolutely no idea what you're talking about."

I take two strides, crowding her space and forcing her

to step backward into the kitchen. As soon as she crosses the threshold, I grab the door and shut it in her face, relishing the satisfying click the latch makes as it settles into place.

"Cassandra Marie."

My mother's voice has warning bells, but I ignore her. I fall onto my bed.

I stuff the pillow against my stomach and curl around it. I can feel a whole wall of tears behind my eyes, just waiting for the dam to break.

On the other side of my door the shower goes off and the radio squawks. "Sunny-Side Up, *come in,* Sunny-Side Up. *Do you copy? Over.*"

Mom's footsteps pad lightly to the navigation center and I hear, "*This is* Sunny-Side Up. *Over.*"

It's Jonah, and I hold my breath and strain my ears, knowing he's going to ask to talk to me. If he thinks he can get me to continue our fight with an audience, he's got a—

But he doesn't ask for me.

In a level voice he asks my mother, "*Are you good with getting under sail in about fifteen? Over.*"

Mom's voice is also steady and belies no trace of our fight as she answers. "*You're not swapping out with Drew? Over.*"

There's a pause and Jonah's voice is quiet as he says, "*Change of plans. Over.*"

I'm sure Mom can put two and two together there. She replies, "*Roger that. We'll be ready. Over.*"

"*Happy sails,*" Jonah says softly. "*Over and out.*"

I hear the sounds of Mom replacing the transmitter and talking to Drew through the bathroom door. Footsteps trudge up the stairs.

Now I will the cry I'm holding in to come. I'd welcome anything to flush out even half of the adrenaline coursing through me, but the dam stays stubbornly in place.

The engine comes to life, and a short time later a second set of footsteps goes above. I can sense us turning and motoring out of the harbor. After a few more minutes the motor cuts off and its sounds are replaced by those of flapping sails, snapping in the wind. We rise and fall over small waves, but it's a familiar sensation now.

Eventually I drift asleep.

When I wake it's middle-of-the-night quiet and the boat sways underneath me. For a moment I forget we're under sail because the motion is no more than the gentle back and forth of being in a protected harbor. But then I hear Drew coughing up above.

I roll over and try to force myself to return to the blissful oblivion of sleep, but I can tell right away it won't work. Everything about the day before is already flooding back in. My stomach rumbles from missing dinner and my full bladder forces me from my covers. I use the bathroom, then make a peanut butter sandwich. Above me, Drew's coughing continues, and I wonder why Mom isn't sending him down for water. Then I register the soft snoring coming from my mother's berth.

Drew is sailing *alone*? In the middle of the night?

I slap together another sandwich for him and fill a plastic cup before climbing the stairs.

"Yum yum for your tum tum's here," I sing softly. When we were little, whenever we ordered pizza or Chinese, my dad would call that out to us as soon as the doorbell rang. Drew and I would push and shove and scratch each other in a race to the door, trying to win the honor of handing over Dad's money to the delivery person on the other side.

He turns and smiles, though it doesn't quite reach his eyes. "Hey. How're you feeling?"

I feign ignorance as I buckle my life jacket. "Me? You're the one coughing up a lung up here."

Drew accepts the water and drinks half of it down in one gulp. He wipes his mouth. "Sorry. Did I wake you?"

I shake my head, looking out over the glassy sheet of water. There's a half moon tonight, and it lights a path that leads straight across the ocean and into the sky. It looks like you could walk over it and right up into the stars. It's beautiful, but the stillness also seems ominous. I've never seen the sea this calm.

Calm before the storm. There's one Jonah could have used against me in our bet. I ignore the tightness in my chest that forms when I think about him.

Drew checks the instrument panel and I ask, "Mom left you alone up here?"

"Only because of how insanely quiet the conditions are."

315

"Still. I'm surprised."

"I don't think she was having a great night." Drew's voice is neutral, but my stomach twists with guilt anyway. He definitely heard some of our argument over the noise of the shower, then. I should have expected that. It would almost be better if he yelled at me for being such a brat to her. He must want to, given the limited information he has to go on. Or maybe even if he had all of it. I don't know anymore.

"Mom told you about the house stuff, right?" I ask.

He nods, his eyes sad. "Yeah."

That's it?

"And?" I prod.

"And what? I kind of figured that was coming, the longer Mom's been out of a job." He shrugs.

I'm not unsympathetic to our family's financial situation, but I refuse to believe that there aren't other options short of selling our home out from under us. Dad could return stateside, for one. They don't have to get back together or anything, but maybe we could turn our basement into a little apartment for him. Save the "two households to maintain" burden.

Even if he wouldn't agree to that, rentals in Pleasant Hill are a thousand times cheaper than what he must be paying to live in Hong Kong. That right there would buy us more time for Mom to find something. If the housing market is so hot, surely the job market isn't as dire as she's making it out to be? Maybe she's just being too picky about what she's applying for. Maybe she should quit looking for a branch manager position and just look for *a* job. Isn't it only fair that *she* be the one to sacrifice for once, instead of asking the rest of us to?

I turn to Drew. "Okay, fine, you saw the writing on the wall. But don't you have any *feelings* about it?"

He shrugs again. "I don't know."

Which I interpret as code for: "Don't feel like talking about it."

Too bad. Maybe if he hears my ideas, I can get him on my side and we can make a case to Mom and Dad. But before I can formulate a plan, he starts coughing like crazy again.

"Geez, at least cover your mouth so your lung doesn't land on me," I say lightly.

He smiles through another cough, and another.

I squint at him. "Are you feeling all right?" I reach out and touch his forehead and it's a little warm, despite the fact that the night is cool.

He grimaces. "It's just a stupid summer cold. Mom's shift is in an hour; I'll be fine till then."

I look out at the glassy sheet of water, devoid of even tiny whitecaps, take a deep breath, and say, "Go get some sleep. I'll keep an eye on things here and wake her when it's time."

He laughs, which makes him cough again. When he recovers, he says, "*You're* gonna sail? Alone?"

I wave my hand over the railing. "Hey, I have mad skillz now, remember? I have sailed into the belly of the beast and lived to tell the tale."

"If you mean Point Conception, I'm not buying it."

I sigh. "Fine, whatever. But a sloth moves faster than we are right now. We're basically sitting in a bathtub, so what 'sailing' are we even talking about? I'll just hang out and watch us move five inches over the next hour, and then I'll call down to Mom. If it'll make you feel better, I'll wake her in half an hour instead. Besides, you refusing to rest now means you're not gonna be any good to her tomorrow, if the wind picks up and she needs an actual sailor's help. Go."

I point at the steps and Drew casts an uncertain look at me, at the water, up at the mast where the sails barely ripple, then back at me again. "I—you're sure you can handle it?"

"You're ten feet and one good shout away if anything comes up. Though what that might be on a night like this, I can't even imagine."

He's struck with another coughing fit, and by the end of it, he's convinced. He gives me a grateful look and heads below.

Leaving *me* alone in the middle of the ocean with my thoughts.

Okay, yes, there are two sleeping people nearby, and though there's enough distance between us that I can't see either of their mast lights, somewhere out there are *Tide Drifter* and *Reality Bytes*. So not all that alone, really. But the last time my loneliness yawned this wide in my belly was the day after Dad moved out and I wandered the rooms of the house cataloging all the small things that went with him.

Now the tears come.

It's so quiet tonight, I know my sobs will carry below easily, so I'm careful to keep them muffled in the armpit of my puffy life jacket, but otherwise I give in to the shaking and the gush of salty water down my face. My cheeks are used to salt these days, though mostly it's been sea spray. None of that to be had tonight.

I cry for normal, happy, carefree Cassie, because at the moment it feels like she's as far away as Dad. I missed her so much and then somehow these last few weeks, she slipped in here and there. Like Peter Pan's shadow. I was just beginning to believe I could finally stitch her back on, but now she's gone again.

Eventually my tears stop and I wipe my nose.

The stage is set a little too perfectly for thinking deep thoughts. Middle of the night, floating on water as free of wrinkles as one of my dad's starched oxford shirts, gentle rocking. But I'm just so tired of thinking, of *feeling* all this heaviness.

Instead I tilt my head and try to count stars. I don't know how Jonah says he finds feeling small and inconsequential comforting. The emptiness of it all chokes me.

Music. I need music blasting in my ears, to chase this melancholy away. Something loud and grating. I'm weighing what could go wrong if I went below for five seconds to grab my phone and headphones when a soft splash sounds over my left shoulder.

I whip my head around, but there's nothing. The noise reminds me of another way I am very much *not* alone. There's an entire ecosystem just below me. Millions—no, billions—of little creatures swimming around, just out of my sight. I hook an elbow on the railing and lean over to squint into the water, trying to see anything that could make a splashing noise, but the moon and the stillness create a mirrored surface, and all I see is a girl with a runny nose peering back at me.

From the corner of my eye I catch a movement off the bow, and I stand and readjust my squint to that section of water. What was it? I wait, perfectly frozen—even my heartbeat stills—as I stare at the surface. And then, in a different spot, farther out, a spout of water arches into the night sky. As I gape, a huge, dark, smooth shadow rolls above the water and slides back below. Several shallow breaths later, an unmistakable shape flicks through the air and slips under the surface.

A whale's tail.

And then another, just to the right of the first one.

Oh my god. Whales! My breath is in my throat and fresh tears form in my eyes, but this time they're of wonder. If I wasn't living this, I wouldn't believe it. It's like something out of a movie. Broken girl has mystical nighttime encounter with pod of whales and realizes the universe wants her to heal.

I'm awed, but I'm not *that* naive. Abigail and Grace have been talking about them this whole trip. I'm well aware this is migration time in these waters for humpbacks, blue whales, and finbacks. There are whale-watching trips leaving out of most of the harbors we're been mooring in. Maybe the real miracle is that we haven't seen any before this.

Still.

I gaze, transfixed.

Within a few minutes their noises are all around me. Not the eerie soundtracks of musical calls that play in spas and yoga studios. These whales are grunting and burping and spraying water in giant spouts. I try to figure out how many there might be, but it's hard to tell if I'm counting the same one multiple times. The most spouts I see at once are three, but I think there might be as many as five or six whales.

There's a creak on the steps and I turn my head.

30

"Cass?"

My mom's face appears, and then the rest of her. She looks around sleepily and steps into the cockpit while whispering, "Why is Drew asleep down there? Are you—?"

I put my finger to my lips and she breaks off. I point to the bow and watch as her eyes adjust to the dark and she realizes what she's seeing in the moonlight.

If we were in a movie, this is the part where the mom would put her arm around her daughter and the daughter would rest her head against the mother's shoulder and, without any words being exchanged, the audience would know they've just forgiven each other. Enya or some other ethereal New Age track with, like, lutes or something would be playing.

In real life, my mother gasps and covers her mouth. "Oh god," she says into her palm. "Oh god. Which direction are they moving?"

When I stare at her blankly, she snaps, "Cassie, *think*. Are they getting closer or farther away from when you first spotted them?"

I blink. "I—um, closer? I think?"

My mother looks around wildly. "Okay, take the wheel and turn off the autopilot."

I continue to stare at her, frozen.

"Cassandra! The wheel!"

"Why? What's wrong?" I ask.

Her sigh is exasperated, as if I should know this on my own. "Do you realize how big these whales are? Can you imagine what it would do to *Sunny-Side Up* if one tried to surface while underneath us?"

My eyes grow as wide as hers. "Does that ever happen?"

Mom nods sharply.

Why didn't I have this on my list of potential catastrophic events at sea? Whales are the gentle giants of the ocean. I had a "Save the Whales" bumper sticker on my binder in fifth grade. I can't get tossed into the water by one!

"The wheel," Mom orders, and I jerk to attention. She races to the bow and peers into the night.

"Should I turn the motor on?" I call, picturing a quick getaway (or a semi-quick getaway, since we're not exactly a speedboat).

Mom shakes her head and moves to the middle of the deck. "No, the sounds from the propellers can actually attract them. Just keep your eyes peeled and get ready to turn hard if you need to."

A shadow rolls across the surface a hundred yards or so off our starboard side, and water rushes down the smooth expanse of black glistening in the moonlight.

What felt meaningful and special and beautiful minutes ago now seems menacing.

I plant my hands on the wheel and stare so hard at the water my eyeballs hurt.

"There!" Mom points to a spout off our port side.

We're surrounded. This is a different kind of fear than what Jonah accused me of running from. This is sharp in my lungs and throat and prickly up my spine.

After all my fears about things that go bump in the night, here I am waiting for a literal one. It's even worse than the abstract.

I have a sudden thought for the other two boats in our caravan. "Should we radio the others?"

Mom crosses to the dashboard instruments and glances at the radar. "Not until we're out of immediate danger. *Tide Drifter*'s at least five miles ahead of us, and I doubt the pod covers a distance that wide. *Reality Bytes* is much farther behind—they're not even showing. They radioed just after we left; they had to go back to the marina to grab a chart Christian left in the harbormaster's office."

I nod and resume staring at the sea. Mom returns to her spot in the boat's center, taking turns peering in both directions.

"I think you should turn us to port," she says a few minutes later. "It's been a bit since I've seen anything there."

I follow her instructions and spin the wheel. Mom ducks under the boom as it swings into place on the opposite side of the mast.

The whale burps and groans begin to recede, as do the spouts of water. I allow myself a deep breath. I think they've moved on.

We're silent, ears strained, for long minutes after that, but the surface is glassy and smooth as far as I can see.

"If I were more religious, I'd be working the rosary right now," she says.

I laugh despite myself, mostly to get the bottled-up relief out.

Mom looks up and offers me a wry smile. "I like when you do that."

I glance away. We may have just shared the terrifying experience of narrowly avoiding becoming whale roadkill, but that doesn't mean I'm ready to hug it out. My anger is lurking about as close to the surface as those whales just were.

Before I can say anything, she holds up a hand. "Stop. I don't want to get into it with you tonight. I need you to stay up here for a bit and help me keep on the lookout for a while longer, so let's just sit here quietly. Please."

My response is to turn back to the wheel and continue squinting into the still, inky waters. Mom is silent.

Long minutes pass where our breathing is the only sound on the deck, and my eyes start to tear up from staring so hard and from wanting to slide back into sleep.

Huuuuuuuuuh.

The sound at my back is like a long, heavy exhale. Like the boogeyman slipping out from under the bed. The air smells like the inside of a slimy bucket, but my brain knows instantly it's whale breath. I'm still turning when the spouting water arcs onto the deck at Mom's feet.

I gasp and spin back, yanking the wheel hard to the left and praying, praying, praying the rudder underneath will respond in time. There's a sickening thud and for a second I'm convinced the whale is under us, that any second now the hull will splinter apart and we'll be dumped into the ocean. But no sharp cracking sound or terrible boat shaking follows, and a second later a spout of water breaks the surface at least fifty yards ahead of us. But if the thud wasn't the whale . . .

I turn. "Mom, I—"

And then I see her.

I raise a hand to my mouth and stare in horror at her slumped form lying motionless on the deck.

The thud was her.

31

I don't realize I'm screaming until seconds later when Drew clomps up the steps, wild-eyed and coughing. "What's going on? I—"

He sees my face and his eyes follow my pointing finger. I'm shaking so hard I can't form words, but he understands immediately and charges over to her.

"Mom!" he yells, right into her face, his voice pleading.

But she's out. A gash in her forehead spurts blood. When he tries to lift her to a sitting position, she's a rag doll in his arms. I'm horror-struck and helpless while Drew whips his shirt off and balls a section up in his hand to press against her cut. It only takes a few seconds for it to tinge red.

The boat turns itself in a slow full circle, causing the boom to swing back and forth. When it nearly catches Drew, I snap out of it enough to lock the spinning steering wheel. Oh god, is that what hit Mom, or did she slip on the wet deck and whack her head when she fell?

"There were whales. They—I— What do we do?" I cry.

This can't be happening. Not all the way out here. Not after everything we've already been through. I'm this close to losing it, hysteria bubbling up from my belly into my chest into my throat, and I fight to force it down.

Mom doesn't move so much as a muscle.

"Radio," Drew whispers. "Mayday."

I moan. We learned how to call for help in the boating-safety course I took and Mom made us practice a drill the first week we were sailing, but that was so long ago now.

"I can do it," Drew says. "You stay with her."

We switch positions and I cradle Mom's head in my lap, letting hot tears fall on her face as I chant, "Please wake up, please wake up, please wake up."

Drew races downstairs, skipping the last few steps entirely, judging from the clatter when he hits the floor of the cabin.

With the hatches open and no wind to distort things, I can hear him clearly as he speaks into the radio. To my chant I add in prayers that he won't have another coughing fit in the middle of his message. It should be me down there instead, but I wouldn't have the first clue how to follow the proper distress call procedures. My stupid stubbornness about this trip has made me useless in this situation, and I hate myself for it.

"Mayday—Mayday—Mayday, This is Sunny-Side Up—Sunny-Side Up—Sunny-Side Up *OR1120. Mayday. This is* Sunny-Side Up. *Latitude 33.694, longitude -118.745. Passenger knocked unconscious, need medical assistance. One adult, two*

teenagers aboard. *Adult has head injury, unresponsive. Boat sea-worthy, capable crew.* Sunny-Side Up *is a forty-foot sailboat. Over."*

I doubt I could've come up with anything beyond "Mayday" right now if you'd paid me. Thank god for his captain's exam studying. Thank god for *Drew.*

There's no response from the radio and he repeats the call before yelling up, "We might be too far from shore for the VHF. I'm switching to the radiotelephone."

But just then there's a reply.

"Sunny-Side Up, *this is catamaran* Emancipator *CA1205. We've relayed your message to US Coast Guard. Assistance is on the way. Please copy. Over."*

Drew answers and the tightness in my chest eases, ever so slightly.

A second later, we hear:

"Sunny-Side Up, *this is* Tide Drifter. *We heard your call and are reversing course to return to you. We're six nautical miles from your position and switching to motor."* Then Amy's clinical voice breaks and she adds, *"Oh god, what's going on over there, Drew. Over."*

"Help is coming, Mom," I whisper, relief coursing through me. "You're gonna be fine."

Wait.

The whales.

"Drew!" I yell down. "Amy and Miranda can't reverse course. What if they run through the pod?"

Drew is calm as can be as he radios *Tide Drifter* and tells them to stay in place. He sounds like a fully grown man as he reassures Amy that we'll be fine now that the Coast Guard is on its way. I wish I felt half as confident.

Just then Mom lets out a low moan and I gasp. "Drew! Hurry!"

He races up, and we both breathe sighs of relief as she moans again, then opens her eyes.

"Wha-what happened?" she manages, her words slow and deliberate.

"Shh . . . just lie still, Mom. You fell. There's help on the way," I tell her.

At this, she starts to sit up, but Drew pushes her gently down. "Mom, stop! Lie back. Your head is cut and you were just passed out for, like, three minutes. You have to lie quietly until the paramedics get here."

She peers at us for a moment, then her eyes slide closed. For a heartbeat I'm afraid she's passed out again, but then she whispers, "Coast Guard?"

I smooth her hair and adjust Drew's T-shirt to place a fresh corner of it against her cut. The gushing seems to be slowing slightly, and that, coupled with her responses, allows my stomach to unclench slightly.

"They're on their way," I say, trying to reassure myself as much as her.

Drew catches my eye. "I need to lower the sails so we don't drift off the position we radioed in. I don't want to move

Mom, but you need to go below and man the radio in case the rescue team needs to communicate with us. I think we should tether her to the railing in a safety harness. What do you think?"

I'm not the one with a fever, yet I'm so not equipped to make any decisions in my current frame of mind; my heartbeat is still hammering in my ears. But I nod and he runs to grab one from the cockpit bench.

Mom adjusts her head in my lap.

"You okay?" I whisper.

"Turkey for library," she answers.

My brow draws down.

"I didn't catch that, Mom."

I watch her closely, but she merely sighs and her eyelids flutter. Her chest rises and falls evenly and it seems like she might be sleeping. Did I mishear her? Drew returns with the safety harness and the two of us work it around her, trying to jostle her as little as possible. We set a cushion underneath her head and recline her on the deck.

"I'll toss up a towel to wipe the water around her," I tell Drew. I'm not sure if it's still considered water, having passed through a whale, but I also know I couldn't give a rat's ass what to term it at the moment. I just want it gone before anyone else gets hurt.

I head below to stare at the offensively silent radio. I can hear Drew's footsteps as he moves around on the deck above, lowering the sails. It's not as if we were actually moving anywhere quickly with the conditions so calm, but I'm still glad he thought of it. A couple of minutes later, he comes down to grab an electric distress lantern to make us easier to spot. I'm blown away that he knows to do all this. Turns out studying for that captain's exam was way smarter than doing the schoolwork he put off.

He's also super calm and efficient. Who knew that mellow vibe of his would serve us so well in a situation like this?

Meanwhile, I stare at the VHF, willing it to broadcast something, anything. A message from the Coast Guard, of course. But one from Christian to say they're coming to us would be equally welcome, even though I know I can't risk tying up the channel to talk to them. My anger with Jonah evaporates in the face of everything that's happened. Right now I just want him here with me.

But all is quiet.

Drew waits with Mom, who continues to sleep, and I sit in the cabin, drumming my fingers on the navigation table.

It feels like a lifetime passes, but it can't be more than a half hour later when we finally hear a noise.

A helicopter.

As the propeller sounds grow closer, the radio finally blasts out a message.

"Sunny-Side Up, *this is the US Coast Guard on scene for a medical evacuation. Do you copy? Over.*"

I swallow and try to keep my voice level and authoritative

as I answer. *"Copy Coast Guard. Over."*

"Please change course to put wind thirty degrees off port bow and provide clear area at stern. Stow all gear, turn off radar, and keep all persons out of the way unless instructed by rescue swimmer. Please advise on survivor's condition. Over."

I reply to the part I understand. *"She came to, but is sleeping now. She's still bleeding slightly from a cut on her forehead. Over."*

"Roger that. Preparing to lower rescue swimmer off your stern. Over."

I yell the other instructions up to Drew, who begins moving us into position instantly. I debate staying by the radio, but I also want to see what's happening above. I settle for standing on the steps, my head in the cockpit, but poised to return to the VHF at the least little screech.

High above, the helicopter circles, shining a bright spotlight onto our deck. When it moves slightly and the light wobbles, I can squint around it to make out the shadow of two bodies in the open doorway.

And then one is dangling midair, at least twenty feet above the water off our stern. He's wearing a mask with a snorkel protruding, a helmet, and a slightly baggy orange suit that covers him completely.

With the dark camouflaging the cable I know he must be hanging from, it looks like he's flying. Like a superhero. That's basically how I'm thinking of him at this point. I mean, seriously, who volunteers for this job? My gratitude at seeing him threatens to get the better of me and I force myself to take a deep breath and stay alert, in case anyone needs me to do anything.

The swimmer unclips from the cable and drops into the ocean, cutting strong strokes to our platform. In less than a minute he's climbing aboard.

"Hello all, I'm Birger and I'll be your rescue swimmer tonight." His manner is friendly and reassuring, but he's focused as he assesses the situation. "How's everyone doing?"

We both mumble "okay" and Drew gestures to my mother. Birger moves to her and drops to his knees, speaking over his shoulder to my brother. "In a minute they're going to lower a trail line to send down the litter. Think you can try to grab it?"

"Of course," Drew answers, and my heart swells with pride.

"Should I be by the radio?" I ask, and Birger darts a glance at me.

"You're good where you are. Stay put for now."

He turns his attention back to my mother, examining the gash on her head. Above us the helicopter lowers a line and Drew is able to lean out over the railing and grab tight. A stretcher with curving sides begins to slide down the cable, like it's traveling along a slow-moving zip line. I'm fascinated, my eyes bouncing between it and Birger.

"Can you tell me your name?" he's asking my mother.

"Twenty-seven motorcycles," she answers.

His eyes slide to me and I climb fully into the cockpit and crouch next to her too.

"When she woke up before, was she lucid?" he asks.

"I—yes. At least, at first. She did say one weird thing, but I thought I misheard her, and then she fell back asleep, so I didn't . . ."

Drew shoots me a questioning look, but I'm more focused on Birger, who offers a reassuring smile.

"It's okay," he says. "You kids did great here. Talking gibberish can happen sometimes with traumatic brain injuries. It isn't necessarily as bad as it sounds."

I must go ten shades of pale at the words "traumatic brain injuries," because Birger reaches over and covers my hand with his. "It's too early to tell anything. Nine times out of ten, cases like this turn out just fine."

What about the other time? I want to ask, but I'm too afraid for the answer.

"Her name's Elise," I murmur, and he nods gently.

The stretcher hits our deck and Birger leaves Mom temporarily to disconnect the cable. He and Drew lay it flat by the cabin opening and Birger returns to my mother.

"Can you squeeze my hand, Elise?"

She must, because he smiles and says, "Good. Okay, do it again if you have any nausea."

I hold my breath. Birger shakes his head and says, "No? Good. What about any dizziness? Squeeze my hand if you do."

He smiles. "No? Great."

They go through the same steps for ringing in her ears and headache and she only squeezes his hand at the last one.

I'm not sure whether to be reassured or not, but Birger is the picture of calm, so maybe things aren't so bad after all.

"Okay, headache we can handle, Elise," he says. "Hang tight for a few secs while I get you set for transport."

He works fast, applying a bandage to her wound and taking a neck brace from his kit. He's quick to reassure us. "Not taking chances. The litter can be jostling."

I glance at the helicopter hovering above, and it sinks in that my mother is going to have to travel through the air all the way up to it.

Oh god, am *I*?

Do we stay here? Do we go with her? Are we *allowed* to go with her? And if so, what happens to this boat that doesn't belong to us? If we abandon ship, what if we're held liable for any damage it sustains, floating alone out here?

While Drew helps Birger settle my mother gently onto the stretcher, I weigh the pros and cons of both scenarios, but I'm relieved when the rescue swimmer takes the decision out of our hands.

"If you have the ability to sail her back to shore, my recommendation would be for the two of you to stay with your vessel. An ambulance will meet us at our base at LAX and transport your mom to Marina Del Rey Hospital—she'll be well looked after until you reach her."

I hate to let her out of our sight, but I'm not in any state of mind to argue with the person most in charge at the moment. If he thinks that's best . . .

When Drew and I both nod numbly, Birger signals for pickup and the cable lowers again. He hooks it to the stretcher and gives a thumbs-up. It begins to rise into the air, and I trace every inch with my eyes as my mother dangles dozens of feet over our boat. As soon as she clears the mast, the helicopter moves back and to the left, and I'm breathless as my mother is pulled inside.

I can't believe this is even my life.

It takes a few minutes for the cable to lower again, and Birger uses the time to make sure we're comfortable being left behind and that we have a plan for getting back to shore. Drew assures him we are and that we have others in our caravan close by who will help. He points out something I hadn't noticed before now—mast lights in the distance.

"They've been coming closer," Drew says, and Birger seems reassured. I desperately want to be too.

Please be Jonah.

The helicopter returns to its earlier hover spot and a cable lowers again. Birger easily grabs it and hooks on. With a reassuring smile to us, he gives someone above another thumbs-up and rises into the air.

Drew and I watch silently as he reaches the helicopter and is hoisted inside. They hover for another few moments, and then they turn to point east. Neither of us says a thing as they disappear from sight, the noise of the propellers fading a few seconds later.

32

I'm at a loss for words over how surreal that all was.

I stare at the ocean in silence for a few seconds, trying to take it all in, but as usual, Drew is already thinking practically.

"We need to radio Amy and Miranda again," he says. "I don't have a clue how to set new coordinates to get us to LA."

I follow him below.

"Tide Drifter, *this is* Sunny-Side Up. *Do you copy? Over.*"

Before they can reply, our radio buzzes. "Sunny-Side Up, *this is* Reality Bytes. *We're approaching off your starboard side. Over.*"

Christian's voice washes over me and I slump in relief. It *was* their mast lights we saw, and they were closing in fast. Thank god. I'm frantic to get to Mom as quickly as possible.

Amy's response comes next and is frazzled. *"We're going crazy here. Give us the update. Over."*

Drew fills everyone listening in, and Amy reassures us that they watched the pod of whales pass by and that their boat is now also pointed our way. We return to the cockpit and stare at *Reality Bytes* approaching. Even though they're gobbling up distance, it's nowhere near fast enough.

I know my mother won't reach the hospital for a bit yet, but I feel so helpless being out of touch with land. It's not like we can radio the emergency room for an update. We have Wi-Fi, but how do you email a hospital?

I can't sit. I can't bear not knowing what's happening with Mom right now. Replaying her nonsensical responses in my head makes my blood chill. People don't start speaking gibberish and then bounce right back. I'm fairly certain of that. What if she *does* have a traumatic brain injury—the actual "traumatic" kind? Or a brain bleed? What if she's taken a turn for the worse already and we have no way of knowing? I should have fought to go with her. Or for Drew to have. We don't both need to be bobbing at sea, completely helpless.

What if that was the last time I'll ever see her alive? It's not outside the realm of possibility.

"Cassie, quit it."

I stop midstride. Have I been talking out loud? But no, Drew gestures to my feet, and I realize I must have been pacing like a mad person. I plop down on the bench.

I can't help it—I start to shake uncontrollably. I know it's a delayed reaction to the shock of everything that just happened, but it still doesn't make me feel like any less of a wimp next to my totally stoic *little* brother. Especially when he disappears below and returns with a blanket to wrap around me.

"Thanks," I murmur. It's not lost on me that this is the second time recently that someone has wrapped me in a blanket during a freak-out.

I steal a glance at Drew. "How come you're so calm? Not just now, I mean, but, like, always. About everything."

"I dunno."

But I need him to know. I need him to have an answer. I need him to feel half of what I'm feeling, because I can't be alone with all these emotions anymore. I stare at him and fight back a sob.

"I'm tired of being afraid and I'm *pissed off!*" I yell at the sky. I lower my head and level my eyes at my brother. "Why aren't you pissed off?"

Drew coughs and shakes his head. "Because this is just *life.*"

I don't have to accept that. It's not the life I used to have. Before this year, a bad day for me would have been getting a B– on my history midterm or losing one of my plants to an early frost.

"Anyway, now I know I can do it," Drew says, so softly I'm not sure he's spoken.

"Do *what?*"

"Get through something like that, if it happens again," he says. "Like the divorce. I thought it would be the crappiest thing ever . . . and it was, but I survived. So now I know that about myself."

I must look like one of the pelicans we saw in Half Moon

Bay, my jaw hanging wide open. Only I don't want fish, I want answers. "So now you *know that about yourself*? What does that even mean? *Why* would you want to know that about yourself? That's a *terrible* thing to have to know. Aren't you furious you were forced to deal with the divorce in the first place? Aren't you scared right now?"

My brother stands and switches off the distress lantern before answering. "I was pissed, a little, but not really anymore. Even if it was under crappy conditions, knowing I could handle it was a good thing to learn about myself, don't you think?"

How has my fifteen-year-old brother figured this out and I haven't? Haven't even come close. I'm about to ask him more when he adds, "And for the record, I'm scared shitless right now."

"Me too," I whisper, wishing he were still sitting so I could lean over and hug him. Or maybe so he could hug me, since our roles as big and little sibling seem to be reversed at the moment. "I just want these horrible things to stop happening."

Drew smiles tightly. "Yeah, except you can't control that, only how you deal with it."

It sounds like what Jonah said. Has Jonah gotten to Drew? Or is this just who Drew is? Damn—he's like a little baby Buddha. How did I not know this about my own brother? I knew he was mellow, but I never knew there was actual . . . I don't know, *depth* to his chill vibe. How did he get this way? Have I been trying to shield him from Mom's cheating this whole time, thinking I was being the protective big sister, and he never even needed that from me?

"You're a totally weird kid, you know that, right?" I tell him, tugging the blanket tighter, but grateful that my shaking seems to be slowing.

He laughs. "Pfft. Whatever. You just can't handle that I'm an old soul. Nana always says it, only you never pay attention."

"I don't remember her ever saying that."

We're both quiet for a second, then I ask, "How come we've never talked like this before?"

Drew cracks a small smile. "Well, usually you don't want to get close to me because of the deodorant thing."

This is true. I roll my eyes at him, but then sober.

"What if I'm broken?" I whisper, scared for Drew's answer. I don't know if I can handle the truth right now.

"You're not broken."

"How do you know?"

Drew glances at me. "Because if you were broken, you wouldn't be fishing with me, or playing Frisbee on the beach, or sticking your tongue down Jonah's throat every possible second."

He makes a face at this last one, and I nearly laugh before I catch myself. That would not be appropriate, given the circumstances. But I'm flooded with relief that at least one person has faith in me.

Drew shrugs. "I think maybe you're just . . . bent."

I can't help it. I laugh. Only a quick one. "I'll give you bent, you brat!"

He smiles, and by unspoken agreement, we both go back to staring at *Reality Bytes*—she's close enough now that I can make out her outline clearly and even see someone moving around on the deck. I don't know what Drew is thinking about now, but I'm trying to digest everything he said. Never in a million years did I think I would be learning life lessons from my baby brother.

As if sensing my train of thought, he suddenly says, "Many of the truths we cling to depend on our point of view."

I groan. "Seriously, Jonah taught you that quote, right? First Mom with all her 'the journey is the destination' crap, and then Jonah with his philosophy mumbo jumbo . . ."

"You don't seem to mind Jonah's mumbo jumbo so much," Drew says. I narrow my eyes at him, but he just grins. "Anyway, it's not something either of them taught me. It's Yoda!"

"Yoda?" *Star Wars*. I should have known.

"The Force is strong with this young Padawan learner."

I make a gagging noise, then ask, "What was it? 'Truths cling—'"

"'Many of the truths we cling to depend on our point of view,'" he repeats.

"So then?" I wait for his brilliant assessment of how it applies to our situation.

He endures a coughing fit, then says, "You think Mom is to blame for all of this, but what if you were going to feel this way about any bad thing that happened, because you're just someone who hasn't learned how to deal with crap yet?"

So, *not* how it applies to our situation. How it applies to *me.* His delivery makes me bristle, but then I pause to take in the words themselves. Could that be possible? Would I have fallen apart in the same way if Dad got sick, or one of my friends got into a car accident, or something else equally terrible had rocked my world? Would any of those have been the thing that pulled the rug out from under me, if Mom hadn't snuck in and pulled first? I swallow. It's a lot to digest, and I'm not sure I can even try right now, with everything else crowding my head.

"What else does Yoda have to say?" I ask, to change the subject.

"Um. 'When nine hundred years you reach, look as good you will not'?"

I look at Drew. "Funny. Though not super useful."

"If you wanted useful you should have said so. Okay, then. 'Judge me by my size, do you?'"

I snort. "Also *not* useful. And clearly a line written by a guy to make underendowed nerdy boys feel better about themselves."

Drew scrunches up his face. "That's gross. Do not even try to ruin *Star Wars* for me, because—"

He's interrupted by Jonah's voice cutting across the water. "Cassie? Drew? Are you guys okay?"

Obviously, in many senses, we're nowhere remotely close to okay, but I'm still flooded with warmth.

It only takes another few minutes for them to maneuver alongside us, and for a second time this trip we tie our two boats together—this time in a sea so calm even I would consider the leap from one deck to another. But I don't have to, because Jonah comes to us.

Before I can get a word in, he covers the three strides across the cockpit it takes to reach me and gathers me to his chest. I exhale a ragged breath and fall apart in the protective circle of his arms.

He strokes my hair gently as the soft words he speaks to Drew make his chest rumble. I can only make out a few of them, but when I hear "hospital" I force my sobs to quiet.

"—on hold with them now," Jonah's saying.

I jerk my head up, the rest of my body still trapped tight by his hands clasped at my back.

"What was that last part?" I ask.

"Christian's got the hospital holding on his satellite phone," Drew answers. "She arrived not that long ago and they're taking her for a CAT scan, but the nurse said Mom was answering questions normally when she got there."

I search Jonah's face for confirmation and he nods, offering a tiny smile. I press my forehead into his shoulder and take a deep breath. Thank god she made it there okay. Thank god she's speaking lucidly again. Just . . . thank god for all of it.

I turn my face and catch my brother's eye. "You okay?" I mouth.

Drew smiles. "Let's get this show on the road; we have a hospital to get to." He unties the cleat hitch keeping us tethered to *Reality Bytes* and calls over to Christian. "All clear."

Reluctantly, I let go of Jonah so he can help, but he tightens his grasp on me and speaks to Drew over my shoulder. "Christian already has the coordinates in his GPS, so we'll stick close to him. It's calm enough tonight for him to handle the yacht on his own, so I can stay with you guys. Can you radio to Amy and Miranda that they should take their time if they'd rather stay under sail and meet up with us there? I'll get our course set and the autopilot on and then I want to talk to your sister for a second, okay?"

Drew clearly gets the message to make himself scarce, because he replies "Sure" and heads downstairs to the VHF. As soon as he's out of sight, Jonah turns to me again. He hasn't released me from his grip and he dips his head to look in my eyes.

"Don't. Move. I'll be right back."

He works efficiently. In less than five minutes we're under way, trailing a hundred yards off *Reality Bytes'* stern, and Jonah has his arms around me once more.

"I'm so sorry," he whispers. "For what happened to your mom and—"

I cut him off. "You don't have to apologize for that. It wasn't your fault."

He removes one hand from my back, the fingers on his other splaying widely to keep me in place. He tucks a piece of my hair behind my ear and sighs. "You didn't let me finish. I was about to add that I'm sorry for everything I said this morning too, although I probably should have started with that. See? Further proof I'm an idiot."

His eyes are filled with his apology, and even if I had been able to summon anger at him in the face of everything that's happened since our fight, his sincerity would be melting it away now.

He takes another deep breath. "I honestly believed what I was saying could help you, Cass, I swear. I only said what I did because I wanted you to see things the way I saw them, because then maybe you could find a way past everything and you could be happy again. You *deserve* to be happy."

More tears threaten. I've been acting like such a brat for so long, and seeing Mom passed out on the deck made me painfully aware of what's really important. She could have *died*. I'd have had to go the whole rest of my life never getting the chance to even *try* to work things out with us. She hasn't been the perfect mother lately, but I can admit I haven't exactly been the model daughter either.

"I don't know what I deserve anymore," I murmur.

"Everything," Jonah answers immediately. "You deserve everything."

I shake my head. "I'm not a nice person."

"Sprite," he groans. "Of course you are. People who aren't nice don't *care* that they're not nice. You're dealing with a ton all at once, and anyone would have a hard time handling it all. I should have been more sympathetic to that. I should have thought about how what I was saying would sound from your point of view—I should have had your back one hundred percent. If either of us is the jerk here, it's me."

His words are so heartfelt that I melt even more. I tilt my chin to see his face.

"Yeah, but do you care that you're a jerk?" I ask, smiling to show I'm teasing and that he's forgiven.

His shoulders relax, but his eyes are intense as they hold mine. "I care about a lot of things," he whispers.

An acrobat inside my belly executes a few aerial moves and I swallow. "Me too."

We stare at each other for a few long seconds, then I raise up on tiptoes to give him a soft kiss on the lips.

His hand at my back tightens. "See? Told you you're a nice person. A very *very* nice person."

He bends his head to kiss me again and I sink into it. It's innocent and sweet and full of promise and hope. It floods me with relief that at least one thing in my life is back in place. When we break apart, we're both smiling.

It's quiet for a long minute, and then I ask, "You know how you just mentioned point of view?" He nods and I continue, "Did you happen to know many of the truths that we cling to depend on our point of view?"

Jonah sputters, and his eyes grow so wide I'm worried for them. "Are you quoting Yoda to me? Because damn, Sprite, that is seriously hot. I know maybe this isn't the time or place to say something like that, but . . ."

Before I can answer beyond a laugh, Drew reappears at

the top of the steps and coughs. It's an "Am I interrupting?" cough rather than the "I feel like crap" one I've heard so much of tonight.

I roll my eyes and smile. "What, are you conditioned to appear whenever *Star Wars* is referenced?"

Drew's eyebrows rise. "Huh? No. You were talking about *Star Wars*?" He pauses, and then his eyes narrow. "What if I *sensed it*? I *told* you the Force was strong within me!"

Jonah laughs, and I giggle too. As much as I know, on an intellectual level, that I can never truly be sure of how things will turn out, right now things feel hopeful.

Which I'll take.

Sometimes it feels good to believe just for the sake of believing.

33

"**If you're feeling** up to it, I think I'm ready to have those fifteen or sixteen hundred talks you wanted to schedule," I say, entering Mom's hospital room and sitting gingerly on the edge of her bed.

It's been a long two days, but she's doing much better.

Turns out Mom was not a worst-case scenario after all. Her CAT scan looked good and she's now acting completely like herself—no more gibberish. She had a minor concussion, but she'll be released later today. Drew is off getting something to eat with my grandparents, who drove up from San Diego, but I didn't want to leave Mom here alone. Besides, this moment has been a long time coming. Like, seven months long.

I've had a lot of waiting-around time to think these last couple of days, and it's possible Jonah might have been right about some of what he said.

I *have* been afraid.

But I don't think I've been afraid that hearing Mom's side

will mean I have to forgive her and accept that it's time to move on. I think my bigger fear has been: What if I hear all the gory details and I *can't* forgive her, because they're too terrible and I won't ever be able to reconcile the person who could act like she did with the mother I thought I knew so completely?

I'm afraid I'll lose my mom for good.

Except, on the boat, I almost *did* lose her for good, in a very real way. And imagining what it would have felt like to *never* be able to have this conversation made me realize deep down that I need to be brave. I need to hear it and deal with this, no matter how bad it is, because I'm not getting anywhere with the way I've been handling things this year.

I've been complaining about not having any control over my own life, but what exactly have I done to fix that . . . to take ownership back? Nothing. I needed Drew to tell me what to do with the whole rescue effort. I refused to learn how to help get us from anchorage to anchorage until Jonah conned me into it.

I've been the sails, filling and deflating, as someone *else* turned me into and out of the wind.

I think I might finally, *finally* be ready to be the one steering the ship.

And since my relationship with Mom is the thing that makes me feel most helpless of all, I'm starting here.

"You want all fifteen hundred talks at once?" My mother's lips curl into a smile, followed by a wince. She touches the bandage wrapped around her head. "Ouch! Remind me not to smile ever again."

"Okay." I answer with a grin of my own, then let it fade. "Maybe not all of the talks at once. Maybe just the big one. Is your brain working enough to handle it?"

She motions for me to help prop her up. I get her situated with a pile of pillows behind her back and move into the chair next to her bed. She wiggles her shoulders to settle in better, then says softly, "Okay, ask away."

Here we go.

I take the deepest breath I can manage. "What happened?"

I know it's not a very specific question, but I think she'll know what I mean. And what I mean is . . . all of it.

My mother tilts her head slightly. "I've tried to talk to you about this, you know. It just seemed like every time I wanted to broach the subject, I couldn't make it past the walls you had up."

We're two seconds into this conversation and my eyes are already hot with tears.

"I know. I'm sorry."

She reaches for my hand and I give it to her. "I'm sorry too, baby. That's the biggest thing I want to say to you. Your dad and I weren't trying to hurt you." She takes a shaky breath and I bite my lip. "Sweet Cassie. It's my job to take care of you, and I should have known how all this would affect you."

A few tears spill over and trickle down my face. Mom releases my hand to wipe them away with her thumb.

I notice she said "your dad and I." I want to push back on how she's lumped him into it when really the divorce is on her. I promised myself before coming in here that I wouldn't dance around the issue of her cheating, but I'm not ready yet. It's something I need to work up to.

Instead I say, "It came out of the blue for me. Not just the divorce. I mean, my reaction to all of it too. I . . . I'm so angry all the time that I don't really recognize myself anymore."

"But *I* should have predicted it." She sighs and catches my eye. "Did I ever tell you what happened when Drew was born?"

I shake my head.

Mom smiles. "Well, you and I were quite the team, even back then. You used to insist on sleeping next to me, between Dad and me, almost every night."

I half laugh, half hiccup through the remains of my tears. "I guess it's a miracle you managed to conceive Drew, then."

Mom laughs, then winces again. "Oh god. I told you not to let me do that again."

"Technically you said not to let you *smile*. You didn't say anything about laughing."

"Touché," Mom responds. "Just for that I should go into specific details about Drew's conception." At my horrified look she starts to laugh again, then claps a hand over her mouth. But her eyes still dance.

This is how we used to joke with each other and my heart loves it, but I'm still bracing myself for what's to come.

Mom continues. "I knew it was going to be a problem

when Drew's arrival intruded, but I never expected you to be so furious. Man, Cassie, you were a little demon. Never with Drew—you were sweet as can be with him. But with me? You let me have it."

"How?"

She looks over my shoulder, remembering. "Mainly you peed, like a cat upset with its owner. Mostly in your bed at night, so that we had no choice but to either get up and change the sheets or to make room for you in our bed. Which was exactly what you wanted, of course. You'd been potty-trained for over a year by that point, so I knew you were doing it intentionally. I really had to give you credit for being a very intelligent and crafty kid. I knew back then I'd be in real trouble when it came to your teen years." She pauses, her eyes filling with sadness. "I just didn't expect any of this to be going on when we got here."

I cringe. "Sorry on behalf of three-year-old me. What finally ended it? I mean, obviously at some point I started sleeping in my bed."

"Oh, you did. The very moment I moved Drew into his crib and told you that you were welcome to come back into our bed if you wanted. You just looked at me, calm as could be, and said 'No, thank you' and we never heard from you again between bedtime and morning."

"What? What the hell!"

Mom manages a smirk without an accompanying wince. "It wasn't the bed you wanted. It was the choice. You wanted to be the one to set the terms and make the decision for yourself."

I hang my head. "Oh."

"I wish I'd remembered that story when Dad and I were talking things through last winter. Drew's like a pincushion— he takes all the needles and then smooths right out again, so I knew he'd be fine. Somehow I deluded myself into believing that you and I could talk our way through it. You're older now, and I guess I stupidly thought we could just sit down and have a heart-to-heart like adults, and I could share all our reasons with you. That . . . didn't exactly go according to plan."

I stand suddenly and face the window. The shades are drawn, but I move them aside to stare out over the city. It's strange to see buildings shimmering in the sun, instead of water. "Now you're making *me* feel like the one who's stupid, because you're basically telling me I wasn't mature enough to talk it out with you."

"I didn't mean it like that, honey. I'm trying to say I was naive for not realizing that seventeen isn't old enough to handle that kind of reasoning."

"That still sounds like an insult wrapped in an apology." Despite all my hopes for this conversation, the cloak of anger that's kept me warm all year threatens to settle back around my shoulders.

"Cassie, stop!" my mother barks, and it surprises me into turning around to face her. She gestures to the chair I vacated. "Please. *Please* sit back down."

I hesitate, but I follow her orders. The agitation is fizzing just underneath the surface though, ready to come back the second I need it. I both hate and love that it's there for me.

"Remember when Nana kept forgetting things this spring and everyone thought it might be the start of Alzheimer's, before we realized she'd been having ministrokes?"

I nod and she continues. "Well, the thought of her not being able to recognize me made me realize that no one is ever too old to need their mom, no matter how mature that person is. I should have focused more on being your mother and less on trying to treat you like a girlfriend."

I swallow. "I didn't even realize you were doing that."

Mom seems surprised. "The spa day I booked that you refused to attend? The dinner I tried for just the two of us? You barely said three words to me between appetizers and dessert."

"Oh. That's what those were all about?"

Mom nods gingerly. She looks at the clock on the wall. "When am I due for more Tylenol?"

I glance at it. "Twenty, twenty-five more minutes. Do you want me to get the nurse now instead?"

Mom moves her head, nearly imperceptibly, side to side. "Nope, I can hold out till then."

My chair is one of those reclining ones, and I fiddle absent-mindedly with the handle. "What would you have said if I had gone on the spa day?"

My mother is quiet for a beat, and her voice is soft when she answers. "I guess I would have told you that your dad and

I had been coasting for a long time."

"What does that mean—coasting?"

She sighs. "Things were *fine.*"

Yeah, they were. Things were so fine I certainly never saw the split coming.

"What's wrong with fine?" I ask.

When I steal a peek at her, she has her eyes closed. Even with her tan that matches the ones we've all gotten, she looks pale, lying tucked among a sea of pillows.

"Nothing's wrong with fine. But nothing's great about fine either. It's just . . . fine. And for a long time, your dad and I had a perfectly companionable relationship, but at a certain point, that's not really enough."

This is it. This is the opening I need, if I can just find the courage. I take a deep breath . . . and waver. They're such ugly words to say out loud. Especially to your own mother.

But I have to know this time. I *have* to.

"So that's why you cheated?" I ask, so quietly I almost can't make out my own voice.

Mom must though, because her eyes snap open and they're full of shock. Mine are too. I can't quite believe I just spoke those words to her, after so many months of forcing them in.

"What?" she asks. "Cass—what—"

I keep my eyes on my lap, squeezing and releasing the chair's lever in my hand. "I overheard you and Dad fighting that last night he was home. He said if you hadn't cheated, you wouldn't be divorcing. I've known this whole time."

"I—good god."

For a long time after that she's quiet, and so am I. Neither of us is looking at the other. Finally, she draws a ragged breath and says, "I didn't cheat, Cass. Not exactly."

34

How does one "not exactly cheat"? I shake my head incredulously.

She exhales and waits for me to look at her before asking, "Remember when I told you about crewing on charter trips in the Caribbean during breaks in grad school?"

I nod.

"Well, I kind of left off the part where I got pregnant my last summer."

The words hang in the air.

"I lost the baby. I was three months along and I had a miscarriage."

I stare at my hands. "I'm sorry."

"Thank you," she answers softly.

"I don't understand how this connects to Dad and you. Was it his?"

Mom shakes her head. "No. But bear with me and I'll explain. The father—sorry, I know it's weird to think of me with someone else besides your dad, but he's part of the story—he . . . wasn't very supportive when I told him. He worked for the charter company too and he was the very definition of a 'grotty yachty.' Told you I was projecting."

She offers me a small smile and I return it.

"He said he had a good thing going that he didn't want to mess up and basically told me if I went through with having the baby, I should lose his number."

"Charming," I murmur.

"Ha! Maybe now you can understand why I had a little bias against Jonah when we first met?"

I bring my eyes to hers and she smiles. "Don't worry, honey, Jonah is *nothing* like Matteo. In fact, I wouldn't be surprised if Jonah doesn't actually need all that long in Mexico to figure out what he wants for his future."

She meets my surprised eyes and winks again. "Especially not with someone so special waiting for him stateside."

If this were Tara and Jess, that comment would have earned an instant "Do you really think so?" followed by an overanalysis of my future relationship with Jonah from every possible angle. But I'm determined to hear the rest of Mom's explanation, so I bite my cheek and keep quiet.

She shrugs, almost imperceptibly. "As long as I'm apologizing to you, let me add that one. I shouldn't have made a snap judgment about the kind of person Jonah is. I hope when you consider the perspective I brought to it, you'll understand why I reacted the way I did initially."

I think of Drew/Yoda's words and bite my lip. Goddamn "perspective" and the number it's done on my life.

"But what happened with Matteo?" I won't let her derail this conversation before I get my answers.

My mother's smile is wry as she continues. "Right. Well, it wasn't the best response on Matteo's part, I'll give you that. In his defense, we were very young back then."

Then she sighs. "Anyway, it was close to the end of summer when I found out, so after that I just . . . went home. Went back to school. And for the seven weeks that followed, between when I learned about the baby and when I lost him or her, I was totally alone. I was too scared to even tell Nana and Gramps because I felt like I'd disappointed them. I refused to confide in any of my friends because I was so embarrassed I'd let myself get into that predicament. Can you imagine being too stupid to reach out to friends who love you?"

I make a sympathetic face, but inside I'm thinking *Only too well*. I know Tara and Jess would have comforted me if I'd confided in them about Mom's cheating, but I also knew there was nothing they could have said to make it any better, and then a very small part of me worried—what if they judged me for forgiving her if I ever decided to? Even then, at my angriest, a tiny, hopeful part of me wanted to believe Mom and I would move past it.

Mom sighs, lost in her own story. "Being pregnant without anyone to talk to was the scariest feeling in the world. Knowing I was losing the baby and riding to the hospital in the ambulance by myself and having to lie there and wait for the doctors to come in . . . It was awful."

My throat constricts and I reach over and grab her hand. She squeezes in appreciation.

"I wouldn't wish it on my enemy. So when I met your dad a few months later, and I fell in love with him, I went from feeling completely alone to latching on to all the safety and security he was offering. And love. Definitely love that went both ways. Your father's one of the good guys, Cass. Despite what's going on with us right now, he always will be."

"Okay, but I don't really understand what this has to do with anything. If you didn't meet Dad until after everything was over and—" I break off as understanding dawns. "Matteo was the guy you cheated with? After what he did to you?"

"No! Well, not—" She sighs again, more deeply this time. "Your father has always had a weird thing about Matteo. He knows everything that happened back then, of course, but I think he also recognized that, before I'd gotten pregnant, my relationship with Matteo had been—"

She breaks off for a second, then says, "I guess you're old enough to hear this. We had a pretty passionate relationship and it wasn't . . . which wasn't the same as what your dad and I had.

"Anyway, last summer, Matteo reached out to me on Facebook."

"I don't understand. How could you want to talk to someone who left you alone *and pregnant*? How could you ever forgive that?"

My mother grimaces. "Because when we grow up, we mature, and we realize that someone could act a certain way out of fear, but it doesn't have to define them for life."

I'm silent as her words hit too close to home for comfort.

Then I can't help saying, "So, what? You went running right back into Matteo's arms."

"I didn't go running into his arms, Cassie. I can promise you, I haven't spent time in anyone's arms but your father's since the day I said 'I do'!"

"But Dad said—"

"Your father was upset I was opening up about things with Matteo in a way your dad and I hadn't done with each other in a long time. He felt betrayed, and I can appreciate that."

I shake my head. "I really, really don't understand."

My mother sighs. "I know, baby. But the thing is, your dad and I had grown apart. Maybe not to the point of divorce yet, but we'd lost a lot of the intimacy our relationship used to have. Not the family part of our relationship and who we were around you, but the adult side of a marriage that's separate from the mother-father part.

"We weren't in a great place, and I wasn't ready to defend my being in contact with Matteo to your dad, so I hid it from him. When he discovered it on his own, I don't blame him for also assuming other things that weren't true and reacting."

"So you didn't—you never—"

My mother shakes her head. "I can't believe that's what you've been thinking this whole time."

Neither can I. This *whole* time. Oh my god.

She. Didn't. Cheat.

Everything I thought about her, the way I acted because of it—I want to crawl under the covers and cry for the last seven months and every emotion I wasted on them.

But no. Those emotions aren't *all* about the cheating. They're also about the divorce itself and how it ripped the ground out from under me, and how she didn't take my feelings into account with this trip, and now, again, with selling our house. It still doesn't change any of those things. I still need more answers.

"Does Dad still not believe you that you were just talking to Matteo? Are you *still* talking to Matteo?" I ask. "Otherwise, why is Dad so angry with you?"

"Dad believes me and, no, I haven't spoken to Matteo since January. Dad's angry because this isn't how he wanted things to play out. But talking to Matteo was just one in a series of events that gave momentum to something that was already building with Dad. Once Matteo and I worked through our unsettled business from back then, we talked *a lot* about that time in our lives. It made me realize how much I'd changed and given up . . . it reminded me of the kind of person I used to be—someone who took more chances and lived with a bigger sense of adventure."

"You're saying you don't like who you've become?" I ask.

Is she implying she regrets marrying Dad? Having me and Drew?

"It's not that. I'm proud of the things I've accomplished

364

with my life. I'm especially proud to be a mom to two such amazing kids."

She pauses and smiles at me. I can't respond. I'm still waiting for the "but."

"But talking to Matteo also reminded me about a lot of dreams for my life that I walked away from—sailing among them—and it made me look long and hard at the ones I still have left for myself. And I realized . . . I wanted *more* than what your dad and I had."

Maybe, *maybe*, I understand a little of what she's saying. But the fact remains, she still acted out of selfishness. There were other people to consider. Dad. Me. Drew. "Why didn't you try to change things *with* Dad? Therapy or—"

Why didn't you fight for our family like I've been doing?

I stand and cross to the window again. The parking garage below is an endless series of cars entering and exiting.

"We tried."

I'm stunned. "When?"

"After your dad moved to Hong Kong. We had virtual sessions with a marriage counselor for several months."

I lean into the windowsill. "Why didn't you say anything to me or Drew?"

When I turn to face her, she looks miserable. "I didn't want you to get your hopes up for some kind of happy reunion between us. I was realizing that wasn't what I wanted. Learning to be an independent person and making my own decisions for the first time in my adult life, it's been . . . empowering.

This is what I need right now."

"But you're not *supposed* to be independent," I say, not loving the whining that creeps into my voice or even the words that leave my mouth. "You're supposed to be my *mom*."

"I *am* your mom. I'm trying to be both. And to be honest, it's a little selfish of you to say that, Cass. You're going off to college next year, and Drew's not all that far behind you. What am I then? Yes, I'm still your mom, but am I supposed to freeze the scene until you return for visits to the family homestead or something? That's not exactly fair, is it?"

I can't deny it's what I'd always pictured. I'd come home for holidays and Mom would have made Aunt Lori's chicken recipe for my first night back, because she knows it's my favorite, and Drew would be on the couch playing video games. Then Dad and I would head to the grocery store first thing Saturday morning for our ultra-competitive version of Coupon Showdown where we divide the list and compete to see whose receipt shows the biggest savings (loser buys bagels and lox). Everything slipping right back to normal, until it's time to leave again.

Maybe that's not fair of me to expect, but she never gave me any reason to think that wasn't a reasonable fantasy until this year. And maybe it is selfish of me, but didn't she act in her own self-interest too? *Was* it really fair to put us all through the wringer so she could recapture her glory days or find her one true self or whatever?

I'm wrestling with this internally when my mother says,

"Maybe it'll help to know that, even though this is my choice, *I'm* scared too. In my darker moments, I feel like I failed as a wife, that my career is currently nonexistent, and now I'm crashing and burning as a parent—especially with you. I know I've taken away your trust in life being inherently good, and I'm so sorry for that. It's like I've robbed you of your innocence."

Before I can answer, she rushes on. "Mostly I'm scared of losing you. I never wanted my independence from *you*. Things between us have been so awful and so cold, and I knew that after this next year, you'd go off to college, and if we didn't fix this between us, you'd be gone and maybe we'd never have a chance to get things back the way they were. I know you never wanted this trip, but it was my Hail Mary."

I don't know how to respond. She should have talked to me. Yes, she made references to "putting our family back together," but she should have spelled out what she really meant by that before we left, so she didn't have to resort to forcing this trip down my throat. She should have—

"You weren't in a place to hear me."

I glare at her, but I smile at the same time. "Get out of my head."

"Can't. They'd have to revoke my mom card if that day ever came," she answers, and smiles, along with a wince that makes me glance at the clock to confirm that medicine time is fast approaching.

I study her for a second. "Why doesn't that go both ways,

then? How come I can never get inside your head? Why didn't I have any idea you were feeling any doubts about Dad or your life or . . . anything?"

My mother's smile fades and her eyes flutter shut for a second. "Because I'm your mom and I wanted to protect you. I've had a whole lifetime of training at putting on a good appearance. But I hate that I'm setting that example for you, because I don't want you to grow up thinking you can't show weakness or that you can't let people in when you're feeling insecure. Except . . ."

She trails off and I wait for her to continue, but she doesn't. "Except what?" I finally ask.

"I don't know how to drop my guard and let all the vulnerable show. I mean, I'm just so used to slapping on a cheerful smile and dealing. I might—I might need your help."

I snort. "My help? I can't even deal with the *idea* of the bad stuff, much less the reality when it actually happens!"

She shrugs lightly. "Okay, so what if I call you out on your b.s. and you call me out on mine? I mean, life's messy, right? It's not like we won't have plenty more chances to practice."

She makes it sounds so easy—the two of us taking on the world. But nothing's that simple, and there's been all this bad blood between us for so long. Even now that I understand things a whole lot better and there's this *massive* relief she didn't cheat—it's still overwhelming. I still need time to process. I still have feelings about how it all went down and her role in that. I don't know if I'm ready to let go entirely and skip off down the garden path with her.

But at least I can *see* the path now, so maybe there's hope for us.

I'm composing my thoughts to answer when I hear the door open behind me.

"If you have drugs in that hand, you are my very favorite person in the world," Mom tells the nurse who enters. I wipe my cheeks and clear my throat, avoiding eye contact with Mom as the woman approaches.

The nurse politely ignores my emotional state and instead chuckles as she drops two pills on the table next to Mom's glass. "That's what they all say. But see if they remember my name come discharge time."

"Knock, knock. Can we come in now too?" Drew appears in the doorway, Jonah hovering behind. Both have their eyes locked on me, even as they wait for Mom's answer. She looks to me as well.

"Had enough for one day?" she asks, quietly enough that only I can hear her.

I nod. I think I have. I'm glad I have so many more of the puzzle pieces to work with. Now I just have to figure out how they all fit together to form the complete picture. I have to turn everything over under the lens of my new *perspective*. I think I might really hate that word.

Mom gives me a lingering look, full of sympathy and tinged with hope, then turns to the doorway.

"C'mon in, my other heroes," she says, gesturing them

over as the nurse slips out.

Drew leans close and gives Mom a peck on her bandaged forehead, and Jonah moves to my side as soon as I stand.

He eyes me carefully, and I know my Irish skin must be betraying my crying session right now, if my puffy eyes weren't enough of a dead giveaway. His eyebrows rise in a silent question and I nod. *Yes, I talked to her. There's still a lot more to do, but it was a really good start.*

As if he understands all this from my expression, he smiles softly, then reaches into the pocket of his sweatshirt.

"Sprite for my favorite sprite?" he asks, handing me an icy soda can. Our fingers brush and the familiar tingles shoot up my arm. He grins, and I know he feels them too.

"Can I please hug her?" he asks my mom.

She looks amused as she replies, "Be my guest."

It feels so good to have his arms wrapped around me. Despite Jonah's advice about creating my own safe to carry within me, and as much as I agree with it in theory, I'm not above admitting that *sometimes* it feels very sweet and comforting to be all wrapped up by a boy you like. Especially one who smells like fresh air and sunshine and fabric softener and . . . chocolate? I'm guessing he has some Ghirardelli on him somewhere.

Jonah turns to my mom, keeping one arm tight around me. "I'm really glad you're out of the woods, Mrs.—er, Elise."

My mother smiles her thanks.

Jonah slides a glance at me. "I'm also really glad I got to

use that phrase so organically, because Cassie here thinks all land-related sayings are good ones, but if you'll kindly direct her to take note—"

"Since when is it not a good thing to be out of the woods?" I protest.

Jonah's eyes dance. "I seem to recall a certain person claiming that 'safe harbor in the storm' was still negative because it implied being unsafe on the water prior to that. Applying that same logic to our woods scenario . . ."

"Oh, blow it out your ass," I mumble.

"Language!" my mother says automatically.

Drew laughs, and just like that, things are back to some semblance of normal.

"Fine," I amend. "Jonah, kindly go gargle a porcupine."

He makes a goofy face before releasing me. I crack open my Sprite and Jonah eyes it. "After all our sailing adventures, I may need to find a new nickname for you. I'm thinking you're becoming way more water nymph than wood sprite these days."

"That could all change back," Mom says, and we each turn our attention to her.

"What do you mean?" I ask.

She locks eyes on me. "I won't force you to continue this trip. The odds of anything like our whale encounter happening again are minuscule, but there are plenty of other things that can go wrong out there, and I can't put you in that position again without your full consent."

"Will the doctors even clear you to sail?" Drew asks.

Mom nods gingerly. "They already have. Christian, Miranda, and I talked about it when they were in here earlier, and if we continue, the plan would be for me to head to San Diego with Nana and Gramps and spend a couple more days resting at their house. The adults would divide up and help you two caravan *Sunny-Side Up* south to meet me. After that I'd need to take it easy to start, but I'd be able to help with most things."

She exhales and slides her eyes back to me. "But if you want to go home tomorrow, I'm fine with that too."

I throw my hands up. "Oh, really? How would the boat get to Mexico? And we'd go home to *what* exactly? Someone else is living in our house. Or . . . their house. Or . . . I don't even know anymore."

My mother raises her chin. "Christian thinks he can find someone to bring *Sunny* the rest of the way to Land's End. As for the house, I don't know what we'll do about that yet, but you get to weigh in on the decision. If I've learned anything these last couple of days, it's that I'm done railroading over you, Cass. And where this trip is concerned, it's your call entirely. Whatever you choose, I'll support you totally. Your turn to boss *me* around."

I stare at her in shock, but she just stares calmly right back.

Do I want to keep sailing when all I've wanted for most of this trip is to get back home to my friends, and my garden, and my life there? I glance out the window, where, although

I can't see it, somewhere off in the distance the blue of the Pacific Ocean sparkles underneath all the Southern California sunshine. It might glisten, but I know the dangers it holds too. Do I want to put myself at its mercy again? Open myself up to all the myriad unknown possibilities?

Or is it time to accept that those unknown possibilities lie in wait no matter where I am? And that not all of them are bad. If I embrace the fact that the exciting *and* the scary could be down either path, then all I have to do is to pick my tack and set my course, until the wind shifts and it's time to adjust the sails. Right?

Which is my tack, then? Drive north or sail south?

Oh my god, I'm so tired of weighing pros and cons and endless loops of questions. Being afraid to let myself fall for Jonah despite all the practical reasons I shouldn't. Being afraid to let down my guard around my mom the times I wanted to, because of all the intellectual reasons I had for feeling betrayed by her. Thinking, thinking, rationalizing.

I don't care that I might look like an idiot. I close my eyes and shut it all down. I take a deep breath, from my core, and slowly exhale it.

Then I appeal to my gut.

I make myself trust what it tells me and I open my eyes.

I know what I want to do.

But finally knowing my own mind clearly and actually acting on it are two different things when other people are involved. I might be making headway in forgiving my mother for forcing this trip on me, but that doesn't mean I can't also learn from her mistakes.

I turn to Drew. "I say we take a vote. You should get to decide too. That's the only fair way to do it, right?"

My brother looks surprised. "Um, yeah, I guess." He recovers quickly and says, "Well, then . . . I vote yes for sailing on."

"Mom?" I ask.

My mother studies me and finally says, "I vote for whatever Cassie wants. Like I said, I'm gonna try taking the backseat on a few decisions where my lovely but headstrong daughter is concerned." She pauses and winks at me before I can take offense to the headstrong part.

"Okay, then. I guess my vote counts for two. Can't say I didn't try, Roo." I draw a deep breath and avoid Jonah's eyes as I say, "Drew, I'm really sorry . . . but we're not sailing on."

His shoulders drop, and beside me, Jonah tenses. I ignore them both and focus on my mother.

I smile at her. "I think I might be ready to try the whole 'sailing in' thing instead."

Mom smiles back, barely even wincing as she does. The pain medicine must be kicking in.

Jonah looks at Drew. "Does any of this make sense to you?"

Drew shakes his head. "I wish I was Luke Skywalker. At least *he* got to reach adulthood before he had to deal with having a sister. Are we going home or not?"

Mom and I laugh, and I say, "Not."

Jonah's grin could light the room, and he squeezes my shoulder. Then he glances at Mom and Drew before saying, "Oh, screw it," and kissing me.

I must say, my gut makes damn good decisions.

I don't know what comes next for us, but if I've learned anything this year, it's that none of us ever know that anyway. Might as well enjoy the present moment. And, uh, *yeah* . . . Consider that box checked.

When he releases me, he says, "I propose a toast!" He crosses to the door and sticks his head into the hallway. "Guys, get in here. We're toasting!"

Amy, Miranda, Christian, the girls, and my grandparents crowd the room. Drew passes my mother her water and the rest of us hold up our soda cans.

"To sailing in," Jonah says, threading the fingers of his free hand through mine.

I lock eyes with Mom.

"To sailing in," we say in unison.

ACKNOWLEDGMENTS

Annie and Alyssa (my own personal A-Team): How did I get so lucky?! I'm fairly certain the three of us would have a better-than-decent time sailing off into the sunset.

Annie, you helped shape so much of this story's concept. When I think back on our early "what if" phone calls, I'm struck by how many major aspects of this book would not exist without your input and your magical idea-sparking abilities.

Alyssa, you swooped in and demanded more Jonah, which was my first clue we'd be simpatico. The fact that your edit letter not only included a picture of the Coreys, but was signed "Frog Brother Enthusiast," well . . . signed, sealed, delivered.

Holly, as always, you're a calm harbor in any storm. You do know I plan to torture you with bad book-specific puns in every acknowledgment from now until the end of time, right? But seriously. I bow to your savvy-with-a-side-of-sweet.

The team at Harper: you beautiful unsung heroes, you. Thank you for the care, pride, and love you put into creating and championing my books. It does not go unnoticed or unappreciated! Special shout-outs to Rosemary Brosnan, Alexandra Cooper, Bethany Reis, Jessica White, Kate Klimowicz, Olivia Russo, and the entire marketing and sales team.

Alison Cherry, Dana Alison Levy, and Gail Nall, thank you times a billion for your early reads. I leaned heavily on you guys with this one, and wow, did you answer the call. Your thoughtful reads (overnight during ALA, Dana? My hero!) and your constant cheerleading were invaluable and I love you guys to the moon and back.

This manuscript took me outside of my comfort zone in more ways than one. I relied heavily on the expertise of those much better versed than me in everything from sailing to medicine to daring rescues at sea. For that I thank (and indemnify—any mistakes in the book are entirely of my own doing):

The very brave Coast Guard men and women who are proud to talk about their line of work and humble enough to not want named credit for it. Beyond gratitude for helping me with the technical aspects of Elise's rescue, an even bigger thank-you for all that you do—and risk—to keep so many safe at sea.

Wade Edwards and the Boston Sailing Center. Thank you for personal tours of differently sized sailboats, answers to ridiculously detailed questions, and "sure, that could work" responses to my many hypothetical "well, could this happen on a boat?" scenarios.

Dr. Lydia Kang. Thank you for the wonderful writerly blog resource that is Medical Mondays, and thank you even more for taking the time to help me solve a critical plot point with regard to head injuries.

Hallie Macdougal. Thank you for lending your boating expertise. I hope you enjoy your summer captaining your very own sailboat, and I'm counting on you to take me out exploring the Maine coast.

Last but never least, a million billion kisses to my patient family, who deliver meals and hugs to the writing cave and provide endless sources of inspiration—all the love to you: John, Jack, Ben, and Caroline. I'd sail away with you anytime.